M000092208

Praise for *Getting Past Anxiety*

"*Getting Past Anxiety* is for you if you've ever wondered why your life was less than satisfying. It will inspire you to conquer your own anxiety and then lead, live, and love your life anew!"

— Seconde Nimenya, MBA and Award-Winning Author of *Evolving Through Adversity* and *A Hand to Hold*

"Want to understand first-hand the pain, fear, and paralyzation of anxiety and also learn how to overcome it once and for all? Then start here and digest this book in its entirety!"

— Patrick Snow, Publishing Coach and International Best-Selling Author of *Creating Your Own Destiny*

"*Getting Past Anxiety* is enlightening and empowering. It unveils the truth and challenges of the effects of anxiety and inspires us to reclaim our life and abundance."

— Nicole Gabriel, Author of *Finding Your Inner Truth* and *Stepping Into Your Becoming*

"Do you feel helpless in affecting change in yourself due to over-whelming anxiety? If so, you are not alone. Read on as one brave woman shares how she transformed from petrified to peaceful."

— Angie Engstrom, Author of *Getting Yourself Unstuck*

"The power of a good story absorbs us as we turn the page.... I was captivated by Stella's journey and transformation. Melissa offers us something beyond a delightful read—she provides hope and a gentle reminder of our own power and grace. As we witness Stella remember and embrace her magic, we are given permission, and inspiration, to do the same. What a gift to read a novel that offers entertainment and healing."

— Vicki Keough, Behavioral Health Specialist

"Through the lives of her endearing and inspirational characters, the author takes you on a realistic journey of healing and restoration. She encourages you to understand better yourself, your feelings, and your knee-jerk reactions to the realities of life's anxieties—the small setbacks of major traumas."

— Susan Friedmann, CSP and International Best-Selling Author
of *Riches in Niches: How to make it BIG in a small Market*

"Stella's unique heartfelt story about her journey into the world of anxiety is a must read! This story will inspire and motivate you to reclaim your life and to be courageous to embrace any fears to grow and enjoy life."

— Karina Taugwalder, Author and Owner
of Online Presence Care

"Once in a while, a profound book comes forth that is deeply introspective, metaphysical, and medically scientific. Melissa Woods has been able to write a book that piques the reader's interest and excitement while delivering a message of huge importance. This message, I believe, will help many who read this book, and at the same time, let them know they are not alone. By the time you finish reading this book, you will realize there is a light at the end of the tunnel and that you have purchased a powerful, healing gift for yourself. A must read!"

— Dr. Michael Gross, Professional Keynote Speaker, Life Coach, Entrepreneur, and Author of *The Spiritual Primer: Applying the 12 Spiritual Laws to Reawaken Your Soul*

"*Getting Past Anxiety* speaks to the very pains that plague our modern society. Melissa A. Woods has created a novel that does far more than entertain. It gets to the very heart of anxiety's sources and educates us on how we can overcome our fears. Readers will find themselves in these pages, and more importantly, find the answers they have long sought. I applaud Woods for this insightful and healing tale."

— Tyler R. Tichelaar, Ph.D. and Award-Winning Author of *Narrow Lives* and *The Best Place*

"*Getting Past Anxiety* is a wonderfully-realistic portrait of a woman in search of her strongest self, which she finds by uncovering and working with the underlying trauma from her past. This book shares the magical journey of spiritual growth."

— Lillian Bridges, President of the Lotus Institute, Inc. and Author of *Face Reading in Chinese Medicine*

GETTING PAST
ANXIETY

MELISSA A. WOODS

GETTING PAST
ANXIETY

AVIVA
PUBLISHING
New York

GETTING PAST ANXIETY

An Inspirational Novel to Reclaim Your Life

Copyright 2017 by Melissa A Woods. All rights reserved.

Published by:

Aviva Publishing
Lake Placid, NY
(518) 523-1320
www.AvivaPubs.com

All Rights Reserved. No part of this book may be used or reproduced in any manner whatsoever without the expressed written permission of the author.

Address all inquiries to:

Melissa A. Woods

Telephone: 206-681-8335

Email: Melissa@MelissaAWoods.com

Website: www.GettingPastAnxiety.com

ISBN: 9781943164967

Library of CongressControl Number: 2016952157

Printed in the United States of America

1 3 5 7 9 10 8 6 4 2

Editor: Tyler Tichelaar, Superior Book Productions

Cover Designer and Interior Book Layout: Nicole Gabriel, AngelDog Productions

■　■　■

"The keys to your happiness are no
longer in somebody else's pocket from the past.

They're in yours."

— Adyshanti

/

To
my spiritual mother, Becky
&
my son, Spencer

■ ■ ■

ACKNOWLEDGMENTS

I am so grateful to the following advocates who believed in me and kept encouraging me to keep writing: creative ass-kicker Philip; my friends Mary, Paula, Sherrie, Susie, Kathy, Leanne, and Paul; my son Spencer; and al mio amore Daniele. Also, all the healers who have assisted me on this journey. A special thank you to my writing coach, Sylvia Taylor, for her encouragement, expertise, and wonderful support of the book, as well as to my publishing coach, Patrick Snow, and my editor, Tyler Tichelaar.

CONTENTS

■ ■ ■

Disclaimer

This book is a work of fiction. The characters and events are fictitious and don't refer to actual persons or incidents. Any similarities to real people or situations are by coincidence only.

The recommendations made to the characters in this book are not intended as a replacement for the reader's individual counseling, but rather as an example of some of the techniques used in therapy. Readers should consult their own physicians or therapists to determine the best program for their individual recovery from anxiety.

ARE YOU READY TO RECLAIM YOUR LIFE?

You're not alone; nearly one out of three Americans can't get on an airplane. Statistically, 6.3 million Americans are diagnosed with a phobia. Perhaps you can't get on an elevator. You panic! You can't stop those thoughts flying around in your head. Perhaps you can't stop worrying! You feel so alone and believe that you will never get on an airplane again. Perhaps you can't sleep at night, and you have an empty feeling in the pit of your stomach while wondering whether you'll ever feel better. You're scared that you will never be okay. You are fed up with this situation, but you have no idea where to turn.

Do you find your mouth dry? Do you feel panic, fear, and uneasiness? Does your heart palpitate like you're dying? Does your chest tighten so you can't breathe? Do you find your hands cold and sweaty? Do you feel irritated and impatient? Do you feel dizzy or nauseated?

I feel your pain, I have been in your shoes, and I know what it is like to go through this experience while feeling alone. I know how it feels to be afraid all the time and not to have any control over your thoughts and feelings. I could not get on a plane for twenty years. But I'm here to tell you it's going to be okay.

Through the story and characters in this book, you will learn about ways to get past your anxiety besides medication. You will discover how certain foods can aid in calming the body, which vitamins and minerals can help you sleep better, how massage can calm your body and nerves, and how to change negative thinking. You will understand how finding a mentor to help you work out the fears can reduce the symptoms of anxiety and get to the root cause of your pain.

I hope you will be inspired by Stella's inspirational path to wellness and by her courage and determination to keep fighting and working to find ways to heal. Stella never gives in to the dark hole and keeps reaching for the light. After reading this book, I hope you can do the same.

Besides my up close and personal experience with anxiety disorder, I have spent years studying anxiety and learning how to heal from it. My formal credentials and expertise include life coaching, therapeutic massage, creative writing, and sales and marketing. I have been a licensed massage practitioner in the State of Washington since 1992 and have worked on numerous clients dealing with anxiety issues. I have a Certificate of Memoir from the University of Washington and have published works in *Memoir Anthology of Writing from the University of Washington*. I am also the proud single mother of a happy, healthy twenty-five-year-old son. I don't, however, claim to have all the answers, and I'm still learning on my journey of life. I can learn from you too.

I understand why you have not pursued all your dreams, goals, and visions. I know you may be suffering from debilitating anxiety, and I can understand why you haven't taken anti-depressants. Your past doesn't equal your future. I want you to know that everything will be okay, and I believe in you.

I want to be your coach, your mentor, and your accountability partner. I want to be the person and resource that you look toward to overcome your anxiety challenges.

Are you ready to begin? Are you ready to step outside your comfort zone and be the person you are becoming? Are you ready to achieve your goals? If so...good; let's get started and make this journey together. It's your time to grow into the person you are meant to be.

1

"Believe that everything happens for a reason."

— Author Unknown

The First Class line at American Airlines wasn't long. As Stella approached the check-in counter, the attendant gave her a professional smile. Her name tag said, "Sally."

"Welcome," Sally said as she scanned Stella's ticket. "Is it just you flying tonight, Stella?"

"Yes, it is. Is the flight on time?" Stella glanced at the clock over Sally's head.

"Yes, we're boarding in a few minutes, but you have plenty of time to get to the gate."

"Okay," Stella said, but she wished Sally would hurry. When Sally handed Stella her ticket, Stella tried not to snatch it. She wasn't sure what she was more anxious about: her dad's hovering, seeing her boyfriend, or taking this redeye flight from Seattle to New York.

Robert, her dad, walked her to the gate, which he didn't have to do. Stella had only asked him to take her to the airport, a big favor already; it was close to midnight and he wasn't used to staying up this late. Maybe he had picked up the vibes given off by Stella's nerves.

Numerous people were at the gate sitting and milling about. Robert found two seats close together and they sat down. Stella's mouth was dry, so it was hard for her to swallow. Her heart began to beat fast.

Stella had been nervous before when she flew, but the feeling always went away as soon as she got on the plane. She closed her eyes and told herself it would be okay.

It didn't feel okay, though. Stella couldn't remember ever feeling this nervous before. Her heart was racing. *It'll be okay; it'll be okay,* she repeated silently to herself, like a mantra. It wasn't working.

A voice came over the loud speaker, "Flight 82 now boarding."

A thought appeared in her mind, as if someone had shot it there like a dart. *I can't get on this plane.*

Stella struggled to her feet. Her knees shook. The conversations around her suddenly muted, as if her head were underwater. Her tongue felt swollen; she was afraid it would shut off her airway. Stella started to pant.

"Okay, honey, have a good flight." Her father's voice sounded as if it were coming from a long way away, although he was standing next to her. He reached over to give her a hug. Stella tried to wrap her arms around him, but they were shaking too badly.

Why is this happening? What's wrong with me? The questions inside her head seemed to be coming from far away too. Stella had no answers.

"Um, Dad," she managed to mutter, "I don't feel well."

He looked at her with concern. "What do you mean, honey?"

"I can't get on this plane," she said, so softly that he had to lean in close to hear her.

"Oh, honey, you'll feel better once you get on the plane. Come on; let's go. Almost everyone else has boarded." As Robert looked more closely at Stella, he said, "Come on; buck up. What's going on with you?"

Time seemed to slow down. Stella couldn't feel her feet, and she was afraid she was going to pass out on the floor in front of all these strangers. Fear of embarrassment mingled with the other, unnamable fear. Robert took her arm. His hand felt strong, almost stern, like when she was a child and he wanted her to go somewhere she didn't want to go. Stella pulled her arm out of his grasp.

"I can't get on this plane," she said again. This time her voice was louder.

Robert stood there for a moment, just looking at her. "But you need to get on the plane," he said, sounding almost as confused as she felt. "It's going to leave."

His words meant nothing to her. Stella started to cry. Robert just stood there looking at her helplessly while she sobbed. People milled around them, but no one stopped to ask what was wrong because the airport was very busy that night. Stella was glad about that because she could not have explained.

Stella walked over to the window and looked out at the airplane. Robert sat in a seat nearby waiting for her. When the plane pulled away from the gate, she began to walk back to the check-in counter, Robert following her. "Stella, you okay?" When he asked her that question, Stella cried all the way back to the ticket counter. She tried to stop, but she couldn't until she reached the ticket counter; then she wiped her tears away with her hand.

At the check-in counter, Stella was relieved to see Sally was still there because she seemed familiar. Stella's tears stopped. Sally frowned when she saw her.

"What happened?" Sally asked.

"I couldn't get on the plane," Stella mumbled.

"Oh, that happens," Sally said, as if it were no big deal. "A lot of people just decide at the last minute that they can't get on the plane."

"But it's never happened to me before," Stella said, and she started to cry again as she moved away from the counter. Sally bent down to grab a tissue and handed it to Stella.

Robert stood at the counter waiting while Sally ignored Stella's tears and began to tell Robert about how the airlines would handle the refund and get her baggage back to her. Stella barely heard her. She was still internally asking, *Why is this happening? What's wrong with me?* And getting no answers. It was midnight, and Sally began to close up for the night.

Robert's voice penetrated Stella's fog as he chatted with Sally. "It happened to me sometimes," he said. "When you kids were little, I had to fly for business between Seattle and Washington, D.C., and I hated it. As soon as the seat belt sign went off, I'd get up and pace up and down the aisle of the plane, up and down, up and down, for nearly the whole flight—five hours! Flight anxiety is no joke," he said with a laugh.

Why hadn't Stella heard that story before? No one had ever told her that her father had suffered from flight anxiety. Maybe knowing that would have helped her feel less alone. The one constant feeling Stella remembered from her childhood was shame and embarrassment because she was so afraid much of the time. Her parents always told her when she was young that she was out of her mind, crazy, weird. They had taken her to a psychiatrist when they first moved to Seattle from the East Coast when Stella was nine because she couldn't talk much. She felt paralyzed, even though she didn't know that word then. The psychiatrist had convinced Stella that the grownups were right because when he showed her the funny black figures that represented her mind and asked her what they meant to her, all Stella could say was, "I don't know." That was her favorite phrase, "I don't know."

Paralyzing fear had been Stella's companion throughout her childhood, but after Michael, her brother, died when she was twenty-three, it had gone away. Suddenly, she wasn't afraid of anything; in fact, Stella became adventurous. She wanted to travel and see the world. She thought about becoming a flight attendant for a while, but then she decided to go fishing in Alaska on the Bering Sea. It had been a dangerous job, but Stella had loved it.

And now the paralyzing fear was back fifteen years later, suddenly and completely, as if it had never been gone. And with it came the familiar thought that she was crazy. Even though Sally had told Stella her panic was common, that didn't make her feel any better. No, Stella was too confused, too terrified—for no good reason. Crazy was the only way to explain what had just happened to her.

Stella was still crying when they got into Robert's car—a BMW that gave Robert the status he needed to compensate for standing 5'7" tall and being bald and geeky with a crooked smile. Stella continued to sob uncontrollably all the way back to her house in north Seattle. The freeway through downtown Seattle barely had traffic at two in the morning. Robert just drove and said nothing while he listened to the local news radio talking about President Clinton denying allegations of an affair with White House intern Monica Lewinsky, the biggest news story of 1998; Stella was deep in her thoughts. In spite of her constant tears, Stella's brain was busy trying to find explanations for what was happening. Maybe it was because she hadn't eaten much that day. She had brought a turkey sandwich with her to the airport, but on the way to the airport, all she could eat were little bits of turkey that she had forced down, thinking protein would be good for her nerves. Stella now realized she had been wrong about the tryptophan in the turkey helping to calm her.

Stella's brain flung up another reason, another excuse. She was nervous about the new relationship with Giovanni; that was why she couldn't take the flight. Giovanni and she had a lot in common: they both worked in the same industry; both were originally from the East Coast; both had kids the same age from previous marriages. Plus, Giovanni made Stella laugh. The differences were there too: he was nine years younger; he lived in New York and she in Seattle. But their relationship had survived a long-distance courtship for two years. They had met periodically when he came to Seattle to visit his daughter. Gabrielle, Stella's daughter, who was nine years old and lived with Stella in Seattle, liked him because Giovanni was funny. Stella loved

Giovanni and had thought seriously about marrying him.

This would have been the first time she went back to New York to visit him. Stella had planned to stay for a week and check out whether it would be a good place for Gabrielle and her to live. There was a lot riding on this visit—maybe too much?

And Stella hated leaving Gabrielle, even though Lucy was staying with her. Lucy was a nineteen-year-old vivacious college student who took care of Gabrielle every day after school. Gabrielle just loved Lucy, and Stella trusted her completely.

Stella and Gabrielle lived in a modest neighborhood in a three-bedroom, one-story home just north of Seattle. It wasn't much, but it was their home. The outside lights were still on when Robert and Stella pulled into her driveway. Her tears had finally stopped, but her face was red and blotchy. Lucy met them at the door. Stella felt more shame when Lucy saw her face.

Robert brought Stella's bag into the house and placed it by the front door as Stella followed him in. He turned around to give Stella a hug. "I'm leaving now to get some sleep. I'll call you tomorrow to see how things are going," Robert said with a quick wave to Lucy as he walked out to his car.

"What happened?" Lucy asked.

"I couldn't get on the plane," Stella said, choking up, knowing she was about to cry again.

"They wouldn't let you on the plane?" Lucy asked while she closed the door.

"No, I just couldn't get on the plane."

Lucy didn't question Stella further, but she gave Stella a strange look as she gathered up her things. Lucy had always looked up to Stella as a strong career woman and a successful single mother. As Stella stood at the window watching Lucy get into her car and drive away, she felt as though she had let her down too.

■ ■ ■

Stella felt ashamed the next morning when she had to call Giovanni and tell him why she hadn't been on the plane. The flight was scheduled to arrive in New York at 8:00 a.m., so it was four Seattle time when she made the call, hoping to catch him before he left for the airport to pick her up.

"Hello," his voice cracked.

"Hi," Stella said, looking down at the floor.

"Baby, what's going on?" he sounded confused.

The tears began rolling down Stella's face again. She was glad he couldn't see them.

"I couldn't get on the plane," she whispered.

"What do you mean you couldn't get on the plane?"

Stella's breath started coming in short gasps. "I just couldn't get on the plane."

"I bought you some flowers; I was so excited for you to meet my friends and see where I lived and worked. I don't understand why you changed your mind and don't want to be with me." Now Giovanni sounded hurt and angry.

"I didn't change my mind; I do want to be with you. I just couldn't get on the plane." As Stella spoke, she knew how weak she sounded, just repeating that same stupid phrase over and over.

"Okay," he said abruptly. "I've got to go. My daughter is calling me now."

And that was it. Stella hoped it wasn't "it" forever. But maybe it was if she couldn't come up with the reason why it had happened. Stella was falling in love with Giovanni, and she didn't know what to say to him.

She stood there with the phone in her hand for a minute, wanting to call him back, but not knowing what to say.

Finally, Stella had to tell Gabrielle. After she got off the call with Giovanni, Stella heard Gabrielle stirring in her bedroom. Stella sat on the side of Gabrielle's bed, waiting for her to open her eyes. Stella stared at the perfectly round pre-adolescent face with long blond hair neatly tucked over the left shoulder. As Gabrielle opened her eyes, she turned to look at Stella.

"Mom, what are you doing here? Where's Lucy?" Gabrielle's energy was always high, even when she first woke up. No sleepy-head for her.

"Lucy went home because I decided not to go to New York after all."

"Why? I wanted Lucy to stay with me." She sat up in her bed, folding her arms.

"Sweetie, Mom is going to stay with you. Lucy will stay with you another day."

"But why can't I stay here and you go to New York? Lucy was going to take me to the aquarium to see the turtles!"

"I'm sorry, sweetie, but I just didn't feel well enough to go to New York right now." Stella hoped Gabrielle would buy that answer, and to Stella's relief, she seemed to, although her little shoulders sagged with disappointment. Gabrielle loved Lucy. She was a good replacement for Stella working long hours, and Lucy took her to fun places. Stella told Gabrielle that she would take her to the aquarium.

The phone rang; it was Robert checking in on Stella. "Hi, Dad," she said, getting up to walk into the hall and closing the bedroom door so Gabrielle couldn't hear the conversation.

"Hi, honey. How are you feeling this morning? Did you get any sleep?"

"I'm okay, really. Sorry I kept you up so late last night," she said, looking out the window at the rain violently hitting the glass. Then, although she hesitated saying it, she added, "Dad, I didn't know that you had problems with flying."

"Honey, I just called to see how you are feeling. I need to go." Stella heard a click, so she hung up the phone. Stella and Robert didn't talk about personal things, ever. Robert wasn't the type of man who shared his feelings at all.

Confusion, suspicion, disappointment, anger—that was what not getting on the plane had brought Stella from the people who mattered to her: Robert, Lucy, Giovanni, and most importantly, Gabrielle. And she still had no idea why it had happened.

But Stella knew she had to find out.

2

"Leap, and the net will appear."

— John Burroughs

Giovanni said she didn't sound like the Stella he knew when Stella called him that evening. "Giovanni, would you come out to Seattle so we can be together?" she asked, sitting down on the kitchen chair. "I really need to see you."

"I would like to see you too, baby."

"Will you be able to come out to see me?"

He came out to Seattle for a weekend visit, a week after the aborted trip to New York. Stella paid for his ticket, feeling it was the least she could do. They hung around at Stella's house, talked a bit about their relationship, but she felt anxious the whole time. Giovanni was always affectionate with Stella. "Baby, it's so good to see you," he murmured as he stroked her hair while she lay in his arms. Stella wasn't herself with him that weekend. She was distant and the sex was nonexistent, though it had always been great up to then.

"Thank you for coming out to be with me," she said, shifting her body so she could sit up on the couch.

Giovanni stared into Stella's eyes. "Do you love me?" he asked.

Stella looked down, not knowing why she felt so disconnected from him. She said nothing. Giovanni was right; she wasn't the Stella he knew. She was the old Stella, the one she hadn't been for nearly twenty years. They had met each other two years before through a mutual friend who was having a party. It was instant attraction for both of them, and they had gone out on a few dates before Giovanni had to go back to New York. Giovanni—tall, slim, with dark wavy hair and deep brown eyes—was very attracted to Stella with her petite stature and wavy, long brown hair. Her eyes sparkled with green and brown hints, and she had a great sense of humor. They had kept up their long-distance relationship for two years, spending time together every five months. Even though Stella still loved him, she was relieved to see Giovanni go home this time, and she thought he was glad to leave too.

Stella and Giovanni talked on the phone less and less after the trip.

She knew something had changed in her and she wasn't the same person as when they had first met.

Stella called Giovanni one night to end the relationship. "Hi," she said, looking out the window at the stars.

"Hey, baby; how ya doin'? I can see the Big Dipper. Can you?" Giovanni had a strong New York accent, which she loved. Stella looked up at the night sky and saw the Big Dipper. She remembered all the long distance phone conversations they had had every night, asking each other whether they could see the Big Dipper from where they were. It was their connection.

Stella felt so ashamed of the anxiety incident. "Yes, I see the Big Dipper here too, Giovanni. I'm not feeling very good." It was quiet for a while as she stared into the sky. Stella cleared her throat. "I don't think this relationship is going to work out for me anymore."

Stella heard him move outside and heard the traffic. "Um, baby, I know you are going through something right now. I don't know how to help you. Do you think you're upset because of the plane incident?" Stella felt a knot in her stomach as she started to cry. She replied, "I don't know what I feel anymore."

She could hear him breathing. "I do love you," she said, "but I have got to figure out what is going on with me."

Giovanni was silent for a moment. "Okay, baby. I hope you figure it out, but I'm tired of waiting for you to figure it out. I think it's best also that we don't see each other anymore." The phone went dead. Stella walked over to her bed and lay down, staring out the window until she fell asleep. It took Stella a few weeks before she told Gabrielle that she and Giovanni had broken up.

■ ■ ■

Anxiety had now become part of the fabric of Stella's being, spiraling deeper into her each day. It affected her work. She held a sales job, which required her to drive, but now driving in traffic increased Stella's anxiety and caused her to break out into a cold sweat. She had to cross busy bridges over Lake Washington to visit her clients in Seattle, but her anxiety was so bad, leading to shallow breathing and sweaty palms, that she found alternate routes, which added hours to her drive time and often made her late to sales calls. She started to avoid all freeways. When she attended sales meetings, Stella sat by the door just in case she needed to exit quickly if she were starting to feel dizzy. She avoided elevators and took the stairs—even in high-rise office buildings. These inconveniences were better than dealing with the panic attacks of feeling like she was going to have a heart attack or die.

Anxiety also bled into her personal life. Gabrielle's dad, Ashton, lived on an island in Puget Sound. He had remarried and had more kids. It was a quick fifteen-minute trip by ferry to Ashton's house, but Stella couldn't get on a ferry anymore. On Ashton's visitation weekends, she had to meet him at the ferry dock instead, which didn't make him happy because he had to pay extra fare to ride the boat, or she would have to drive around the Sound, an extra hundred miles. Stella withdrew from her family and friends. She couldn't sleep through the night. She ate little; food tasted like sawdust. She didn't want to leave her house. All the normal conditions of life had turned into enemies. Any outside influence like socializing sent Stella plunging into an anxiety attack. Her skin felt like it had been turned inside out.

They say you can get used to anything, and Stella thought this was true because she lived in this skin-shriveling anxiety for about three or four years before she finally had enough of feeling awful. Stella kept her anxiety a secret from her friends, and she used the excuse that she was tired whenever they wanted to visit with her.

Gabrielle showed her concern by hugs. Stella wanted the anxiety to go away quickly, so she made an appointment with her GP, Dr. Brown, to see whether she could help her. Stella drove all the back roads to her doctor's appointment. The nurse took her to a private room and took out a green gown for Stella to wear after she undressed. The nurse left the room while Stella put on the gown. Then Stella sat patiently waiting for her doctor in the examining room. She was looking at a magazine when the door opened.

"Hi, Stella," said Dr. Brown as she looked at Stella's chart.

"Hi," Stella said as she folded the magazine and laid it on the chair.

Once they were inside her office, Dr. Brown asked Stella to sit on the examination table.

"I understand you are suffering some anxiety," she said while she poked around Stella's lymph nodes.

"Yes, I wasn't able to get on an airplane. I guess I had a panic attack."

"Have you ever had a panic attack getting on an airplane before?" asked Dr. Brown, leaning against the counter.

"No, never."

Dr. Brown looked at Stella for a moment. Then she said, "I know a psychiatrist in Seattle, Herman Smith, who deals with anxiety issues. If you like, I could make a referral to him for you."

Stella took the referral and called Dr. Smith's office the next day.

■ ■ ■

Dr. Smith's office was in a high-rise with elevators, which was a bad start because Stella had anxiety about getting on elevators. In the lobby, she pushed the button for the elevator. When the door opened, she stepped into the elevator and pushed the twelfth floor button. She closed her eyes the whole time and tried to breathe slowly. As soon as Stella walked into Dr. Smith's office, she was reminded of the time her parents took her to see a psychiatrist when she was ten. Dr. Smith didn't show her a bunch of weird-looking black and white pictures like the last psychiatrist had, but his voice was the same—a monotone that sounded like a recording.

"Why are you here?" Dr. Smith asked, looking down at the pad of paper with pen in hand.

"I have anxiety attacks and can't get on an airplane."

Dr. Smith looked up at Stella and said, "When did these attacks start?"

Stella paused for a minute before she answered.

"I want to find out why this is happening." She felt like she was having déjà vu because this wasn't the first time she had experienced anxiety episodes, but those had eventually gone away. Why were these new and stronger anxiety attacks not going away, but lasting for years?

Dr. Smith listened to Stella without comment. Stella explained how she wasn't able to drive in traffic and told him about the airplane incident when she'd first had a panic attack. At the end of the hour, Dr. Smith wrote her a prescription for an anti-depressant that he said would help. Then he asked that she call him in a few weeks to schedule a follow-up appointment. Stella reached out and took the piece of paper. She didn't argue with him, but she did feel let down.

"I really want to understand why I feel this way. I don't want to mask the symptoms with an anti-depressant," she said, walking to the door.

"This prescription will help with the panic," he repeated, while Stella walked out of the office. Stella went home and took the pill. The psychiatrist told her to give it a few weeks, but after three days, her anxiety was worse. She developed more episodes of stomach aches, and she couldn't sit still. Stella stopped taking the medication and never called him again. She didn't even let her GP know. Instead, she called her astrologer, Philip.

Philip had been an intermittent part of Stella's life for fifteen years since he'd done a reading for her that was right on in every detail. Stella had met Philip through her friend, Stacy. She and Stacy had known each other for thirty years, since Stella moved out to Seattle when she was nine years old. Stella initially met Philip in Seattle and had a reading in his home, but after he moved down to Arizona, Stella had had her readings by phone every few years. Once, at the end of a reading, he had said, "When we're done here, I want you to go down to your beach. You're going to find a beautiful eagle feather, a gift for you." Stella didn't know what the gift meant, but when she went down to the beach in front of her home, there it was—an eagle feather lying on a piece of driftwood.

Gabrielle and Stella lived in a small beach community surrounded by houses that had a seaside feel. From their small, yellow, two-bedroom loft house, they would often walk down to the beach and look for special rocks. Stella was very isolated from her parents and friends, so she focused most of her time on parenting her daughter.

Stella was often confused by the stories Philip told from Native American traditions. They were stories full of myths from the Hopi tribe that she had never heard of. Stella also wasn't too good at following his advice, which was always the same every reading: She needed to do some serious healing work. She didn't know what he meant by "healing work."

Stella made an appointment with Philip, and the day of the call, she felt relaxed and calm for once. She knew she would have to tell him what was going on in her life, but Stella decided not to disclose the struggles she was having with anxiety. She felt ashamed and was too embarrassed to tell anyone, which was why she had kept her attacks a secret for years, ever since the incident at the airport. None of her friends or family knew about the airport scene, except for Robert. As far as Lucy, Gabrielle's babysitter, knew, it had been just a one-time thing.

"Hey, Stella," Philip greeted her when the call began. "What do you want out of the reading today?"

Stella just said she had quit her sales job and started working part-time at a local bookstore.

"Well," Philip replied, "you're coming into some big changes, emotionally."

"What do you mean?" she asked, looking out the window.

He started out with where Stella's stars were and how they were aligned, but the reading came out exactly like all the others—she really needed to do some serious healing work.

Philip's deep, calm voice went on. "You will find someone to help you with the healing you need to do. A shaman or a shaman-like person like you, but with more experience," he went on. "You'll do some incredible healing work with this person."

Stella didn't know what he meant, so she asked, "Am I a shaman?"

"Well, are you?"

Stella sat for moment and didn't say anything. She wasn't sure what a shaman was, and what did he mean by 'more experience' than her? Was she supposed to find someone like her? "Philip, what is a shaman?"

"It's a person who helps in the healing process of the soul and is connected to the spiritual realm," Philip replied. "Why don't you research and learn more about the role a shaman plays for someone who is suffering and needs some help healing?"

Stella felt desperate. Philip had seen through her, just like he always did. She was hanging on to the last thread at the end of her rope. She needed help, she wanted help, but how could she find help when she didn't know where to look? She had isolated herself from her family and friends because she felt so ashamed about the anxiety.

Stella didn't know that people don't need to "look" for what Philip called shamans—at least not "look" in the aggressive, take-charge way people usually mean. They simply showed up in your life, and if you were open, you would recognize them.

After Philip's reading, Stella called Robert to see how he was doing. She hadn't spoken to him for a few months since the incident at the airport, which was pretty common between them.

"Hi, Dad. How are you doing?"

"Hello, honey. I'm just getting ready to fix dinner. How are you?"

"I'm getting ready to fix Gabrielle and me some dinner. I'm making some tacos tonight."

"Oh, that sounds good. How are you feeling, honey?"

"I'm doing good, Dad. I just wanted to touch base and see how things are going," she said, pulling a pan out of the cupboard.

"Things are good," Robert said. They chit-chatted for five minutes about the weather and the news; then they hung up.

After the phone call, Stella started cooking dinner. As she waited for the taco meat to brown, she thought about how she still felt confused about how to find this person who was going to help her.

■ ■ ■

Weeks passed. No shaman appeared for Stella, but her anxiety attacks continued. She was looking for some hope. Her chiropractor referred her to a massage therapist, named Wendy, for the tension in her neck. Stella felt at ease as soon as she walked into Wendy's massage room, which was about the size of a walk-in closet and almost like a warm and cozy cave. Wendy's smile was warm too, and her hands were kind. Stella melted away under them, and the massage also helped with the tightness in her chest and to relax her mind. Stella, however, didn't mention her anxiety to Wendy since she had just met her.

After the massage, as Stella was getting dressed, she saw a sign on the wall about Wendy's "Energy Work." When Stella asked her what energy work was, Wendy smiled and said, "I work with the chakras." Stella had heard of chakra work, but she had never had it done. She knew the chakras came from Eastern spiritual beliefs and were spinning vortexes of energy located in the body. *Is a chakra worker a kind of shaman?* Stella wondered. *Could Wendy be the person Philip told me I'd find?* That night, Stella felt calm and relaxed in her body, and she slept well.

Wendy and Stella worked together twice more, and it helped with some of the pain in Stella's neck, but her secret anxiety attacks were still causing havoc in her life. She would wake up at one in the morning, unable to breathe, feeling light-headed, and with her stomach hurting. She _ime visiting her friends and family, and Gabrielle was spending a lot of time in her bedroom.

One day during a session, Wendy began telling Stella about a woman named Rachel who had helped Wendy's son when he was just a toddler.

"Why did your son need to see Rachel?" Stella asked while sitting in the chair.

Wendy looked over at Stella while she placed a pillow on the massage table. "He'd had a traumatic birth, so Rachel helped him overcome some issues with fear. Her expertise is in working with people with pre-natal shock and trauma."

"Does she only work with children?" Stella asked, taking her jacket off.

"No," Wendy replied. "Rachel works with adults too, but she doesn't work with everyone. In fact, she doesn't even advertise. She doesn't need to. When people are ready for her, they just find her."

Like a shaman, Stella thought.

After the massage, Stella got dressed, asked Wendy for Rachel's number, and scheduled an energy healing with Wendy. Stella went home and placed Rachel's number on her bedside table.

The following week, Stella went to her first chakra session with Wendy. She was a bit nervous, but for some reason, she felt excited too. She relaxed into the massage table, adjusting her jeans and fleece jacket to be more comfortable; the room was warm and dark, except for a few candles. Wendy lit some sage to cleanse the room and pulled out a pendulum, which she said measures the chakras and how they are spinning, if at all.

"Close your eyes; you don't need to watch the session; you can just pay attention to what happens," Wendy said, holding onto Stella's feet. Wendy's hands were very warm, which felt good on Stella's cold feet. Other than a few twinges and some grumbling coming from her stomach, Stella found the session very relaxing. When Wendy placed her hands on the heart area, Stella felt a surge of heat penetrate her whole chest cavity, and then she felt a weight lifted. It helped Stella release some of the tightness she always felt in her chest when she had anxiety. Afterwards, Wendy left the room for a minute while Stella became more aware of her surroundings. Then Wendy reentered the room to discuss the session with Stella.

"Most of your chakras were shut down, but the seventh and fifth chakras were spinning backwards, so I balanced them out and got them all back on the right track," she said. Wendy explained how the chakras spin in a clockwise direction and are shaped like a spinning fan. Every chakra spins at its own frequency, ensuring that the life force is being drawn into the body to keep it balanced.

Stella just lay there, listening to Wendy explain the chakras' components and also what guides were in the room. "You must have eagle as some kind of totem because there was a very strong eagle energy in the room as well as jaguar energy."

"What I found interesting was your fourth chakra, the heart," Wendy further explained. "It wasn't spinning vibrantly, but it wasn't shut down either. The heart chakra represents love. It is the core of the human energy field and works with the upper and lower chakras to determine our health and strength. Have you called Rachel yet?"

"No, not yet," Stella confessed.

"This could be the indicator that you are ready to do your work, your serious work," Wendy said. "Your guides are clapping. You've an audience of love and support in the universe to encourage you to do this level of work."

"I know. I really want to tackle my demons and be the best mom

I can be for Gabrielle. I think Rachel could help me get there," Stella said with conviction.

"Go for it. You deserve happiness, peace, and love, Stella."

"Thank you," said Stella, smiling.

"Thank you for the lovely session," Wendy replied. "I really enjoy this work and would like to work with you again soon."

Stella paid Wendy and drove home, noticing that the trees were greener and the cherry blossoms were in full bloom. It was a nice sunny spring day, and she didn't have to pick up Gabrielle from school for a few hours, so she drove into the garage and walked through the family room to the kitchen. She opened the refrigerator and poured herself some cold water. She took her jacket off and draped it over the dining room chair, and she walked into her bedroom where the sun shone brightly on the bed. She closed her blinds down a bit to block the sun and lay down on the bed to take a little nap.

■ ■ ■

When Stella woke up, she went into the family room where the computer was and researched information about the heart chakra. She found a site where she read about how the heart is central to unconditional love for self and others. When people have a balance in their lives through this chakra, they are healthy and strong. This chakra drives the energy of emotional development. Life crises that have issues with love at the core, like divorce, death of a loved one, abandonment, and abuse, can cause illness. It is important that individuals heal themselves emotionally. Confronting the demons within their psyches and healing the wounded children within them all starts with loving themselves. If unhealed, their wounds keep them in the past. Forgiveness and self-love allow them to pardon people in their past so the wounds can no longer damage them. With this forgiveness, and by releasing their old attachments, individuals can move out of their childlike relationship with the Divine into a spiritual maturity where they can act out of unconditional love and compassion.

It takes great effort to commit oneself to healing all the way to the source of the pain. It takes great courage to go inside, excavate, and understand the wounds, and to observe how you have used them in your life to control the people around you and even yourself. This understanding allows the psyche to release the victimhood and live in appreciation and forgiveness.

Stella went into her bedroom and took Rachel's number off her nightstand. She looked at it for a moment. *Could this woman really help me heal? I have had so much therapy, and I am still anxious and lost; this has to work. I don't know what else to do.* Stella walked over to her cell phone and started dialing Rachel's number.

"You've reached Rachel. Leave a message and please leave me your phone number." Rachel's voice was medium-toned and calming, which put Stella at ease. "Hi, Rachel. My name is Stella. Wendy referred me to you," she said and left her phone number. *Okay,* Stella thought as she hung up the phone, *that was the hard part, maybe.*

Stella's stomach started to hurt, and she needed to pick up Gabrielle from school so she motioned to Tiger, who was their two-year-old family dog, a golden retriever Gabrielle had picked out, to come for a ride in the car. He loved riding in the car with the window down. The song "Drops of Jupiter" by Train was playing on the radio, and once Stella started driving toward the school to pick up Gabrielle, she noticed the pit in her stomach had disappeared. Stella felt better if Tiger and Gabrielle were near when she had anxiety. On the way home, Stella stopped at the grocery store and bought her and Gabrielle a pizza to eat while they watched one of their favorite movies, *The Lion King.*

Later that evening, the phone rang.

"Hello," Stella answered.

"Hi, is this Stella?"

"Yes, this is," she said with a smile.

"This is Rachel. Let's schedule a time for you to come and see me," she said. They chatted for a bit about why Stella wanted to see her while they nailed down a day and time.

"I am really excited to meet you and see if we can work together," Rachel said. She explained how to get to her house. "Are you familiar with Seattle?" Stella knew that area well, so Rachel only had to give her instructions on where to park. "I have a place in front of my house next to a six-foot fence. Go ahead and park there." Stella wrote down the directions. "First, you ring the bell; then enter the studio and place your shoes on the carpet next to the wicker chair."

"Okay, I have the directions written down and I'll see you in a week," Stella said, hanging up. She felt scared and lonely. What if Rachel couldn't help with her anxiety? She felt really weak and vulnerable and was hanging on a thread. She had nowhere else to turn. She had a week to prepare or cancel the session.

3

"Only when we are brave enough to explore the Darkness
will we Discover the infinite Power of our Light."

— Brene Brown

Stella couldn't see Rachel's house from the street, although she lived in an old neighborhood in Seattle with brick Tudor homes and neighbors all around. There was a six-foot fence wrapped around both sides of the house, and as Stella pulled open the gate, she was blanketed by grape vines stretching over a wooden trellis leading to the cottage in back of the house. Prolific tomato plants grew along the path, their reddening globes swelling with juice. Tibetan bells hung on the porch column of the cottage. This was Rachel's studio where she did her work. Stella didn't know yet what that work would be since Rachel hadn't gone into detail about it during their phone conversation.

Stella rang the bells as directed, alerting Rachel to her presence. She took off her shoes, also as directed, by a handwritten sign posted on the clear glass French door. Entering the room, she placed her shoes on a small brown rug next to the door and stood for a minute looking around.

The ceilings were high, with a wood fan slowly rotating the air, which had a natural clean smell. Off to the side by the door was a small, faded green wicker chair, not big enough for an adult to sit on—perhaps it was for a child. Over the chair was an orange and white afghan. It looked soft, fluffy like a baby's blanket. In a corner across from the door was a cast iron black stove to heat the room, and next to the stove, a futon mattress lay on the floor, covered with many pillows and blankets. A small side table on the stove's other side held little trinkets and art objects. Off to the right was a massage table draped with a Mexican wool blanket, colorful in turquoise, black, and yellow. Just above the massage table were hooks, one holding a little boy's jean jacket and another holding a stethoscope. A bookshelf against the other wall was filled with books, pictures, dolls, and seashells.

The last thing Stella noticed was the big green beanbag chair, sitting right in the room's center. Once she did, it dominated the room, and she wondered how she had managed to miss it before. Stella felt her anxiety fluttering in her stomach. She thought about sitting on the beanbag, but then she thought it must be where Rachel sat during the sessions with clients, so Stella sat on the futon mattress and waited until she heard footsteps coming down the path, walking up the steps and across the porch to the door. While Stella waited for Rachel, she thought about the drive to Rachel's house. She had been anxious about having to cross a bridge, not knowing how the therapy would be for her, and whether it would even help.

A short, fifty-ish woman with shoulder-length gray hair entered the room. She smiled at Stella; her smile was wide and genuine, as if Stella were the person she most wanted to see right then. She took her hand.

"I'm Rachel," she said. "I am so happy to meet you." Her voice was soft, yet clear and penetrating. Letting go of Stella's hand, she plumped down in the bag chair. *Thank God I didn't sit in it*, Stella thought. Stella had looked up the name Rachel. She was very interested in the meaning of names. The definition was from the Bible, meaning, "ewe" or "little lamb." In the Bible, Rachel had been a beautiful and cherished wife of Jacob, and the mother of Joseph and Benjamin.

Stella's anxiety increased and her mouth became dry. Her heart started palpitating. She had been in therapy before, but it felt different now. This wasn't an office; there weren't any desks or chairs to sit in while Stella discussed her problems. *Maybe this form of therapy isn't for me*, she thought; then she answered herself immediately. *The other forms didn't work either, did they?* And she knew her anxiety was getting more and more out of control, to the point where her normal life had vanished. She'd had to leave her sales job; she was always anxious when she left the house by herself and it was hard for her to be alone at any time. She had to be willing to try anything. Had to.

While Stella had this internal dialogue sitting on the futon, Rachel spoke softly. "Stella why are you here?"

"Well, I am afraid and anxious all the time," Stella said while Rachel busily gathered objects from the room, placing them on the floor next to her. "I have always felt this way since I can remember, but it seems like the apprehension is getting worse." She watched Rachel spread a white blanket on the floor, big enough for a person to lie down upon.

On top of this, Rachel arranged a shawl that had a deep eggplant-color background with a delicate design in lighter purple woven through it. It had long slender fringes, making her arrangement look like waving fronds of purple seaweed in a white ocean.

"Oh, that looks good," Rachel said.

As Rachel wandered around the room, she explained how she was building a space for Stella, and she continued to gather up items like a doll and a pink flower; then she went outside and took a piece of bark off her cedar tree. Back inside she picked up a purple cord, like something used to tie back curtains. She placed the objects around the perimeter of the eggplant shawl.

"Okay; that's good," she said.

Stella sat on the futon and stared at the space Rachel had created. She didn't get it. *This is weird,* she thought. *What does she want from me?* Rachel was silent, gazing at her creation on the floor. Was she meditating?

After what seemed like a long time, but was probably just a minute or two, Rachel smiled and Stella heard her warm soft voice say, "This is your space. I've created it just for you, a womb if you like. When you are ready, you can enter it."

Stella immediately froze. Her arms and legs felt like they belonged to a robot. Not knowing what else to do, she got up and placed herself inside the circular space on the floor. She lay down on the purple shawl. Her head and her toes lay on the white blanket.

It was quiet, but Stella did not feel peaceful. She felt uncomfortable; she was probably doing this—whatever *this* was—wrong. Rachel wasn't saying anything, so Stella just lay there. She closed her eyes. After a while, she had a vision—she guessed it was a vision; she didn't know what else to call it. Stella was a bird, a big bird like an eagle with a huge wingspan. She was flying, soaring over the mountains. She felt the lift of the wind. She could see rivers below; she even saw ripples on the rivers and fish in the depths—her eyesight was that keen. Stella perched on top of a mountain just to look around, and then she heard a voice.

"Where are you?"

"Huh?" Stella asked. She was herself again. The eagle was gone.

"Where did you go?" It was Rachel's voice. Stella didn't answer because she didn't know what to say.

"Are you comfortable in this womb?"

"Not really."

"You can get out if you want to." Rachel's voice was calm, peaceful, like an angel's voice.

Stella got up and went back to the futon. They sat in silence for a few minutes, and then Rachel asked Stella to describe her experience.

"Well, I felt like a bird flying around," Stella said.

"Was this a new experience for you?"

"No, when I was younger, I would dream about being a bird, but I haven't had those dreams in a long time."

"That was your way of detaching from your environment," Rachel said matter-of-factly.

"Oh, okay," Stella said, not really understanding what it meant. Still, she felt tears start to build in her eyes. But Stella couldn't allow herself to cry because she was afraid she wouldn't stop. She had just met Rachel, and she couldn't cry in front of someone she had just met. She shifted around on the futon. She didn't want to talk about flying anymore.

Rachel said nothing for a while. They just sat there in silence. Stella heard the birds chirping outside and the wind blowing through the trees. It was springtime and the buds on the grapevines were starting to unfurl into leaves; she gazed at them through the glass door. They were that pure spring green, so fresh, so new.

"We're almost done for today," Rachel said. "Here is what I picked up. I think your mom probably drank alcohol when she was pregnant with you. She didn't want to be pregnant. She didn't want another baby at that time. That's why she drank.

"You know, Stella, not being wanted is one of the deepest wounds a person can have. This wound is responsible for your loneliness in this world, and it's also responsible for your toughness, your ability to survive. You had to be tough to survive in your mom's womb."

As Rachel talked, a picture rose in Stella's mind. She saw her mother, Shirley, sitting at the kitchen table, wearing a camel-colored dress and smoking a cigarette. A brownish drink in what Stella thought was called a "lowball" cocktail glass was in front of her. Her rounded belly pushed against the table.

Stella wanted to cry; she could feel the tears pushing their way forward, but she clamped down hard inside so she wouldn't. It was hard for Stella to cry in front of people she didn't know.

"It's okay," said Rachel. "You'll cry when you cry. You will learn to let go of all this grief. This is the start of your healing work. You will replace all your old beliefs with new ones."

Somehow, Stella had held the grief in, but she knew she was on her way. And underneath the grief was an odd sense of relief—she wasn't crazy, she wasn't wrong; everything she had felt her whole life was true: the feeling of being a burden, abandoned, not important, not loved. It was all true because her parents had not wanted her. They still didn't.

Stella got up to go. Rachel picked up the eggplant-colored shawl from the floor and handed it to her. "This represents a womb," she said. "It is yours now." Then she gave Stella the purple cord. "This is our connection to each other," she said. "Wear it whenever you feel anxious, and bring it to our next session."

"Thank you," said Stella as Rachel hugged her goodbye.

Stella walked out the gate onto the street and back to her car. Her tears finally began to fall as she sat in her car. She thought how unusual this form of therapy was. Stella had never experienced anything like it before. She felt comfortable with Rachel and was optimistic.

On her drive home, Stella passed by her old high school and saw that it was being torn down. She smiled and thought, *The death of an old script!*

Stella didn't stop crying until she picked up Gabrielle from school. The eggplant shawl was around her neck, and the purple cord was tucked in her purse. Stella wasn't sure what to make of these items that Rachel had given her. She waited in the car to pick up Gabrielle as her head began to swirl. She felt very anxious immediately, so she pulled the cord out of her purse to hold on to it. She felt stupid sitting in line with all the other parents holding on to that piece of fabric to try to end her apprehension, so she placed it between her legs on the seat, just in case Gabrielle surprised her by sneaking up alongside the car. Stella continued to hold on to the cord for dear life as she breathed and tried to take her mind off the pit in her stomach and her dizziness. Suddenly, Gabrielle opened the door.

"Hi, Mom."

"Hi, honey; how was school today?" Stella asked, starting the car.

"Well, my friend Alex and I teamed up today for a science project," she said, fastening her seatbelt.

"What did you learn in school today?" Stella asked, pulling out onto the street.

"Just how to construct the volcano Alex and me are making." Gabrielle looked out the window while they drove home. Even if they didn't say much else, having Gabrielle with her helped with the anxiety, and soon Stella forgot she had had an anxiety attack.

■ ■ ■

It was time for bed, so Stella went to say goodnight to Gabrielle. Gabrielle loved it when Stella rubbed her back so she could fall asleep. Stella thought about the session with Rachel and how different it was compared to the other forms of therapy she'd had in the past. *I have come to my last piece of rope. I'm hanging on for dear life. I don't have any other tools in my arsenal to heal this anxiety. This time it has to work.* Stella was so tired from the day and especially from the anxiety attack that she went to bed earlier than usual. She laid the purple shawl over her pillow for closeness and wrapped the cord around her waist. It went around three times before she could tie off the ends because she had lost more weight from the anxiety.

This is my chance to change the way I mother Gabrielle, she thought. Ashton and she had divorced when Gabrielle was three years old. It was very important for her to be a good mom to Gabrielle and want more for her than she ever got from her mother. She saw the similarities from her past behavior with Gabrielle that indicated wounds from her own childhood; she wanted to change the course of parenting so Gabrielle didn't have to suffer from all the generations before her with the abuse, neglect, and lack of love and respect that Stella had been subjected to by her mother. She wanted to confront her truth and heal.

Stella turned off her light and tried to fall asleep. She started feeling a pit in her stomach. It was heavy and felt like a knife cutting the inner layer. It was a very familiar feeling, a constant companion for most of her life. She knew it was a symptom of anxiety. Stella got up to search the house for Tiger and brought him into her room so she could cuddle with him. Stella had learned to soothe herself as a child by cuddling with her family's dog. Even as an adult, it always brought so much relief from the anxiety. Tiger brought a sense of safety to her, helping with the loneliness and the stomach aches that came with it.

Stella had done some research on the positive effects an animal can have on anxiety, and by having Tiger as a family pet, she felt very safe. She felt all the love Tiger had for her, and having him close to her to help calm her anxiety and ease her loneliness.

Stella lay there for a bit, going over the day and how she had seen her old high school being torn down. She knew it was probably just a coincidence, but it felt symbolic to her. She eventually fell asleep with the cord wrapped around her waist, the eggplant shawl draped on her pillow, and Tiger snuggled next to her.

4

"Without memories of childhood, it is as if you were doomed
to drag a big box around with you, though you don't know
what's in it. And the older you get, the heavier it becomes,
and the more impatient you are to finally open the thing."

— Jurek Becker

Stella wore her purple cord all day every day for the next
week. After all, Rachel said to wear it when she felt anxious, and that was nearly always. Stella wrapped the cord
around her waist, hidden under her pants. Stella tied it in a knot close
to her belly button where she could feel its reassuring presence. Most
of the time, she felt more secure and calm whenever she wore the cord.
Then she didn't feel alone.

■　■　■

The day before Stella's next appointment with Rachel was a busy one. She hadn't seen Rachel in a week. She spent time with Gabrielle after she picked her up from school, attending her soccer match and running to Costco to buy dinner since she didn't have time to cook.

Stella went to bed early, but when she took off her clothes, she discovered that her cord was gone! Panic rushed through her. Where could it be? She looked all over the house and checked her car, but no cord. She retraced the day in her head—somehow, it must have fallen off when she was at Costco; it must have come untied and slithered down her leg and out through the bottom of her pants. With that thought, Stella's panic was replaced by embarrassment; she saw herself with the purple cord trailing behind her as she walked through Costco, looking ridiculous as the other shoppers gawked.

Stella tried to shrug off both the panic and the embarrassment by laughing at the incident, telling herself it didn't matter; it was just a string of material. By the time she got to Rachel's the next day, the purple cord incident was stowed safely away in the back of her mind, where Stella often put things she didn't want to remember.

Instead, Stella talked to Rachel about how she wanted to break the cycle of the past so Gabrielle could have a better childhood than she'd had.

"My grandmother neglected my mom, and Lynn neglected her daughter, so it's very important to me to be Gabrielle's mom, a healthy mom," Stella said.

"I see a young girl always present with you," Rachel replied. "You love her very much. Your ability to love is a miracle because you received little of it when you were young—where do you think you got this ability to love?"

Tears welled up as Stella thought about how much she loved Gabrielle and how lucky she was to be her mom. If she could love her daughter so much, then the ability to love was a part of Stella, and Rachel was going to help her reclaim it so Stella could love herself too. But all Stella said was, "I thank God every day that I get to be Gabrielle's mom."

Rachel explained to Stella that when children are born, what they need most is love from their parents, all the basic needs like affection, care, protection, attention, kindness, and communication. If these needs aren't met, the child will have a lifelong yearning to fulfill these vital requirements, which will show up in that child's relationships with other people. The void is there and ready to be filled. Stella knew she had that void, and so did her sister Lynn, because of how their mother had often neglected them.

Stella didn't have a relationship with Lynn because she lived a live full of drugs—probably her way of trying to fill that void. Lynn was five years older than Stella and had lived in Nevada since she was eighteen. Shirley, Stella's mom, had gotten pregnant with Lynn nearly three years before she met Robert. Shirley had come from a Southern Baptist family and lived with her grandparents. When she became pregnant, her grandmother threw her out of the house because she was just like her mother and they didn't want to raise her bastard child. Shirley moved to New York when Lynn was two years old, and she met Robert three months later at the grocery store. Shirley looked like a model; she was tall and walked with a swag that captured Robert's attention. He was a financial advisor at a prestigious firm right in the heart of New York City. They married soon after their first date. Lynn had olive skin with coal black hair so she didn't look like Robert at all, but that was okay with Shirley; she needed someone to support her and Lynn.

Stella didn't want Gabrielle or herself around Lynn's behavior. Stella also had a hard time being around her mom, Shirley, because her anxiety increased with each visit. Thankfully, now Stella had Rachel;

she knew she would not leave her alone as she began her journey toward healing.

Rachel and Stella agreed that Stella needed to cut the cords that bound her to her dysfunctional family. "To do that you first have to accept them as yours and see your family as they really are," Rachel said. "This is the work of healing. First you put your protection in place, and then you go on a journey to the real world that lives just under what we show on the surface."

Stella instinctively knew that Rachel was the person who could accept her for what she was, who could give her protection, respect, sympathy, and the understanding she needed to realize how she became what she was. And with this guidance, Stella could begin to experience love for the child she once was. As Rachel spoke, Stella began to feel almost as if she had been adopted by Rachel. She felt her mothering warmth and sensed that she could reveal to her all the horror and indignation that arose when her emotions exposed themselves to her. She thought about how her inner little girl agonized, what she went through all alone, fearing impending danger. *Rachel's got me and my little girl*, Stella thought, *and we will not be ignored anymore.*

As the session progressed, Rachel prayed that she could shed Stella's symptoms of anxiety, help free her from depression, and help her regain happiness in her life. She said she wanted to unshackle Stella's condition of constant exhaustion and replace the repression of energy in Stella's body—from denying or playing down her memories and the strong emotions hidden in her body—so she could experience a restoration of spirit in the light of her own truth.

After Rachel said all this, Stella looked at her and said, "I have a memory of a matrix right now that is dark and lonely like a steel cage suffocating every breath. I feel like I'm suspended in air surrounded by fluids that are poisoning my very being. I'm afraid to move, to make myself noticed. It's better that I stay frozen; that way maybe I could survive the term to remain in this space."

Rachel asked Stella whether she would like to be born again. At first, Stella wasn't sure what she meant. Rachel meant it literally. They took a journey together, a journey in their minds that she narrated. They lived in a remote Cherokee village, a long time ago. Rachel was heavily pregnant with Stella. For the birth, they traveled by canoe to the birthing place, where they labored together and Stella was born. Was it a past-life experience? Did it happen in some kind of alternate universe? Did Rachel just make it up? Stella didn't know—Rachel said it didn't matter.

"There are all kinds of realities, many different forms of energy," Rachel said. "Some professionals say a child's emotional development starts in the womb around the sixth month of pregnancy. After birth, if basic needs are met in a rather consistent manner, then the child learns to love, trust, feel secure, and gain a sense of confidence and self-worth."

Stella opened her eyes and stared at Rachel. "That was so cool. I feel like I get a second chance with my life and how I will be raised. I know that sounds weird, but I get to start over with my birth so I can proceed with my life now."

"No, it's not weird, Stella. You do get a second chance, and working with me will give you a different perspective on what you didn't receive as a child and how you can heal those wounds."

"Where's your cord?" Rachel then asked, catching Stella by surprise.

"Um…I lost it," she stuttered, startled by the abrupt change of topic.

"When did you lose it?"

"Just yesterday."

"Why didn't you call me?"

"I don't know." Stella felt ashamed, like she had done something wrong or disappointed Rachel. She didn't want to disappoint her and make her mad at her, but she tried to convince herself that the cord and Rachel's opinion didn't matter. *Who cares?*

Rachel just looked at her for a moment. "Do you have anything to do after this appointment?"

Stella looked up at her. "I need to pick up Gabrielle at 3 p.m."

"Okay then," Rachel said briskly. "There's a fabric store not too far from here where you can get another cord. Do you know where the fabric store is?"

"Uh, no."

"That's okay; you just follow me—it's just across the Ballard Bridge. I'll go get my purse and meet you in the driveway."

Stella hadn't told Rachel her little secret about being afraid to drive in traffic, cross bridges, or go anywhere unfamiliar. She wasn't used to talking about her fears to anyone. She was still ashamed and embarrassed by all these stupid fears she had; she didn't want anyone to know about them because she didn't want to be judged. So although Stella was afraid, she got in her car and followed Rachel. When they came to a stop sign, Stella expected Rachel to go straight, but Rachel turned left and soon disappeared in the traffic. Stella's anxiety started to build. Her hands gripped the steering wheel tightly, and she tried to breathe slowly so she wouldn't hyperventilate. After a moment, Stella recognized Rachel's car up ahead. She didn't take her eyes off Rachel's car as they worked their way onto the Ballard Bridge. Stella tried not to think about being on a bridge. She turned on the radio and found a song she really liked to drown out her thoughts and fears.

Finally, they pulled into the fabric store parking lot. Stella got out of her car and continued to follow after Rachel, who seemed to know right where she was going. They went straight to the aisle where all the cords were. There were lots of different colors, but they didn't see any purple ones.

"Maybe the purple ones are in a special place," Rachel said. "Let's find someone to help us." She went off looking for someone to help. Stella followed closely behind her. The helper told them that those were the only colors they had, so they went back to the cord aisle. Stella just followed along, amazed that Rachel was going through all this trouble just to find her a cord.

"What color do you want for your cord?" she asked her.

Stella still couldn't believe that Rachel was spending so much time on this. As she looked at the cords, she became overcome by a feeling she couldn't name—a feeling that sat deep in her heart. Stella's body tensed up as the feeling spread; she didn't want to lose control, but then she saw a beautiful pink cord, not an intense pink, but one that reflected softness and love.

"This is the color I want," she said, reaching out for it.

"Okay," Rachel said.

"How many times do you wrap this around?" she asked.

"Three times."

Rachel took the spool off the shelf and asked Stella to hold the container while she wrapped the cord three times around Stella's waist to measure it, and she pulled off some extra from the spool so they would have enough material to tie it. The helper cut what they needed, and then they went up to the register to pay for it. Rachel handed the clerk the string of cord. While they were in line, Stella reached in her purse for her wallet, but Rachel placed her hand on Stella's arm and said, "I'm buying this. It's my gift to you."

"Oh, no, that's all right; I'll buy it," Stella said, feeling uncomfortable.

Stella earned enough money to pay for Rachel's fee; it was very reasonable.

"I'm buying this for you; nothing else to say," Rachel said serenely, and she smiled at the check-out person as she handed over her money.

Stella just stood there feeling confused. *Why is she doing this for me? I barely know her, and she is spending her money for this cord that I'm going to wear.* Stella couldn't believe that someone would care for her that much—to go to this length just to make sure she had her cord.

"Thank you, Rachel."

They walked out to their cars in the parking lot. Then Rachel gave Stella a big hug. "This is our connection to each other," she said. "When you get home, be sure to burn both ends to fuse them so they don't unravel." And she got into her car and drove off.

Stella sat in her car and began to cry. It didn't take long before she wiped away the tears and started the car to head home. After she burned the ends of the pink cord, she wrote in her journal about the day. Stella had kept a journal for the last ten years. Most of the contents were affirmations she had collected over the years, thoughts on past boyfriends, and some writings on her past therapy experiences.

Rachel didn't have to be so kind to me. Therapists don't take clients to the store and buy something for them. They just don't. But she isn't just any therapist, is she? She is the shaman-like person Philip told me I would find—the person who would help me heal. Rachel is more than a therapist; more even than a shaman. She is my re-mother. She is giving me a second chance at being mothered, something I have never had before. And I have a pink cord to prove it. It's symbolic.

The pink cord that attached Stella to Rachel was real in many ways other than their ordinary reality. It was not just a length of pink fabric, but a string of loving energy. Stella had a new birth memory.

5

"The wound is the place where the light enters you."

— Rumi

Stella had been working with Rachel every week for the last year. During one of their conversations, Stella mentioned that her brother, Michael, had died in a tragic car accident nineteen years before. "He died in 1983 when I was twenty-two years old. I was living with my mom and Michael while working at a local automotive store."

"What happened?" Rachel asked.

Stella explained that at the time of his death, Michael had been an eighteen-year-old senior in high school, so she didn't see him much. Lynn, her sister, was still in Nevada, using and dealing drugs at the age of twenty-seven while living with her little girl and the boyfriend whom she hadn't married yet.

Stella saw Lynn at times, but not too often, and her mom was busy with her career as a wedding planner, so she wasn't around much either. Her parents had divorced in 1981, and soon after, her dad had moved to San Francisco with his new girlfriend, Susan. He'd started his own financial consulting business. Stella had visited him a few times after he moved. In late spring of that year, he'd called to say he'd had a heart attack and needed open heart surgery. He asked her to come so she could be with him before his surgery.

Stella guessed he was scared he might die. So she made arrangements with work to take the time off. Stella asked Michael if he wanted to go with, but he wanted to stay home and hang out with his friends. Michael wasn't close to their father. His high school graduation was only a few weeks away, of course. He didn't seem too concerned about the situation. Their mom, of course, didn't care one way or the other. Stella thought maybe she didn't care if her father died.

"When did you go to California?" Rachel asked.

"I flew out the night before my dad's surgery, and the next morning we woke up early so I could take him to the hospital to be prepped. I took my suitcase with me because I was scheduled to leave the next day; I figured I would just stay the night in the hospital with my dad.

Before the surgery, my dad lay in his hospital bed reading the Bible; I remembered thinking that was weird because I had never seen him read the Bible before."

"Well, some people are private with their beliefs around religion." Rachel said.

"My mom and dad were career-driven," Stella continued, "so most of their time was spent working. When I was younger, we went to Mexico for a family vacation, but as Lynn and I became teenagers, we were basically left on our own. My mom paid a lot of attention to Michael, and my dad was working all the time."

"How was it for you to see your dad in the hospital?" Rachel asked.

"During his surgery, I stayed in the waiting room, and I thought I might have fallen asleep because the only thing I remember was the nurse coming in to tell me that my dad was going to be all right. She told me that I could go see him in the Intensive Care Unit if I wanted, although it might make me uncomfortable because he had a lot of tubes coming out of his body. I just shrugged because I had lots of practice detaching from my feelings and pretending everything was just fine.

"I didn't even recognize my dad when I came into Intensive Care.

He didn't look like himself anyway; he was all swollen and unresponsive."

"After sleeping in the waiting room all night, I left California and flew home to Seattle. My boyfriend, Bradley, picked me up at the airport. We had plans to spend the weekend together just hanging out at his house. That night I was sitting on the couch when suddenly I felt really sick, as if someone had punched me in the stomach."

"What did you do then?" asked Rachel, looking Stella in the eye.

"It was so bad I leaned over my knees and rocked back and forth for what seemed like hours. The deep pain and nausea gradually went away, and by that night, the stomach ache was gone, except that I felt hollow and still wrong somehow, like I was waiting for the pain to come back."

"What did Bradley say to you?"

"He really wanted me to stay the night, but I wished I could go home. However, I'd promised to spend time with him, and I missed him."

"The next day, some friends came over; it was one of those unusually hot spring days when you could wear a bathing suit in Seattle. We lazed around in the sunshine, listening to music and laughing, but underneath, I couldn't get over the feeling that I wanted to go home."

"The phone rang and Bradley ran to answer it. He was gone for a long time so I went in to see what was going on. When he saw me coming, he dropped his voice to a whisper, and he looked guilty, like he was hiding something. I could hear a girl's voice coming from the phone, so I sat down at the kitchen table and looked at him until he hung up."

"What did you think was going on with Bradley?"

"I didn't know. That's why I asked him who he was talking to.

"Instead of answering, Bradley knelt down on one knee by my side and grabbed my hand. He stared at me and opened his mouth, but he said nothing. I saw his Adam's apple jumping in his throat. *Maybe he's going to dump me for another girl,* I thought, as that same feeling I'd had the night before started to come back into the pit of my stomach. Then I heard him whispering, but at first, the words made no sense.

"'There's been a terrible accident,' he said. 'It's your brother—that was your neighbor; they're trying to get hold of your mom, but they can't find her—your brother is dead.'

"I felt like I was a long way away, and Bradley's words were all mixed up with the music coming from the backyard, faint and fading in and out, like I was going deaf. Even after Bradley stopped speaking, his words seemed to continue, echoing in my head. Then I heard screaming ripping through the kitchen, and it took forever before I realized the screaming came from me."

"'We need to get you home,' Bradley kept saying. 'They can't get hold of your mom; you need to find her and tell her about Michael.' Those words repeated over and over in my head, all through the time it took to get my things, get into the car, and drive the two hours back to my house. Those words were all I was aware of, lodged in my mind like a pebble in a shoe. I had to tell my parents that their only son was dead. Me. I had to tell them.

"But I knew I couldn't. By the time I was home, I'd remembered that my mom had gone with her current boyfriend somewhere for the weekend; they were sailing in the Puget Sound, but I knew she'd be home soon because it was Sunday afternoon and she'd be going to work the next day; my mom never missed work. *I can't tell her, I can't tell her*, kept thundering through my head. My mom adored Michael; she would hate me forever for telling her he was dead."

"Did you have any other support from friends besides Bradley?" Rachel asked.

"Our neighbors were still at my house, trying to be there for me, but I hardly noticed them. When Stacy, my friend whom I'd known forever, hugged me, it felt weird, as if a total stranger had just thrown her arms around me. I was consumed with fear. Soon my mom would be home and I would have to tell her, but I couldn't tell her, and I didn't know what to do.

"Finally I had an idea. I found my mom's address book and found the numbers of her best friends and therapist. In fact, my mom had met her friends in group therapy with this same therapist. I called them and told them what had happened and asked them to be there for my mom and tell her when she got home.

"Then I called Susan in California and told her what had happened. I asked her to tell my dad, but she couldn't do it, so I asked his doctor to tell him. He was still in Intensive Care, but I couldn't worry about him now.

"Just after it got dark, me, Bradley, Stacy, and my mom's friends heard her car pull up in the driveway. I immediately ran downstairs into my bathroom, where I sat on the toilet with my arms hugging my stomach. I heard the front door shut and muffled voices, and then I heard my mom say, 'No. No. No.' Each 'No' was getting louder, and then I heard a deep animal-like scream like you hear on the nature programs when an animal is killed. I was alone in the bathroom, crying and wishing it was me who was dead."

Rachel reached over to grab a tissue for Stella.

"Thank you. That night after everyone had finally left, my mom went to bed. She was exhausted and looked awful. I thought she'd take something to make her sleep, so I was surprised to hear her calling me to come into her room and sleep with her so we could comfort each other.

"I got out of bed and walked down the hall and climbed into bed with her.

"My mom commented on how this must be rough for me, but I was just worried about her. It's funny, but I thought it was really my mom who needed comforting. It was the only time I could remember my mom showing me the nurturing side—the only time I had felt she needed or wanted me.

"The next day when we woke up, my mom told me, 'I need you to go to the coroner's office in Seattle with me to identify Michael.' I told her I would.

"It had been only a few days since my dad's surgery. He had gotten the okay from his doctor to fly to Seattle for the funeral, but he hadn't arrived yet. Nobody suggested asking Lynn to come; I wasn't sure if she had even been told yet. So there was only me and my mom. She seemed almost back to her normal self—all business, all orders, no feeling. Only her face looked like she had aged ten years in a night.

"Both Michael and his friend Steve were in the morgue. They had been in the backseat of the car, which had been traveling eighty miles an hour in a residential zone where the speed limit was twenty-five. The driver, who didn't go to the same high school, lost control of the car and it hit a tree, flipped upside down, and landed in the front yard of someone's house. There were small children living in that house, but luckily, they weren't playing outside at the time. Michael and Steve died instantly; the driver died on his way to the hospital, and the one other passenger walked away without a scratch. They had been partying all day down at the beach close to Seattle. Michael didn't even know the driver of the car; he'd just met him that night at a party. He and Steve had caught a ride home since the people they'd originally come with had already left. They were only a mile away from their home when they crashed. It was six o'clock on Sunday evening, the same time I got my sudden stomach ache.

"I didn't have to identify Michael in the morgue. I went into the room with my mom, but she was the one who looked at him. My mom told me to stand by the wall.

"Then my mom went over to the body and looked down. 'Yes, that's my son,' she said, as she walked back toward the door.

"'Mom,' I told her, 'I don't feel right about leaving him in this cold, empty place all by himself in that awful drawer.' I was crying. I had never thought much about death, about what happens after you die— whether anything or nothing happens. To leave him there felt like abandoning him forever.

"'Stella, let's go,' my mom said, grabbing my arm.

"My mom decided, without consulting my dad, to cremate Michael, and his body was sent to the local funeral home in Seattle. Making the decision, she stayed calm and authoritative like she was at work. Just before his cremation, we were allowed to go in the room to say goodbye. My mom went in first. She was only in there for a couple of seconds before she came out again, saying that the body in the room wasn't her son. After a lot of confusion, they found out that when they went to identify the body, the coroner's office had shown them Steve's body instead because both bodies were so mangled they weren't sure who was who. I was shocked that she had mistakenly identified the body they showed her as Michael.

"Michael's body was actually at another funeral home, and it took another day for the funeral homes to switch the bodies. Again we were allowed to say goodbye to Michael before he was cremated. I went in after my mother. I had never seen a dead body before and was nervous. I sat by Michael's side and stared at him. It didn't look like him. He was all swollen and gray, and there was a white sheet drawn up just underneath his chin. They had to do that because he had been decapitated during the car accident. I couldn't quite believe that that body was really my brother, the brother who'd lived in our house for eighteen years, whom I had known through all the stages of his life. I was suddenly overcome by the love I'd had for him that I didn't know was there, but that had probably been there all the time. I begged God to bring him back and made all sorts of promises like I would be a good girl and take care of my brother if only time could be pushed back. I felt so guilty that he was dead and I was alive and that I hadn't loved him enough when he was there. I ran out of the room sobbing."

Rachel had been quiet the whole time Stella spoke about her brother's accident. "Stella, at the age you were, you showed so much courage and made some serious decisions regarding contacting your mom's friends to give her support."

"Thank you," said Stella. "At the time I felt like it was my entire fault. It sure has made an impact on my life for a long time. I want to heal this time in my life. It was very painful," Stella said, wiping her tears.

Rachel slid over to Stella and wrapped her arms around her. "You will heal this when you're ready. Let's schedule next week."

6

"I do not at all understand the mystery of grace—only that it meets us where we are but does not leave us where it found us."

— Anne Lamott

A week later, Stella arrived at Rachel's a bit early, so she lay down on the futon since she was feeling very tired. "Hi, Stella," Rachel said, as she walked in the door.

Stella sat up. "Hi, Rachel."

Rachel came over and gave Stella a hug. Then she sat in her chair. "You can lie down if you need to."

Stella lay back down on the futon, placed her head on a white pillow, and pulled a yellow fuzzy blanket over herself.

"I'm really tired today," Stella said.

"Why are you tired?"

"I've been thinking about our conversation in the last session and it really helped me to release some anxiety over the incident. Is it common to have feelings after nineteen years?"

"Oh, certainly—especially if you haven't dealt with them. If I remember correctly from our last session, you didn't talk about what happened after you and your mom identified Michael."

"My friends started showing up at the house to give me comfort and I called work to let them know I wouldn't be in for a week."

"Where did you work?" Rachel asked.

"I worked at a local grocery store so they had someone to pick up my schedule. My mom and I drove home from a long day in Seattle at the funeral home making arrangements for Michael's cremation. I was still openly upset and my mom was very quiet. When we arrived home, several cars were parked in the driveway. When we walked in the front door, there were friends standing around chatting and bringing dishes of food out to the table so everyone could eat. My mom said she needed to call Lynn, so she went into the bedroom before she talked with her friends. My mom asked me to come into the bedroom with her for the call, and she put my sister on speaker.

"We all exchanged hellos, and then my mom just came out and told Lynn that Michael had died in a car accident on Saturday and the funeral would be the following Saturday.

"Lynn sounded surprised but didn't say much after that.

"My mom asked Lynn if she would be at the funeral, but Lynn was hesitant in committing and said she would try to make it. She also commented on not liking funerals.

"I went downstairs to my bedroom and lay down on the bed. I listened to the muffled voices coming from the kitchen and wondered who all those people were. I had never seen them before. I didn't really know how to feel. I just had a pit in my stomach that felt empty and nervous, and it was hard for me to breathe—like I couldn't catch my breath. I rolled over to see if that would help with breathing but nothing changed. I thought about Michael and how I would never see him again. Something inside my stomach gurgled and shook, and I thought I had eaten something that was going to make me throw up. A tingling feeling started at my feet and worked up my back. It felt so tight on my back that I couldn't stand the pain and started to cry. Sobbing uncontrollably, my body froze for what seemed like forever. Then I let out a scream, but I couldn't hear anything. Nothing came out, but in my mind, I was screaming at the top of my lungs. I stood up and paced the room in hopes that it would alleviate the pain. I knelt down on my knees and cupped my head in my hands and cried silently. I felt guilty for having all this emotion, so I stood up, wiped the tears away from my eyes, and went into the bathroom to blow my nose. Once I got myself together by breathing and telling myself I was going to be okay, I went upstairs to join the crowd of people."

"Did your mom come down and check on you?" Rachel asked.

"No, eventually everyone left and my mom's friend took my mom out for a drive. I cleaned up the dishes and prepared myself a plate of food. Even though I wasn't hungry, I realized I hadn't eaten all day. I went into Michael's room and lay down on his bed for a while. I must have fallen asleep because the phone ringing woke me up. It was Lynn. I hadn't spoken to her since a few months before Michael's death, except briefly on the phone with my mom.

"She asked me to do a big favor for her. She didn't mention our phone conversation earlier about Michael's death.

"I said, 'Okay' and asked what.

"Lynn told me to go into Michael's room and look for a pound of pot for her and then told me to look for a bunch of money.

"I couldn't believe what I was hearing from my sister. She kept repeating to me to go into his room and look for the pot and money before our mom found it. She said to look in the closet or around the headboard of his bed.

"I couldn't believe what I was hearing and had no idea that my sister was giving Michael pot to sell. I had no idea.

"She told me that she had been supplying him with pot to sell at school to make some extra money. The only thing she was worried about was the pot and the money."

"What did you do?" Rachel asked.

"I looked in Michael's room and found the pot stuffed in the headboard, but although I looked everywhere I could think of, I couldn't find any money. I called Lynn back and told her there was pot but no money. Lynn wasn't happy. Or maybe she didn't believe me; I don't know.

"I asked Lynn, 'Why Michael? He was our little brother. Why would you put him in this situation?'

"She said to just keep looking for the money and then she hung up.

"The money never did turn up as far as I know. Maybe my mom found it and said nothing. Maybe Michael gave the money to someone else. Maybe there was no money because he hadn't sold the pot yet. I never knew what happened to it.

"My sister and her boyfriend lived in Nevada with their daughter and sold pot for a living. She rarely had any contact with our mom, dad, or me, but she must have convinced Michael that he could make a lot of money selling marijuana at his school and my sister and her boyfriend could make a living off what Michael sold. Lynn must had mailed the pot to a P.O. Box so our mom didn't know what Michael was doing.

"I went back to bed but stayed awake for a while, my mind still reeling from my conversation with Lynn. I woke up early and went upstairs to find out what needed to be done before Michael's funeral. It had been a week since I flew home from California; the last time I had seen my dad was in Intensive Care. My dad and Susan were arriving that morning, and one of my dad's friends was picking them up at the airport to drive them to the church. My mom had left early to gather some things for the service. I was alone in the house feeling so guilty. I should have made Michael go to California with me; then this never would've happened. I felt it was my fault. Or maybe I shouldn't have gone to be with our dad. Maybe I should have stayed home to take care of Michael. I knew my mom was mad at me. I knew she thought it should have been me in that car."

"It's good you're talking about your brother's funeral. Was your boyfriend with you?" Rachel asked.

"Bradley went back home after my mom found out about Michael, so he drove out early the morning of the funeral to pick me up. The church was already packed, but there was a seat up front for Bradley and me. So many people showed up at the church that day that they filled the foyer and outside. We sat in the pew just diagonal to my mom, dad, and Susan, but most of people were from the high school.

"Most of the service was a blur to me. It was like my body wasn't there. I didn't feel attached to anything. Bradley held my hand, but I couldn't feel my hand grasping his. There was beautiful music from the movie *Terms of Endearment*. Lots of people I didn't know stood up to say something about Michael, and I thought how brave they were to stand in front of all those people sharing their stories and crying. I could never do that; I didn't have the courage. Neither one of my parents stood up to say anything. At one point, I looked over and there wasn't any emotion on their faces. Once the service was over, it took a long time for everyone to clear the church so some of my friends from high school came over and talked with me for a bit. My mom, dad, and Susan stood together for a while talking about the fact that Lynn wasn't at the funeral, and Bradley and I sat in the pew until everyone left.

"Everyone shuffled up to our house to say one last goodbye, and of course, my mom had the event catered. So many stories were told about how Michael was a kind friend, a true friend, and that he would do anything for his friends. How he was such a great athlete and how all the girls wanted to be his girlfriend. They told my mom how much he spoke of her and told his friends how much he loved his family. How he wanted to go to college. He just wanted to spend the summer making money at the automotive store, working on his car, and hanging out with his buddies. There was lots of laughter, lots of tears, and people just joining together for one last goodbye. People stayed for a long time. Some left and came back with other people who weren't at the funeral. I wished that

Lynn would've shown up, but I knew the reason why she didn't—she couldn't face the fact that she had put Michael in a position to sell pot for her.

"My dad looked really gray and tired; he was leaving on the plane the next day to go back to the hospital because his doctor only allowed him to be out of the hospital for two days. He owned his own business as a financial advisor, which was where he had met Susan.

"It was ten o'clock in the evening and everyone had been standing in the dining room drifting around the table talking and eating the last of the salads and sandwiches and saying their goodbyes. My dad was sitting in the chair next to the window watching as people moved to him to give their condolences. He and Susan were staying at the airport so they could catch their flight early in the morning. I went over and hugged my dad and told him that I loved him.

"I had just seen him in California having open heart surgery with tubes all over his body in the Intensive Care Unit a few days before. I felt so sorry for him.

"My mom had gone to bed, so I cleaned up what was left in the kitchen and sat with Bradley for a bit in the dark living room. He consoled me as best he could and we fell asleep on the couch.

"Before Bradley left to go back home, we went down to the beach. He asked me how I was feeling and hugged me as we sat in the sun looking out over the water. He brought me back home and then he went home."

"You know, Rachel, I have one distinct memory from my brother's funeral. My mom bought balloons for Michael's friends and family to hold when they gathered at the house. She told us the balloons represented Michael's soul, and she asked everyone to go outside and release them at the same time, which would be like releasing Michael's soul so he could be free. I stood slightly apart from the rest of the group, in the lower part of the backyard, holding my white balloon. My mom gave the signal for everyone to release their balloons. I let go of mine, but it wouldn't fly away. It fell to the ground and stayed by me, just sitting at my feet. Someone came by and said all the helium must be gone in it and that's why it wouldn't float away. But I felt marked—the only one who wouldn't let Michael go."

"I'm surprised your mom made such a gesture with the balloons," Rachel said.

"Me too. But this was Michael, her beloved son.

"The weird thing, though, was couple of nights later, I was sleeping when the phone rang about two in the morning. My mom answered it, and a few minutes later, she came into my room and said she was going over to her friend's house for a while. I was only half-awake, so it didn't seem odd to me that she'd go visiting at that hour.

"After my mom left, I fell back asleep and dreamt that my brother had come to visit me. In my dream, I was asleep. I saw myself in Michael's bed with my eyes closed, and then I saw Michael come into the room. He was smiling. He told me not to worry about him, that he was in a good place, and that he was not alone. He came over to the bed and lay down next to me. I was lying on my side, and he put his hand on my back and rubbed it up and down my spine, all the while whispering that he was okay and not alone.

"The most profound feeling of peace and love swept over me as he rubbed my back. It felt as if all the pain I'd ever known was gone forever.

"I heard the front door open and my mom's footsteps coming down the hall. It seemed like I was awake, not dreaming, and it felt so real that my brother was there with me."

"It sounds like you were never able to tell your story and how painful it was for you to be alone in the death of your brother," Rachel said.

"I was never able to talk safely to someone about the events and how I had to push my feelings aside for so many years. I just kept living life the best way I knew possible."

7

"Trauma is personal.
It does not disappear if it is not validated."

— Danielle Bernock

Mother's Day, 2007, when Gabrielle was eighteen years old, Stella invited Shirley and her husband David over for brunch. Shirley had remarried ten years before. They were sitting outside on the patio when the phone rang. The phone was in the room on the other side of the sliding glass door to the patio, so it took only a few steps to reach it. After saying hello, Stella heard Lynn's voice.

"Happy Mother's Day."

Stella hesitated before replying. Shirley was sitting just outside the sliding glass door and she'd hear her. Feeling awkward, Stella took the phone and walked quickly out of the room and out the front door on the other side of the house. She shut the door behind her before she answered.

"Hi, Lynn. Happy Mother's Day to you too," she said, but quietly. Maybe Shirley had followed her—probably not, but Stella didn't want to take the chance of Shirley overhearing her.

"Are you okay?" Lynn asked. "You sound funny."

"Just tired today," Stella said.

"So how are you? What are you up to?"

This was unusual. Lynn never asked how Stella was; her conversation was always about her.

"I have company over and it's not a good time to talk," Stella said.

"Is everybody okay?"

"Yeah, fine."

"Well, I'll let you go then," Lynn said finally. "I just wanted to say Happy Mother's Day."

"Okay. Thanks for calling. Bye."

Stella hung up and sat on the front porch for a bit, feeling sick to her stomach. She was caught in the middle between Lynn and Shirley again, forced to choose between them. Lynn was still a mess, with drugs and alcohol, but she had called Stella and asked about her this time. Maybe she was getting better; maybe they could repair their relationship after all. But Shirley would have a fit. Shirley hadn't talked to Lynn in over fifteen years because Lynn was on drugs.

Stella walked back to the patio and sat down at the table.

"Who was that on the phone?" asked Shirley.

"Oh, just my dad," Stella said.

"What did *he* want?"

"Just to wish me Happy Mother's Day."

■ ■ ■

Stella had a session with Rachel the next day.

Rachel began the session by asking, "How did yesterday go with your mom?"

"My sister called me while my mom was there. It was really awkward," Stella replied, reaching for a Kleenex.

"Tell me why it was awkward." Rachel took a sip of tea.

"I couldn't talk to her while my mom was there, so I didn't respond much to her and the whole conversation lasted less than five minutes."

Rachel placed her cup of tea on the floor next to her bean bag chair and reached over to grab a white blanket to wrap Stella's feet in.

"If I could do it all over again and Lynn called to wish me a Happy Mother's Day, I would behave very differently. I would talk up a storm with her, and if my mom was in the room, so what?" she said, wiping away her tears with the Kleenex. "I wouldn't be afraid to talk with my own sister. I abandoned her, just like my mother did. I allowed myself to be ashamed of her, of her lifestyle, and how she treated her daughter."

Stella's healing had let her recognize that Lynn abused, abandoned, and neglected her daughter just like Shirley did to her.

"Lynn didn't have a chance to raise a healthy daughter because she wasn't raised by a healthy mother herself," Stella said.

Rachel sat back in her chair and picked up her tea. "Stella, you were put in a place with your mom to choose sides. You learned this at a young age."

Stella sat up and leaned against the pillow to support her back. "I'm still angry that I felt I had to choose between my mom and Lynn. I'm ashamed that I chose our mom. But most of all, I'm sad that Lynn and I lost our sisterhood at such an early age," she said, weeping, snot running out of her nose. Stella blew her nose and grabbed another Kleenex.

"We have no relationship and haven't had one for decades. When I watch my friends interact with their sisters, it's a constant reminder to me of what I've lost. I don't know if Lynn and I could start a relationship as sisters now. There is so much time and so much hurt between us. When I call her, she doesn't return my calls, and when she goes to see our dad, I'm not invited."

Rachel moved over to Stella on the futon. She wrapped her arms around her and held her for a long time. Stella's memories tumbled out in her session with Rachel, and the more she talked, the more she remembered.

They scheduled another session in a week. Then Rachel asked Stella if next week she would bring in some pictures of her and Lynn so she could see them as they were then.

■　■　■

The next week, after Rachel and Stella greeted each other, Rachel immediately got down to business.

"Did you bring in photographs of your family when you were a child?" Rachel asked.

Stella reached into her purse and pulled out a photo of her and Lynn when they were four and five years old. Lynn was facing the camera, but her eyes were closed. Stella was standing at her right side, looking at her, so Stella's face was in profile. Rachel looked at the photo for a moment.

"Why did you pick this photo to bring in?"

"I don't know." Stella was trying not to use that phrase anymore, so she said, "I don't have very many of just me and Lynn."

"What's the first thing that pops into your mind when you look at this photo?" Rachel asked, holding it up in front of Stella.

"Open your eyes," she said immediately, no hesitation at all.

"And what do you want Lynn to see when she opens her eyes?"

She was silent for a minute. "I want her to see what's going on in our house," Stella whispered. "I want her to see all that abuse and neglect and unhappiness. I want her to see what I see.

"Lynn knows nothing about my healing over the last several years. She doesn't know that my relationship with my mother has changed; she doesn't know that I have burnt the ends of the cord that used to hold us together. Lynn still thinks that my mom and I are a team, so if she deals with me, she'll have to deal with our mom, too. I don't blame her for not wanting to. Losing my sister validates the feeling I have of being an orphan with no family. Lynn is the only sibling I have left. We are the only survivors of a disaster, and I so wish we could talk again. I wish I hadn't lost the cord that tied us together. The only good thing about my relationship with Lynn today is that it reminds me not to let this happen with Gabrielle. I am continuing to break this cycle right now—today and every day."

■ ■ ■

Gabrielle and Stella had planned the high school graduation party together, inviting all Gabrielle's friends from school and some friends of Stella's, like Maggie who had been her friend since Gabrielle was in kindergarten, and Jeff, Stella's friend for almost ten years, and some family, including Shirley and her husband. A few months prior to the party, Shirley had called to tell Stella that she wanted to buy Gabrielle a computer for her graduation present. However,

Stella told her that Gabrielle's dad, Ashton, and she were buying her a new computer for college, so she needed to think of another present. They left it at that.

Ashton and Stella had now been divorced for fifteen years. He had married Carina just a year after he and Stella divorced. Gabrielle had been four years old when her father remarried. Ashton and Carina now had two children of their own—Julia, who was five years younger than Gabrielle, and Jake, who was a year younger than Julia. They lived an hour and a half north of Seattle in a small town along the water. Throughout Gabrielle's childhood, she spent every other weekend with her dad and his family.

During the party, Stella noticed that Shirley had not given Gabrielle a present, and she was beginning to wonder why she hadn't. Toward the end of the party, while Stella was cleaning up outside, out of the corner of her eye, she saw Shirley secretly pull Gabrielle into the house so she could speak to her privately. Stella had been waiting for this. Immediately, she entered the house and saw Shirley facing Gabrielle and talking to her urgently. Gabrielle looked uncomfortable when she saw her. Stella positioned herself between them, forming a triangle.

"What's going on?" Stella asked.

Shirley rounded on her and said in an angry voice, "We are talking." Then she turned to Gabrielle, her back to Stella.

"Gabrielle, I bought you a computer for your graduation present," Shirley said, ignoring Stella.

Stella stood there for a minute until she couldn't take it any longer and walked into the kitchen. Shirley turned around and walked outside. She left the party without saying goodbye.

In a moment, Gabrielle followed Stella into the kitchen. "Grandma bought me a computer," she said nervously.

She always does this to me, Stella thought, *undermines me in front of my child.*

"I already told you, and Grandma, that your dad and I are buying you a computer," Stella said.

"I don't know," Gabrielle said defensively. "Grandma said she already bought it."

"You knew we were buying you a computer; why didn't you tell Grandma that?" Stella's voice was getting louder. She was shaking, but not with fear, with anger.

"I didn't remember," Gabrielle said, looking down at the floor.

"Don't you see what Grandma is trying to do here? She is undermining me."

"Mom, this is all in your head," Gabrielle said impatiently.

"Gabrielle, this is real! It is not in my head. Why can't you see that?"

Gabrielle gave an exasperated sigh and walked back to the party. Stella stood in the kitchen, not knowing what to do. She realized that Gabrielle was caught in the middle of a pattern that had been going on with her mother for a long time. Stella knew Shirley was trying to drive a wedge between her and Gabrielle. She had been working on Gabrielle since she was young by not respecting Stella in front of Gabrielle.

Stella felt like crying, but before she could, Gabrielle suddenly walked back into the kitchen. She gave her a big hug and said, "Thanks for the party, Mom." Stella's heart lightened. The wedge hadn't been driven between them yet.

"Mom, I'm sorry I said those things to you," Gabrielle added, kicking her toe on the floor. "Thank you for making this day wonderful. I love you," she continued.

Stella reached out and wrapped her arms around Gabrielle. "Honey, you're welcome. I love you."

After the party, Gabrielle left to go out with her friends. Stella's friends, Maggie and Jeff, stayed to help Stella clean up. While they were cleaning, Maggie told Stella she'd overheard the conversation between her and Gabrielle in the kitchen. When she came out of the kitchen, Maggie had asked Gabrielle to go back and apologize to Stella because she'd put together this beautiful party for her. Gabrielle had a lot of respect and love for Maggie. She'd known her almost her entire life since Maggie had been her kindergarten teacher. Stella was glad that Gabrielle had taken her advice.

After they'd cleaned up, Jeff, Maggie, and Stella sat down at the kitchen table. Both Jeff and Maggie had wanted to talk with Stella before about Shirley, but they were both waiting for a signal from Stella that it was okay. Tonight was the night. They told her they'd seen Shirley use her money to control and manipulate both Stella and Gabrielle for a long time; they'd observed Shirley's disrespect for her and her obsessive need to compete and win at any cost. As Stella listened to these trusted friends validate the thoughts and feelings she'd had for so long, she began to cry with relief that she was not alone and not crazy like she had sometimes felt.

"Could you talk to Gabrielle too?" Stella asked them after she'd calmed down. "Maybe it would help her to understand if she could hear it from someone other than her mom." They both agreed to do so.

When Gabrielle got home that night, Maggie asked her whether she and Jeff could talk to her. They went into the family room and closed the door.

Stella was in the kitchen emptying the dishwasher. She could hear muffled voices coming from the family room, so her curiosity became too much for her. She crept up close to the door and listened. She couldn't hear everything, but what she did hear made the tears start again. Maggie and Jeff were sticking up for Stella—to her, an unbelievable thing.

"Gabrielle, your grandma needs to see that you and your mom are a team and that nothing comes between you," Stella heard Maggie say.

"...your grandma has stepped over the line with me too—she's dissed your mom to me, and I felt she wanted me to join her against Stella.…"

"…your mom mothered you so well even though she wasn't mothered herself.…"

"…your mom knows what it's like to be controlled by your grandma's money.…"

And the last thing Stella heard was Maggie saying with a tremor in her voice, "I admire your mom. She's sacrificed a lot for you because you are so important to her. Your happiness is her main priority; she loves you so much.…" Stella couldn't listen anymore because she was crying and was afraid they would hear her. Back in the kitchen, she started drying dishes that were already dry, while her body shook all over. Through Stella's sessions with Rachel, she'd learned about trauma and how the body releases shock by shaking. Stella went back to the door to listen.

"…when your grandma wants to give you money or things and you're not comfortable with her gifts," she heard Jeff say, "just tell her you will talk to your mom about it, and leave it at that."

"Okay," said Gabrielle, her voice solemn. "I understand now.

Thank you for talking with me." There was a silence and then a rustling noise—Stella knew they were hugging. She went into the living room when she heard Gabrielle going down the hall to her bedroom. When Maggie and Jeff came into the living room, she hugged them, "Thanks, guys, for supporting me."

"Oh, I love you and Gabrielle," Maggie said, hugging Stella back.

"I feel that Gabrielle gets what Maggie and I said to her. She's a smart girl," Jeff said, hugging Stella back.

With Jeff and Maggie's help, Stella felt that she and Gabrielle could now both be free.

8

"Children will not remember you for the
material things you provided
but for the feeling that you cherished them."

— Gail Grenier Sweet

They left at 6:00 a.m. on an early autumn morning in 2007. The sun shone and promised the last of summer warmth. Gabrielle was eager and nervous; Stella was anxious and nervous. Gabrielle was leaving home for college, and although Eastern Washington was only a two-hour drive away over the Cascade Mountains, this would be the first time she had not lived with Stella—a new experience for both of them.

"Mom, did you remember to bring my paperwork for financial aid?" Gabrielle asked.

"Yeah, I have it in my purse. How are you feeling about leaving home for college?"

"I'm really excited to live in a dorm with other people. Even though I enjoy my space, I'm going to enjoy having roommates."

"I think that will be good for you too. You've had a lot of space at home just with me and you."

Although they'd left early so they'd have lots of time to move Gabrielle into the dorm, the campus was filled with excited energy from parents and students. Were the other parents feeling the same way as Stella was—a mix of pride and fear?

As they walked into the dorm, a smell of mold met them, lingering in the halls and up the stairs. It was an old building, probably built in the early 1920s. It had very high ceilings and a wooden staircase wrapping up to the second floor, like an old Western-style hotel. Gabrielle's room was on the second floor. Across from the second floor landing was a touch of modernity—a big common games room.

Gabrielle's two roommates, Sarah and Jenna, strangers to each other, were already in the room, putting stuff away.

"Hi. Are you Gabrielle?" one of the girls asked.

"Yeah," she said with a smile.

The girl reached out to shake Gabrielle's hand. "My name is Sarah, and this is Jenna." The other also walked over to shake Gabrielle's hand.

Stella reached out her hand. "Hi, I'm Gabrielle's mom, Stella. Nice to meet you girls."

Like all dorm rooms, it was small—just three rooms, including the tiny bathroom that was only a shower and toilet—the sink was in the bedroom along with three captain beds and a rod to hang clothes on. The front room held three desks and chairs, a small microwave and refrigerator, and a tiny couch with a stained cover and some holes showing the foam rubber beneath. The girls didn't seem to notice how small the space was. Stella thought it felt closed in, but the girls didn't plan to spend much time there.

The three girls were soon off. This move-in weekend was a time for socializing and activities the school had planned for the freshmen. Stella was staying the whole weekend at the Country Inn close to the campus; she wanted her daughter's move-in to be as smooth as possible, so she spent the weekend fixing up the room. Gabrielle and Sarah had taken the two beds by the window, leaving Jenna the bed by the sink. Stella had brought the same kind of green sheets for her bed here that she'd had at home—she liked them and she thought they'd make her feel less homesick, although Stella hadn't seen any signs of homesickness yet. Gabrielle's dad had given her a light green comforter that went well with the green sheets. After making Gabrielle's bed, Stella folded her clothes and put them away in the built-in drawers. Then Stella arranged Gabrielle's books and her desk.

Stella saw Gabrielle at fleeting moments; she seemed to be happy—and busy. Mostly, they communicated by texting, a form of communication that was new to Stella. There were events planned for parents the whole weekend so Stella participated in speaking forums from faculty on what to expect the first year to be like for their kids. She had planned to leave on Monday, but by Saturday night, Stella had nothing left to do, and Gabrielle was too busy to spend time with her. Stella texted her and asked whether it was okay if she left on Sunday instead. While waiting for Gabrielle's reply text, Stella thought about when she was eighteen, about the time she would be going off to college. Shirley and Robert had never discussed college with Stella, so she had never thought about it. Stella had told Gabrielle when she was eight years old that she was going to college no matter what. Stella really wanted Gabrielle to have that going away to college experience that she had never had. She was happy when Gabrielle wanted to go away to college too.

"Yeah k—going 2 b really busy tomorrow w school activities," Gabrielle texted back.

"Ok, I'll stop by 2nite & bring u ur door panel, see how ur doing."

"We r busy 2nite w our neighbors. Can u come in the morning 2 say goodbye?" Her return text came immediately. Stella felt a twinge in her stomach. Gabrielle had already let go.

But she texted, "Sure, sweetie. I'll b by around 8am. U want me 2 bring anything?"

"No, just come by & bring the panel & then u can go hm. Just park in the 15-min parking spot." Stella's heart sank. *My baby is on her own,* she thought. And the thought in back of that one was: *I'm all alone.*

Again, she sucked up her real feelings and texted, "Ok, see you at 8. Have a good sleep."

Whether Gabrielle slept well or not, Stella did not. She blamed it on the hotel mattress, but the real reason was that she was going home without her baby. She only had one thing left to do for her daughter—

Gabrielle wanted more privacy between the bedroom and front room, so Stella told her she'd get her a rod and a panel to separate the two rooms. She'd bought it on Saturday at the local mart, and in her hotel room she'd ironed the panel to get all the wrinkles out. Now all Stella had to do was hang it in the dorm room and then she would leave.

The next morning, only one fifteen-minute loading/unloading spot was available in the parking lot of the dorm, so she grabbed it and called Gabrielle from her cell phone to tell her she was downstairs.

"'Kay, Mom. I'll be right down." Gabrielle's voice sounded as if she'd just woken up. Stella waited for five minutes until she showed up at the door of the dorm to let her in. Gabrielle gave Stella a hug. As they climbed the stairs, Stella saw new banners and flyers tacked to the walls, reminders about the dorm's rules. When they entered Gabrielle's room, she noticed that it smelled stuffy. The drapes were drawn so it was dark, but Stella could see crumpled potato chip bags and empty pop cans on the floor, and a lump in the bed in the corner; it must have been Jenna asleep. She laid the panel and rod on the couch. "Do you want me to hang this for you?"

"No, my roommates are sleeping. I'll do it later," Gabrielle said, standing in the middle of the room and shifting from one foot to the other.

Stella walked over to the couch and sat down, slowly sinking until her knees were parallel with her armpits. "How did you sleep?"

"Good," Gabrielle said shortly, seeming agitated. She didn't like drawn-out goodbyes. Over the years, they'd had many goodbyes—from the time Gabrielle was three, she'd gone off to see Ashton for holiday trips or visitations. She'd gone on school mission trips to do charity work, sometimes for a month or more when she was in high school, so Stella and Gabrielle had long goodbyes and short ones. But this goodbye was different; it wasn't a weekend or summer vacation goodbye. This was an unfamiliar goodbye that meant that from now on things would be different. When Gabrielle came home, she would come home as a visitor.

They sat there, Gabrielle on her desk chair and Stella on the foam rubber couches, trying not to look at each other. Stella wanted to cry, to hug Gabrielle for a long time, to tuck her back into bed—but Stella knew she couldn't do any of those things. At one point, they did make eye contact for just a moment, and in Gabrielle's beautiful blue eyes, Stella could still see that little girl who stole her attention and her whole heart. But now Gabrielle was a young woman. Finally, Stella stood up and wrapped her arms around Gabrielle. She leaned down to hug Stella back and turned her head so Stella could kiss her cheek.

"Well, I'll let you get back to sleep, sweetie."

"Okay, Mom."

"I'll call you when I get home."

"Okay, Mom."

"I love you, Gabrielle."

"I love you too, Mom."

Stella walked out of the room and down the stairs and got into her car, feeling numb the whole way. She'd been dreading this day for many years, ever since Gabrielle was born. *This is just a short goodbye,* Stella lied to herself, in order to detach from the raw emotions she felt swirling inside. On the drive home, Stella kept repeating to herself, *This is just temporary; she'll be home soon; it's just like a weekend away at her dad's.*

■ ■ ■

As the next week dragged on, Stella was still telling herself she was okay because this was just like a vacation away for a couple of weeks. But when two weeks had gone by, reality set in. She had to see Gabrielle. She'd go out the next weekend, just for a day, just a Sunday. Stella texted Gabrielle to let her know she was coming, and then a few days later, she called her to firm up the plans.

"Hello, Gabrielle. How are you, sweetie?"

"Good," she said. She sounded hurried. Stella imagined her sitting on her desk chair, wearing pink gym shorts and a white T-shirt, her long brown hair with the widow's peak slightly messed up, surrounded by books and board games.

"I'll be there this Sunday," Stella said happily. "Do you need me to bring you anything?"

"No," she said slowly. It sounded like there was an echo on the phone. Stella had never heard that tone before. "Why are you coming out to visit me?" Gabrielle asked abruptly.

Stella paused a moment to find her heart before she could answer. "Well, I want to see you."

"Mom, it's only been two weeks since I've been here."

Stella couldn't say anything for a moment. It didn't feel like only two weeks to her; this separation was different from anything before. It was longer than mission trips with her high school or weekends at her dad's where she visited every other weekend—she was away from her, building her own community without Stella. The pause seemed to last for an eternity, but finally, Stella was able to say, "Do you want me to come out and visit you?"

"No, I don't want you to." Her voice was full of confidence, but somehow soft, like her pink baby blanket. Stella's image of the young girl in gym shorts faded. Instead, she saw a young adult with strength in her bones and love in her heart.

Stella was stunned and speechless for another moment, but then, reluctantly, she said, "Okay, sweetie.…"

"Bye, Mom."

Stella hung up the phone and walked into Gabrielle's old bedroom. The walls were bare except for her flat screen TV and the cross above her bed, which Gabrielle had gotten when she attended a Christian-based school. All the family photos were gone. The closet held just a few items of clothing. Her old down comforter was still on her bed, but Gabrielle was gone. Stella felt rejected and alone.

I'm not going to call her ever again, ran through her mind. *I won't give her any more money; she's on her own from now on. Forget her.*

But then these thoughts washed away and the mantra that Stella had been practicing for years came up instead. *Those are my mother's words, not mine. This is my mother speaking, not me. That's what she always did. If she didn't get her own way by controlling or manipulating people, she eliminated them from her life. That is not what I do. That is not who I am.*

Stella called Rachel and scheduled a session with her. Rachel had a cancellation the next day so she took the appointment.

■ ■ ■

The next day at the session, Rachel began by remarking, "You mentioned in your voice mail that a phone conversation with Gabrielle didn't go well, in your eyes."

Rachel sat in her chair and took a sip of tea while waiting for Stella to respond. It had been a few weeks since Stella's last session.

"Yeah, I wanted to drive out and see Gabrielle this weekend, but she told me no."

Rachel smiled. "Why are you so upset, Stella?"

"Because I want to see her," she replied, crying.

"You just saw her a few weeks ago. Give her some space. She's exploring who she is. This is what college does for you."

"How would I know? I never went away to college," she said hastily.

Stella sat for a minute thinking about what Rachel had said. Then Stella added, "I remember when I was eighteen and living with my best friend, Claire, in our first apartment. I remember how much I loved the feeling of freedom, how much I loved having my own things, my own space. And I remember how my mother abruptly demanded I come home and live with her because she said she needed me.

"I moved out when I was eighteen, after graduating from high school. I got an apartment with Claire. Claire and I had met in our freshman year of high school, in PE class. None of my other friends were in this PE class, and Claire had no friends because she had just moved to the area. Claire got teased because she was legally blind and wore very thick glasses. I didn't like people making fun of her so I asked Claire to be my friend; I knew what it was like to change schools and have no friends."

Rachel looked up at Stella. "How's that?"

"When I was younger living on the East Coast, we had moved a lot because of my dad's work, and then they transferred our family out to Seattle. Claire and I became really close, almost like sisters, especially when my sister moved away to Nevada with her boyfriend. I felt very lonely."

"Tell me about your apartment with Claire."

"Our apartment was a few miles from the neighborhood where our families lived, but it was close to the beach—a big deal in the summer for me and Claire because we both loved sunning on the beach. Heck, we were only eighteen. Claire and I also worked together at a downtown bank in the Accounts Receivable processing center. It was a twenty-mile commute, but that was okay because we drove in my car that my mom had given me for my sixteenth birthday."

"We loved that apartment. It was only 650 square feet in a building right next to a bowling alley. Orange shag carpet and a kitchen with no window. We had to have the lights on even in the daytime in order to see. I had my own bedroom, although the only furniture was a mattress on the floor. I kept my clothes on the floor too. But in the living room we had a twenty-seven-inch TV that Claire's parents had given her, and a fold-up chair that we found at the local thrift store. It wasn't fancy, but it was ours."

Stella started crying so Rachel moved over to her and sat next to her while she talked about the apartment and her friend.

"I loved Claire. Claire hung in with me through all the years that followed. I didn't treat Claire very well at times when we were at parties with other friends. I would ignore her. Claire knew about my childhood, my mom yelling at me and hitting me, so Claire was forgiving when I ignored her or when I got angry when I didn't get my way. Claire didn't let me manipulate her; she would just walk away and call me later."

"She sounds like a good friend."

"She was a very good friend. By the time we were twenty-three, Claire was married with two kids. I used to call her up and talk to her on the phone for hours while her kids played. She never told me that she had to go. All our conversations were all about me, my problems, and my boyfriends. I never asked Claire how she was doing. I just didn't get it then; I didn't get that Claire's life was just as important as mine."

"How long did you live together, and why did you move back home?"

"We lived together for eight months until my mom called one day, telling me that she was leaving my dad and she needed me home."

"Why did your mom need you home?"

"Because she was working and she wanted me to be home for her and Michael. You know what I did next when I hung up the phone? I told Claire I was moving out the next day. Just like that. I didn't care how that would affect Claire or the rent. My mom wanted me home, so I left Claire in a difficult situation. Eventually, she got a roommate, but that wasn't cool—what I did to her."

Rachel didn't say anything to Stella, just allowed her to purge her story.

"I remembered how angry I felt that I had to take care of my mother, although I never said so—in fact, I was afraid even to think about being angry. What if I had said no to my mom? Would my life have been different? Would it have been better?" she asked, wiping her tears.

"The best part of this memory is that you can now let it go and have an understanding of the kind of support Gabrielle needs from you," Rachel said, while kissing Stella's forehead.

Stella's anger at Gabrielle disappeared, replaced by a sense of connection and understanding. The immense love she felt for her rushed back into her heart, and with it came the knowledge that she had done a good job of raising her. Pride in Gabrielle, pride in herself, filled her. *That Gabrielle doesn't feel it's her job to take care of me—that shows good parenting,* she thought.

That evening, she texted Gabrielle: "Hey, sweetie, thx 4 telling me not 2 come over 4 a visit. I really appreciate ur honesty. Mama loves you much!"

Gabrielle responded faster than she'd ever texted Stella before.

"I love you too, Mama."

9

"There is a crack in everything.
That's how the light gets in."

— Leonard Cohen

While the world was watching Apple's big launch of its iPhone in 2007 and a Seattle native was being held in an Italian prison for murder, Stella was adjusting to Gabrielle being gone and being home by herself. Even though Gabrielle was off to college studying economics, some of her things were still nicely arranged in her room, so Stella still had a bit of denial that she was completely moved out. Stella was still reeling about the graduation party and the incident around Shirley and the computer. She hadn't spoken to her since June, and now it was October. Shirley had reached out to her several times with phone calls and emails, but Stella had ignored all the attempts and requests for visitation. Stella was done! Shirley had crossed the line with Gabrielle, and even though Shirley hadn't bought Gabrielle the computer, Stella wouldn't reconcile with her mother and risk a wedge then being created by her mother between her and Gabrielle. One day, Shirley reached out to Stella in an email, saying she wanted to talk with her about their relationship. Stella knew what that meant; Shirley would only add to her anxiety if they met. Stella was at an all-time low of feeling isolated, not sleeping, and having a loss of appetite, all symptoms of her anxiety; she couldn't face Shirley.

■ ■ ■

In Stella's next session with Rachel, they spoke about honoring her feelings of not contacting Shirley.

"I usually don't do this with clients," said Rachel. "I'm all about not severing relationships with family, but it would be good not to contact Shirley so you can work on the anxiety."

Stella looked up at Rachel and said, "Thank you." Stella knew that Shirley brought a lot of anxiety into her life. After working with Rachel for seven years, Stella had seen the healing at work in her relationship with Gabrielle and increased her commitment to being a good mother. She really wanted to have a solid, healthy relationship with Gabrielle, so it was important to Stella to uncover the root of her anxiety. After all these years, she had still not figured out the primary cause of it, but she thought her mother might be the cause.

They then talked about how Stella could learn to handle Shirley since she still felt she would want to have a relationship with her mother in the future. She just couldn't deal with her at this point in her life. They began with Stella telling Rachel more about her mother's background.

"My mom is ambitious, intelligent, and mean. She's a beauty to anyone's eye; she possesses a charm that can lure anyone into her web. She was born on a farm in Oklahoma to parents so poor they couldn't afford to feed my mom and her brother, so at the age of ten, she was farmed off to live with her granny while her brother was to be raised by a neighbor. She's independent and angry; my mom had already known how to take care of herself and others. At the age of five, she was sent down to the local store to buy the family milk and bread. She would walk for miles alone to fend for her brother because her mom was timid and her dad was the town drunk. My mom hated her dad and mom for not taking care of the family, so when it was time to live with her grandmother, she was relieved.

"My mom's outlet was school because she was so smart. She only had a few friends, all of them from affluent families in the area, so she became very resentful and jealous of their status. When she became pregnant in her junior year, her grandmother wasn't happy about it, so once my mom graduated from high school, her grandmother kicked her out of the house, telling her she wasn't going to raise her child. She left the next day with just enough money to pay for the train ride to New York, and she found a job as a secretary at a local accounting firm. She married my dad so she could have security. She then took on the role of a dutiful wife and mother, only to be left with an emptiness and regret. After my parents' divorce, she had dreams of becoming successful in her career and one day being able to care for herself. All that resentment went toward me and Lynn. She was strict and disciplined us like a heartless tyrant. Because of that discipline, I grew up fearful of her and always tried to please her to escape her wrath.

"I've never confronted my mother before," Stella told Rachel.

"I don't want to have a conversation with my mom about what happened at Gabrielle's graduation party, and I most certainly don't want to be manipulated by her words."

"Rather than have a phone or in-person conversation with her," Rachel suggested, "why don't you send her an email to tell her how you feel?"

"I admit that I would feel more comfortable doing that, but I would still be really scared to send the email. I always obeyed my mom and felt obligated to stay in that unhealthy relationship with her, even if it was at the cost of my own health. I suffered immensely at the hands of my mom. How could I confront my mom with the truth—the truth that I was sacrificing my life to my mother's dysfunction—her abuse?"

Stella's work with Rachel had scratched the surface in revealing how individuals learn to cope when they come from abusive backgrounds. Their bodies keep a complete and faultless record of everything they have ever experienced. Rachel showed Stella a healthy way of mothering through the pink cord and the window to view her emotions. Stella was no longer doomed to pass the legacy of abuse on to Gabrielle. She was able to confront her childhood in a safe place and to see her parents in a realistic light, but the chains that bound her to the past still resonated within her cells; she still felt she owed her parents the love and gratitude that had been instilled in her being from the beginning. Rachel had worked extensively with Stella in changing the script that was handed to her in childhood, but the residue that still existed in Stella's body craved the nourishment she needed so badly from her mom that was never given and was the source of her suffering and distress. Stella understood that she believed she needed her mom because despite all the disappointments she had experienced, she quietly hoped for some proof of genuine affection from her.

Since Stella was afraid to send an email, Rachel tried to help her with the best way to word it. "What would you like to say in the email?" Rachel asked.

Stella turned away and looked outside at the purple grapes hanging on the vine. "I want the email to state that I need a break from our relationship for a while."

"Then say that," Rachel confirmed.

■　■　■

Stella got up the next day and crafted an email response to Shirley. "Hi, Mom. I appreciate you reaching out to me. I have been doing some healing work around our relationship, so I am not interested in getting together and talking at this time. I will contact you when I'm ready."

As Stella pushed the send button, she could no longer deny the truth.

She had a witness in Rachel to help her unlock the repressed suffering—someone who could accompany her on the road to her own truth. To assemble the things always denied to her, like trust, respect, and love for herself, Stella knew she needed to integrate the story of her childhood.

Stella knew that staying in contact with Shirley would not allow her to look at the source of her anxiety honestly. She now had a chance to liberate herself from her destructive attachment to her mom. She didn't hate Shirley; she wanted to take her life into her own hands, to be free from the chains of the past. She had to learn to see and judge everything she felt through her eyes instead of her mom's. She felt handicapped in her ability to feel her own needs. It took her some time to realize that staying connected to her mom was doing her some serious harm.

Stella sent the email and didn't check her inbox for a few days. When she did, she saw that Shirley had sent a short response saying that she understood that Stella needed space to work through some of her issues. Stella shrugged her shoulders and closed down the computer. There was a sense of relief that she didn't have to respond to any questions on why she needed some space. It felt truly liberating that she could say what she needed and have it be honored.

Stella wasn't talking much to Robert these days, either. Through all her work with Rachel so far, she realized that her parents had systematically driven the trust out of her from birth, and she knew now that they had not wanted her. She knew her dad had wanted a boy, and her mom had been unhappy in her marriage. Stella had spent most of her adult life compensating for the death of her brother and trying to fill in the blank spaces with her dad from his pain over the divorce and death. Stella wasn't willing to live her life that way anymore. She scheduled sessions with Rachel every week in an attempt to excavate, understand, and heal the wounds that bound her to the past.

■ ■ ■

A few weeks after Stella had sent the email, she was in a session with Rachel when Rachel said, "I have witnessed how much more you are in touch with your emotions about your mom."

"What do you mean?" Stella asked.

"You are more in touch with the memories of your mom's cruelty to you when you were younger," Rachel said.

"I don't feel hatred for my mom. I don't need to hate her because I don't feel emotionally dependent on her anymore," said Stella. "I didn't need to suffer from pretending that I have feelings for Shirley. I don't have feelings for her. That's why I don't feel any hatred for her."

"It was always the hatred of you as a dependent child that kept the circle going between you and your mom," Rachel explained. "It didn't matter before if you broke off contact with your parents or not; it was really about the process of separation from being a child to an adult."

"I never truly grew up," Stella said.

Stella was now becoming much closer to Rachel due to the separation from Shirley, and through that trust, she was able to expose her anxiety and deal with its symptoms and episodes as they arose.

■ ■ ■

At the end of 2007, Stella landed a full-time job in technology sales—a good way for her to focus on something other than Gabrielle being away at college. She also wasn't all alone in the house since Tiger was still a source of comfort and companionship for her. They would take day trips out to the college to visit Gabrielle every other week. Stella also dated a few guys during this time, but it never amounted to anything. She was focused on doing her healing work and figuring out how to manage the symptoms of anxiety when they presented themselves. Gabrielle came home for holidays and summer vacation. Even during the summer, Stella didn't see much of her because Gabrielle worked full-time as a barista to earn some extra money.

That fall, the first black president in U.S. History, Barack Obama, was elected. Stella fell back into her routine of eating alone and spending more time at the office once Gabrielle returned to school. Stella didn't like it when Gabrielle left. It always left such a void in her daily routine. She loved having Gabrielle around. At least she knew Gabrielle would always come back home.

To cope with her loneliness, Stella fell back into some old behaviors with alcohol. In the past, when she had needed some numbing and something to fill the void, it was either guys or alcohol. She had so much anxiety around relationships with men that she didn't trust herself to communicate what she needed in a relationship or in the process of getting to know someone. She didn't want to fill the void with these devices. When Stella was young, she'd learned to suppress her feelings of fear, anger, and pain. She wasn't allowed to have her feelings out of fear of being hit or abandoned. So Stella developed the skill in controlling and restraining her feelings. In their next session, Rachel and Stella addressed the anxiety and why she had the need to avoid the symptoms and not walk through to the other side.

Rachel had asked Stella in their last appointment to bring her pink cord so they could do some "feeding" through the rope. Stella arrived the next day very exhausted because she had drank too much alcohol and not gotten much sleep the night before. She felt scared about the session because sometimes the sessions made her anxious the next day. Rachel picked up on Stella's apprehension and sat next to her while they talked a bit about why she was drinking more alcohol than her occasional drink.

"I don't know why. It's really hard that Gabrielle is gone. I feel so alone," she confessed.

"Stella, sometimes alcohol is used in an attempt to fill the void," Rachel said. "Maybe you've been trying to fill the emptiness you had as a child. You were not given the nourishment needed from your mom, so you've tried to find a substitute in alcohol, but alcohol doesn't work as a substitute."

Rachel went on to explain that the body will always look to fill the vacancy that developed since childhood. "Your body urgently needed something, something that was withheld since infancy. You're simply trying to substitute the alcohol for the emotional nourishment you really needed. Where is your cord?"

"Um, it's in my purse," said Stella.

"Pull it out and give me one end while you hang on to the other end," said Rachel. "Let me feed you."

They sat there for most of the session with their eyes closed. Stella felt a sudden flush come through her body, starting at her hands and working its way all around. Suddenly, an image came into Stella's mind. She was lying in a hole dug out in the ground. She was surrounded by trees, birds singing, and the sun was shining. The hole slowly started filling up with crystal clear turquoise water. It was very warm and it covered her body like a baby being swaddled. Stella opened her eyes and told Rachel about the vision she'd had with the pink cord. Rachel explained that her adult person needed to develop empathy for the little girl she had once been, the little girl whose sufferings went unnoticed. "Talk to that little girl inside of you and tell her that I have her. I am protecting her."

Stella started to cry because she knew she was reverting back to her old way of dealing with her emotions. Rachel reassured her. "Stella, this process with the cord is a process to unleash the memories and to look at how far you've come. The pink cord nourishes you with safety, love, and support so you can get in touch with your wounding and release the negative energy that has been in your system from birth. It gives you a way to look within and feel the void, release the emotion, and replace it with the cord attached to loving nourishment; then you can have a new belief about who you are and the support that is given through my love."

■ ■ ■

Gabrielle was going up to Camano Island to her dad's for Christmas break. She had just come home for a couple of days to see her mom before going.

"Gabrielle, what time in the morning are you leaving?" Stella asked during her last night there after they had finished dinner.

"Just after nine to avoid the rush hour traffic," she said. She cleaned up the dishes and went into her room to pack.

Sensing Gabrielle didn't need help packing, Stella decided to reach out to Robert in a phone call. She hadn't spoken to him in six months. "Hi, Dad. What are you doing for Christmas Eve?"

"Hi, honey; it's good to hear from you. We're going to be here so you and Gabrielle can come over."

"Dad, Gabrielle is going to her dad's for Christmas Eve, so it will just be me. I don't want to stay home alone."

Robert was all that Stella had in terms of family. Robert and Susan had moved back to Seattle when Gabrielle was born and lived a twenty-minute drive from Stella's house in North Seattle. She always felt awkward going over to her dad's house. There was always a feeling of disconnect between her and Susan and her kids. Susan and Stella were close when it was just them together, but when her kids were around, Susan seemed distant and her kids didn't talk much to Stella or Gabrielle. Consequently, Stella rarely visited her father's house. She also still wasn't speaking to her mother and had no contact with Lynn, even though Lynn had recently moved back to Seattle. Gabrielle was her family.

Stella knocked on the door and waited until someone yelled, "Come in!" Then she opened the door and walked inside. She was greeted by Susan, a tall blonde, slender figure with a great smile. "Hi, Stella," Susan said, as she closed the door behind Stella. "Your dad is in the family room watching sports." She led Stella into the living room where her kids were. Stella said hello to Alex, who was the oldest, tall, and athletically built, then to Stu, the middle child, who was short but also athletically built, and to Jessica, the youngest, who was short and plump, sitting with her newborn baby. They had come over to visit their mom for the holiday. Stella briefly exchanged holiday greetings with them and then walked down the hall to see her father.

"Hi, Dad," Stella said as she walked into the family room.

"Hi, honey," Robert replied, slowly getting out of his chair to hug Stella.

Stella sat down in the chair next to Robert. "Dad, it's good to see you. Did Lynn call to wish you a Merry Christmas?"

"She did. I invited them over for dinner, but she is staying home."

"How is she doing?"

"Good, working at her job as a hair stylist."

Conversation was superficial at Robert's house. Mostly, he and Stella sat in the family room catching up on news about family members in Massachusetts and also how Lynn was. Robert had contact with

Lynn, and he told Stella that Lynn and her daughter now had no contact. The situation reminded Stella of how both she and Lynn had no contact now with their own mother. In fact, she had come to visit her dad hoping to fill her empty feeling of being alone without Gabrielle or any other family.

After a while, however, Stella realized her dad was behaving more distant than usual, as if something were bothering him.

"Dad, you seem preoccupied with something," Stella said, while fiddling with her phone.

"No, honey. Everything is fine," Robert replied, staring at the TV.

So much for filling the void, Stella thought.

While Stella drove home that night, she decided to plan something with Gabrielle over spring break. She really wanted to attempt a trip where she could fly on an airplane. She wasn't sure whether it would ever become a reality, but at least it was a step in the right direction. Even thinking of wanting to travel on a plane showed her that she had made some leaps. She remembered when the thought had never entered her mind.

■ ■ ■

After Christmas that December, Seattle had a snowstorm of eight inches that brought the city to a standstill, not helped by record low temperatures in the teens. Greyhound, Sea-Tac airport, and Amtrak to Oregon ground to a halt. Drivers were trapped in vehicles on I-5, I-405, and I-90 for over eight hours. Luckily, both Gabrielle and Stella didn't have to endure the situation because they were home watching it on the news while eating leftovers from their Christmas dinner. Stella was concerned about whether Gabrielle would be able to drive over the pass back to college once Christmas break was over. Fortunately, the snow had melted and the pass was clear to travel in time for Gabrielle to go back to school.

It was a new year and Stella was excited to plan a trip with Gabrielle over spring break and fly on an airplane—that is, if Gabrielle would be onboard with this spring break plan. Stella had done some deep work with Rachel over the past two years, dealing with neglect, abandonment, and the physical abuse she had endured from Shirley as a child. She felt that she had really gained some ground by working on her grief over her childhood not being nurturing. Now she was ready for some relief from her anxiety symptoms.

10

"Though it is difficult when life presses you down,

Still if you make the effort with strong determination,

You will triumph over every challenge."

— Paranahensa Yoganda

tella received a phone call on a Wednesday in February 2009 from Robert. "Honey, I have some bad news," he said, his voice emotionless.

When Stella had received bad news calls in the past, she instantly thought someone had died. "Is Lynn okay?" she asked, holding the phone with her left shoulder while she finished drying her hands.

"Um, yes, she is okay. Honey, I have cancer—in the lungs—and it doesn't look good," Robert said.

Stella placed the towel on the kitchen counter and leaned against the stove while she listened to Robert; she was in shock; she didn't know how to respond to his news. She was thinking how he was the only parent she had left because she didn't feel she would ever see Shirley again.

"Stella, are you there?" he asked in a panicky voice.

"Yes, Dad, I'm here. I don't know what to say. How serious is it?" she asked, looking down at the floor.

There was silence on the phone. "Stage four," he said.

"Does Lynn know?" Stella asked, starting to chew on her fingernails.

"Yes. I called her just before I called you," Robert said.

"My oncologist suggested chemotherapy to try to shrink the tumor. He will need to see if the cancer has spread to the brain, so I'll be going into the hospital tomorrow to have a CT scan."

"Oh, Dad, I'm sorry this is happening to you. What can I do?"

"Well, I've an appointment with my oncologist to go over the results on Monday. I would like for you to be at that appointment."

"Of course I'll be there. What time?"

"The appointment is at 10:30 a.m.," he said, hanging up the phone.

Stella hadn't spoken to Lynn in two years so she called her just after she hung up with Robert. Lynn didn't answer so Stella left her a message to call. Lynn called the next day.

"Hi, Stella, how are you?" Lynn asked in a raspy voice.

"Hi, Lynn. I'm okay. What do you think about Dad's situation?"

"Yeah, that's tragic. He seemed really upset when I talked to him," she said. "I'm really busy at work, so I can't deal with this right now. I've all kinds of customers wanting me to—"

"Lynn, will you go to Dad's doctor appointment with me? I don't want to do this alone. I can pick you up too if that helps," Stella asked in a pleading voice.

"You know I don't like doctor offices."

"Yeah, I know, but I really need your support. And so does Dad."

With some convincing, Stella got Lynn to commit.

■ ■ ■

The day of Robert's appointment, Stella picked up Lynn at the beauty salon where she worked in Lynnwood. Stella hadn't seen Lynn for a long time, so it was awkward being in the car listening to her talk about her job as a hairdresser.

"Yeah, this job is so good, and I love the people I'm working with," Lynn said, looking out the window.

"That's good," Stella said, looking out her driver window to merge onto I-405 to Bellevue. Stella lived ten miles away from Lynn and twenty miles from Bellevue where Robert and Susan lived. Stella really wasn't listening to her sister; Lynn always talked about the same thing: Lynn. Stella was still reeling from her conversation with their dad and not knowing what to expect from the appointment.

When they arrived at the clinic, they went up to the second floor to meet Robert and Susan.

Robert grabbed Lynn the moment he saw her. "Hi, honey. Thank you for being here." Stella was used to being second to Lynn around her father, so she went over to hug Susan, who was standing behind Robert. Then he turned around and hugged Stella. They all found a place to sit together while waiting for the appointment. The tension in the waiting room was so thick. Stella reached down to her belly button and touched the pink cord through her T-shirt. When the nurse called "Robert Maris," Robert waved his hand to identify himself and they all shuffled into the examining room. While the nurse took Robert's vitals, Stella sat quietly next to Lynn. *It seems really weird to me that we are all here,* Stella thought. *It's been a long time since Lynn, Dad, and I were together. It's a shame that our dad's diagnosis has to be the incident to bring us all together again.*

After ten minutes, Dr. Chin finally opened the door and sat down next to Robert. "Hi. My name is Dr. Chin. How are you doing today, Robert?" he asked while looking at his chart.

"Well, under the circumstances, I feel okay," Robert said, holding onto Susan's hand.

Dr. Chin explained that the cancer hadn't spread to the brain or anywhere else, but there was a tumor in the right lung. "I would like to prescribe chemotherapy to try to shrink the tumor and keep the cancer at bay," he said.

"How long will the treatment be?" Robert asked.

"We'll do one round and then give you another CT scan to see whether the tumor has shrunk," Dr. Chin replied, writing on the chart. "If so, then we'll apply maybe two more treatments."

Robert and Susan were very quiet. The doctor wanted Robert to start chemo the following week, so he gave him the phone number to schedule the times.

"The cancer being a Stage Four, you could have nine to twelve months to live," Dr. Chin added. "Does anyone have any questions they would like to ask?"

Stella pondered for a second. "Dr. Chin, what caused the tumor?"

"Well, your dad was a smoker in the past," he said, looking at Stella.

"I get that, but some people smoke their whole lives and don't get lung cancer. Can you explain that?" she asked.

The doctor searched for his words and said, "Some people are just less fortunate that the cells turn into cancer."

Lynn and Susan sat quietly while the doctor answered Stella's question and gave Robert the phone number to call and set up the chemo treatments.

The elevator ride down was very quiet. Stella was lost in her thoughts: *Cancer will eventually take my dad's life. I don't have a relationship with my mom or my sister. I can't imagine not having my dad in my life.*

Stella and Lynn hugged Robert and Susan inside the elevator because they had to go down another floor where Stella's car was parked. Stella didn't know how to feel, so she kept walking to the car. When she opened her door, she turned around to see Lynn smoking a cigarette.

"What didn't you understand about the appointment we just had with Dad?" Stella asked.

"I'm going to quit right after this cigarette," Lynn announced, taking a drag.

"I can't stand the smell of smoke, so make sure you stand outside for a bit before you get into the car so my car doesn't reek like smoke. Gross!" Stella opened up her window for some fresh air.

Stella wasn't very talkative driving home. She was still thinking about Robert and how his cancer would affect his life. *Will he die from this? I don't know much about cancer. What will be his quality of life while on chemo?* So many questions with no answers.

"Stella, I need to let you know I won't be able to help you with Dad," Lynn said.

"Why?"

"I don't do well around hospitals and death, and I'm too busy with work."

Stella stared straight ahead as they pulled into Lynn's parking lot. She turned to Lynn. "Just like you to bail out on me. I really need you to be there not only for Dad but for me, too. I'm really scared, Lynn."

Lynn just stared ahead and didn't say anything.

Stella reached out to touch Lynn's arm. "You're the only one in the family left to support me. I don't have a relationship with Mom, and most likely our dad will die from this. I don't want to be alone."

Lynn turned to Stella and didn't say anything, just her goodbye, and got out of the car.

As Stella drove away, once Lynn was no longer in sight, she started to cry.

■ ■ ■

Lynn and Stella were five years apart. As kids, they had shared the same bedroom and the same friends. Photographs of them as children showed them wearing matching pajamas, matching shorts, and matching T-shirts. Lynn's eyes radiated the color brown like a button, and her black hair fell to her collarbone. Stella's eyes embodied a deep green like the sea, and her hair was the color of sand as it flowed down her back. But despite that, they were sisters. Lynn was older, so she had been more protective and told Stella what to do.

Lynn had trouble going to the bathroom. She would have to go, but her bowels would freeze up; she would sit on the toilet for hours, trying to go. Sometimes, Lynn and Stella would try to play Barbies together, but Lynn would leave Stella setting up the Barbie house and playing by herself for hours while she was in the bathroom. Or Stella would ride her trike around the block several times while Lynn was in the bathroom, and by the time she appeared and said, "I'm ready to play," Stella would be done.

Lynn and Stella often got into the ugliest fights. Lynn was so mean to Stella, always bossing her around. Lynn was older, stronger, and much bigger. If she didn't get her way, she would punch or scratch Stella with her long fingernails. Stella was a nail-biter so she didn't have any nails, which gave Lynn another advantage, and she used it frequently. From the time Stella was eleven and Lynn sixteen, until Lynn left home, there wasn't a day that went by when they didn't have a fight. Shirley and Robert never intervened. Once in a while, Shirley would make them go to their room, but that never lasted. One time during their fight, Lynn came into the bathroom while Stella was cleaning it and shoved her head in the toilet.

Stella never knew why Lynn was mad at her that time—she always had so many reasons that Stella couldn't keep them all straight. She thought all sisters fought like that. Lynn never fought with Michael because he was nine years younger than her, but Stella did fight with him at times.

The fights continued until Stella was about twelve. Then she finally stood up to Lynn. Stella was talking to a friend on the phone when Lynn demanded she hang up because she wanted to call someone.

"I'm not done talking yet," Stella said and told her to go away.

Lynn screamed, "Tough" and grabbed the phone away to hang it up. But Stella fought to take the phone back, and they struggled violently. It took everything Stella had to fight against her sister. The fight ended when Stella saw an opening, swung her arm, and punched Lynn in the face with all her might. Stella almost broke her nose. Lynn never bugged her after that.

■ ■ ■

When Stella got home, she went into her bedroom and continued to cry until she fell asleep. When she woke up, she called Rachel to schedule an appointment; it had been a week since their last meeting. Stella unwrapped the pink cord from her waist, kissed it, wrapped it in the white lace handkerchief, and gently placed it in the Chinese box sitting on her dresser where she stored it.

At Stella's next session with Rachel, Stella's pink cord was securely wrapped around her waist three times. The two women sat quietly for a few moments, peacefully watching the sunbeams dance over the pillows on the futon. Stella felt protected and safe.

"Tell me about the beatings," said Rachel, in her soft, calm voice. "I'm getting an image of your mom beating you."

An old, old feeling flooded Stella. She had felt this feeling constantly as a child—it was like being paralyzed with shame and fear. And embarrassment. *No one must know.* She had to keep these feelings secret. But Stella saw Rachel looking at her with those clear eyes, and she saw no judgment there; Stella realized that here it might be safe to tell; it might be safe to remember.

"The waiting was the worst," Stella said.

The anxiety built with every minute Lynn and Stella waited in their bedroom, waiting for their mom to come in with the belt. Shirley was the main disciplinarian in their family, and it was always the same: They would be told to go to their room and wait for her to come in and beat them. In the bedroom, Stella's stomach hurt from fear, and she was always afraid she would throw up. Lynn and Stella talked about who would go first, although it didn't really matter because either way they had to watch each other get beaten; even if Lynn were first, Stella had to watch while her sister would scream.

"I can't remember what Lynn and I did that made our mom beat us. I felt so powerless and shameful wondering what was wrong with me," Stella said, looking at Rachel. "I was just a young child wanting to be loved, nurtured, and cherished for just me. I couldn't understand why my mom hated me so much. I felt that way most of my life."

Rachel grabbed a tissue for Stella. "When Gabrielle was born, I couldn't imagine spanking her, let alone hating her. I love Gabrielle so much. I don't remember how many times my mother would hit Lynn and me; it felt like it went on forever. How I detached from the incident was to pretend I was a bird—a bird that flew away, trying to escape the pain."

Rachel talked to Stella about how child abuse and neglect can have lasting effects upon a child's sense of self, and his or her ability to have healthy relationships, and even the ability to function at home and at work. As well as showing the lack of trust in relationships, the feelings of being worthless led to trouble regulating and identifying emotions. All those effects could contribute to anxiety.

Rachel reached out to massage Stella's foot to help soothe her tears. Stella began to shake, so Rachel got up and went to sit next to her. She placed a yellow blanket on Stella while she wept. Rachel didn't say much—just let her be in her grief. Then an incident popped into Stella's mind from when she was just three years old.

"I remember packing my Barbie case with my clothes since I had no other suitcase. I'd walk to the end of our street, about three houses away, where I'd sit on the corner and wait. I don't know what I was waiting for, but I had that running away feeling most of my life," Stella said, while wiping her tears.

Rachel sat close and allowed Stella to tell her story.

"Even though I tried to run away, I was terrified of being alone, especially alone without my mom. The thing that really scared me was that I believed my mom was going to die. It didn't matter that she wasn't sick; I was sure she was going to die and I'd be left alone. When I was around eight, we moved to another house and my sister and I each got our own bedroom. I hated it. It was a two-story house, and when I'd go to bed, I was so scared of being alone that my mom would bang a broom handle on the ceiling from downstairs to signal that she was still in the house and had not left me alone."

Stella adjusted her position on the futon to allow Rachel to adjust her position.

"Even later when I was nine or ten and we had moved from the East Coast to Washington, I got to the state where I didn't want to go to school or leave the house for any reason, even to play with a friend, for fear that my mom would die when I was gone. What would I do without her? I was afraid of her, but afraid to be without her," Stella said, looking down at her hands folding the tissue.

Stella sat up and wiped the tears from her cheeks with the tissue. She began to tell Rachel about the image that came to her while she was lying down. "I could see why I always wanted to run away, to detach from people and my surroundings," she said.

Rachel explained, "The beatings, not being nurtured, and not having a safe and loving environment can all contribute to the anxiety and having the urge to run away."

"It's so true. I have had trouble connecting and trusting relationships with guys too. I don't remember a time when anxiety was not present in my life. When I became a teenager, I started to drink a lot, which numbed the anxiety somewhat."

"I also discovered I could stuff it away if I slept around. Alcohol made me feel less fearful, and promiscuity made me feel loved and wanted, at least for a little while. After a while, I cut down on my drinking, but I continued to sleep around for years, using sex as my 'drug of choice.' I wasn't into real drugs; I was afraid of drugs. They would make me more anxious and I would lose myself. I was afraid that if I took drugs, I would never find myself again."

"Stella, you just did some good deep work. Your truth to the situation was really profound," Rachel said, sitting back on her bean bag chair. "I know it was tough for you to share these feelings, but this was a great breakthrough in connecting with how you dealt with the pain."

Rachel hugged Stella goodbye and told her that she loved her. They scheduled another appointment a few weeks later.

When she got home, Stella made herself some soup. Most of the time when she had a deep session with Rachel like the one she'd just had, it was hard for her to eat and her stomach would hurt. After the soup, her stomach settled down and she prepared to go to bed early. Stella decided to keep the pink cord wrapped around her waist, so she slipped into her pajamas and crawled into bed. Stella was feeling a bit anxious, so she kept the cord on while she slept. The session with Rachel rolled around in her head so she focused on how much she loved Rachel, how much she felt supported by her, and how she truly felt loved by Rachel.

■ ■ ■

Stella woke up to her phone ringing around 8 a.m.; it was Robert, so she answered it. "Honey, I want to take you out for lunch today; are you available?" he asked.

"Yes, Dad, I do have some time today; where do you want to go?" she asked.

"I'm coming down your way, so we'll go to the waterfront. I'll be there around noon," he replied.

"Okay. What is the special lunch for?"

"Just want to spend some time with my daughter, if that's okay."

"Sure, Dad. It will be good to have lunch with you," Stella said, as she hung up the phone.

Stella felt bad for Robert because Lynn had disappeared after the oncology appointment and had also told him she wouldn't be around while he had his chemotherapy, so Stella agreed to go to lunch with him on such short notice. She took a shower and did the usual ritual of putting a small amount of geranium essential oil in her belly button and then taping a cotton ball to her skin so no energy could penetrate that area. Rachel had taught her to protect herself when visiting her parents. In the past, Stella would wear her pink cord when around her parents—not so much with her dad, but she always did that ritual when she visited her mom. Stella hadn't had to do the aromatherapy ritual for a while since she was not having a relationship with Shirley right now, but today she did because she was feeling very vulnerable after her session with Rachel, and she knew her dad was in a very vulnerable place too.

11

"There is a place for everyone in the big picture.
To turn your back on any one person,
for whatever reason, is to run the risk of losing the central piece
of your jigsaw puzzle."

— Johnna Howell

It had been four months since Robert had visited Stella at her house. Not knowing what to prepare for, Stella grabbed her coat when she saw her father pull into the yard. He got out of his vehicle and met her at the front door. She offered to drive and he picked a waterfront restaurant in Stella's neighborhood for lunch. Then after they got in the car, before Stella even started the car, Robert began to cry. Stella put her arm around his shoulder to comfort him. She knew it was hard for him, not knowing if he'd live or die, and her heart went out to him as he cried.

Suddenly, he started pouring out his heart. "I met this woman named Spring. She was like the season, warm and exciting. Spring is not her real name; she has an Asian name, Jiaying."

Stella started the car, trying not to hear what Robert was saying, and sat idling in her driveway.

"Stella, do you think someone can love two people at once?"

Stella turned to Robert and said, "Sure, depending on the type of love."

He started crying. "I love this woman; she's my soulmate."

Robert had met Spring through a mutual friend a few years ago and he started going to her restaurant in Chinatown in Seattle. He would frequent the restaurant at least once a week and got to know Spring's husband. They all became good friends. It was not a physical relationship but Robert was attracted to her and Spring was in a bad marriage, so Robert gave her advice. He was a good listener. Susan had many of her own friends and spent a lot of time with her kids and grandkids so he was lonely and had enjoyed Spring's company.

When he began confessing his love and connection with this woman he had met a few years ago, Stella didn't have time to respond.

"I really believe she is an angel who will help me to heal this cancer." Robert filled the car's atmosphere with descriptions of how Spring was his soulmate.

Stella cracked the window; his words were suffocating her. "Dad, I have never heard you use the word *soulmate* before." She thought he had gone mad dealing with the cancer. "Dad, don't you think this could be a result of you not wanting to deal with your situation?"

He didn't respond.

The conversation took Stella back to when her parents had just divorced and Robert had moved to a suburban neighborhood just thirty minutes from Seattle in an apartment. Stella would visit him on occasion because she felt very sorry for him being alone. She needed to make sure he was okay; her life had been consumed by feeling responsible for her dad's happiness.

One day, her father began to tell her about a gal he was dating. It was almost like he was bragging that the girl he was dating was only a few years older than Stella.

That he would date someone so young made a lot of sense to Stella because when he was drunk, he often looked at Stella in a way that made her uncomfortable. Sometimes he'd take her to a restaurant, just the two of them, which made it appear like they had a close relationship, but they didn't. At the restaurant, Stella would sit there and watch Robert get drunk. If they ran into a friend or acquaintance of his from work, he'd never introduce her as his daughter; instead, he'd just say, "This is Stella." She didn't know what they thought—that she was his girlfriend or what. When he was drunk, he sometimes told her he wished she wasn't his daughter. Then he'd give her kind of a leering smile. Stella found that creepy. She wondered whether Lynn had ever had any situations like that with their dad.

Stella put the car in reverse and proceeded to drive to the restaurant. She didn't say anything to Robert on the way.

After they arrived at the restaurant and ordered their food, it was quiet for a minute until Robert asked, "Stella, do you want to meet her?"

"No, Dad, I don't," Stella said firmly.

Stella felt very conflicted. Even though she didn't condone her dad's behavior, she understood how he had come to have an affair. Robert and Susan had been married for thirty years, but they didn't spend much time together. Every winter, Robert would go down to

Mexico alone, and Susan spent most of her time with her kids. Stella didn't understand why they stayed married.

When the food arrived, Robert just looked at Stella for a minute before he began to eat. "I'm going to beat this cancer and turn my life around for the better," he said, shoveling food into his mouth.

Stella looked up from her salad and stared out the window at the water. The restaurant was a popular food chain with lots of seafood to choose from. It had a rustic beach look that really appealed to the area. She hadn't seen her dad so excited about something in a long time. He used to have an optimistic attitude before her parents' divorce and her brother's death. Maybe the Spring girl gave him hope.

"Dad, just concentrate on your healing," Stella said.

Robert paid the bill and then Stella drove them both back to her house. They said their goodbyes and Stella watched Robert drive away. She went back into the house and called Rachel.

■ ■ ■

Rachel had worked with many cancer victims, helping them to labor through the end of their lives, so she brought some good wisdom to their next session together.

"It's not about you helping your dad through this journey; it's his transition; he picked this route, so it's up to him, if he can, to heal," she said.

"I know; I just don't know how to help him," Stella said.

"You can't; it's not your job to make this better for him. All you can do is be present and keep your heart open." Rachel always had a way with words. *She's right,* Stella thought. *It isn't my journey; it's his. It has always been his journey, but I've always made it my own—to try to take away his pain and make his life fulfilling and happy.*

"Stella, life is about embracing this gift of being able to say good-bye to your dad."

"I know you're right," Stella said, while tightly wrapping the blanket around her.

"You didn't get that chance with your brother, so here is the opportunity to let go of all that you need to let go of so you can heal your relationship with your dad."

"Yeah," Stella agreed. "I get to let go of what I didn't get from him and to love him with a healthy open heart."

"Stella, you've worked so hard on yourself and coming to terms with your childhood and the anxiety."

"I have, haven't I? Rachel, you've helped me do so much healing; that's why I can be present with my dad."

"Let's schedule for next week. Bring in some photos of you and your dad then so we can do a ritual around letting go."

■ ■ ■

Stella wasn't a big gatherer of items or photos, but she had two snapshots of Robert and one of her and Robert when she was three years old. At their next appointment, she pulled them out of her purse and Rachel looked at them for a while, smiling at the photograph of Stella and Robert.

"What a precious picture of you and your dad," she said. "He looks very relaxed in this photo with you," she continued while adjusting in her chair. "You look content too, Stella."

Stella looked up at her and smiled. She didn't remember much about her childhood so Rachel's words were very comforting. "I wonder when the shift came—when your dad started looking at you differently. Dads have a hard time when their daughters grow up and start becoming women."

Stella looked at Rachel while she explained why her relationship with Robert became unhealthy. "The discord and inappropriateness can come when a guy doesn't develop emotionally into a man, so he is left to his own devices with boundary issues. You didn't cause any of this inappropriate behavior from your dad when you were young, Stella. This is who he is."

It was good to hear this, and Stella trusted Rachel with every inch of her being. Rachel held one end of the pink cord while Stella held the other. They did this ritual at times during their sessions so Rachel could literally pass her loving, mothering energy through the cord to Stella.

■ ■ ■

Eight months had passed since Robert's diagnosis. Stella spent some time with Robert every few weeks during the chemotherapy treatments. She would go to his house because it was easier for her— sometimes he was too ill—and she didn't have any anxiety driving anymore. Stella hadn't seen Robert in a few weeks when she received a call from him one morning.

"Honey, I wanted to let you know that the last round of chemo didn't shrink the tumor."

"Oh, Dad, I'm so sorry. Does Lynn know?"

"I'm going to call her after we hang up."

Stella started to cry. "Can't they try another kind of chemo?" The conversation went silent for a bit. "Dad, I don't have much going on tomorrow. I would like to come over and spend the day with you."

"I would really like that, Honey," Robert said. Then he hung up the phone.

■ ■ ■

Stella arrived to find Robert slouched in a tan leather chair with his feet on the footstool. He looked preoccupied, not noticing Stella looking at him. Susan was helping Robert change his T-shirt, which revealed how his body had changed so much in the last few weeks. Stella could see his boney ribcage, the remnant of a potbelly, and his muscles stripped away to uncover bones. It was painful for Stella to witness this decay. She felt so bad for him, his life ending like that. He had fought this battle for ten months, but the chemotherapy had not shrunk the tumor. His doctor had now told him to put everything in order before his passing. Robert did so and began to receive counseling from a hospice therapist named Marsha.

When Susan finished helping Robert get dressed, she excused herself to go see about making lunch.

"Dad, how are you today?" Stella asked, putting her purse down on the bed.

"Not good," he said, getting right to the point.

"What's wrong?" she asked, sitting down on the couch and rubbing his leg.

"Spring wants to come over to visit, but Susan won't let her," he said, sounding like a small child who had been told he couldn't go out to play.

Stella had a good relationship with Susan. She was always decent to Stella and Gabrielle when they visited. Stella had known she and Susan would be in this journey together from the beginning of Robert's diagnosis. Susan was a retired nurse and Stella was Robert's daughter. Susan was all Stella had for support besides Rachel.

Before Stella decided how to respond to her father's remark about Spring, Susan reappeared and asked Stella to come into the kitchen so she could speak to her. Stella began to wonder then whether Susan knew Spring was more than just a friend to her dad.

Keeping secrets was routine in Stella's relationship with her dad, but she felt it wasn't her business to tell Susan, even though she wanted to desperately. She would have to tell her dad he needed to be honest with Susan about his relationship with Spring, but when Stella got to the kitchen and saw the look on Susan's face, she knew Susan had already figured out the truth.

"Stella, I can't stay here and take care of your dad," said Susan, her eyes fixed on stirring the soup.

"Why do you want to leave?" Stella asked, dreading the answer.

"I can't be here if Spring is going to come over. I just won't do it," she said, stirring the soup.

"Susan, I can't take care of him. I'm working a full-time job and don't have the skills to do this," she said, reaching for a bowl. "My dad needs you here to help him through this. I need you here to help him through this."

Robert was sitting in the family room listening to their conversation. "I'll just move over to Spring's house," he said loud enough for them to hear. "She'll take care of me."

That's going to really help the situation, thought Stella as she shook her head and rolled her eyes. Stella asked Susan to come back into the family room so they could all talk about it. She agreed. Stella was surprised by how much Susan knew about Spring already.

They settled in the family room. Robert was propped in his chair while Susan sat on the couch on the opposite side of the room with her arms crossed, staring at Robert. Stella stood at an angle between them.

Susan pushed on. "I'm not going to stay in this house if *she* comes over."

Something in Stella felt sorry for both of them. *What a matter to have to confront at this time in their marriage,* Stella thought. *They should be spending this moment together grieving their loss, sharing their love for one another. Instead, they tolerated the distance over the years, letting unspoken words separate them and spoil the foundation that was created years ago.*

"Dad, is there any way Spring can come to visit another day?" Stella began. "Susan is very upset with her coming over, and I feel you two should resolve this." The room was silent except for the clock ticking on the wall. No response. "Would you just call Spring and say that you will need to reschedule?" she asked in a calm, quiet voice.

As Robert and Susan stared at each other, Stella looked nervously out the picture window. The clouds looked gray and troubled. She hoped they would resolve this issue themselves. She had been picking up the pieces for her father most of her adult life as if she were responsible for his happiness. Where was the parent to help her through this situation? As she sunk deeper into that thought, she realized she had become the parent.

Then she remembered that Robert had a hospice therapist, Marsha, now. Robert had already met with her a few times, really liked her, and opened up to her regarding his feelings for Spring.

"What do you think about calling Marsha to help us figure this out?" Stella said, with authority.

Susan perked up with her reply, "That's a great idea. I'll get you the number so you can give her a call." Stella followed Susan into the kitchen. Susan grabbed the piece of paper with Marsha's number and placed the phone in Stella's hand. Stella clutched the phone, watching Susan clean up the kitchen. Susan seemed content, as though she knew Stella would take care of the situation. Oddly, this was Stella's own insight. A thought appeared as Stella dialed the number. *You're his wife. You should handle this.*

After Marsha's visit, Spring never did come to visit Robert.

■ ■ ■

Stella didn't realize that Robert worried about her. She always felt that he was so distant, so non-observant when it came to her life. The day that all changed for Stella was the next day when his hospice bed was delivered. Stella arrived early to Robert's house so she could be there to help set up the bed downstairs in the family room. This was the final indicator that Robert wasn't going to beat the cancer. He had been sleeping upright in his chair in the living room because he couldn't walk up the stairs to his bedroom.

Susan didn't know what time the bed would arrive so Stella called to find out what the plan was for delivery and negotiated the time. When she hung up the phone, both Susan and Robert were astounded by her assertiveness to get results, in this case a delivery time commitment. Stella shrugged her shoulders and said, "What's the big deal? I always talk like this."

"I never thought you had it in you, Stella. I always thought you were this timid, sensitive child who didn't like confrontation," he responded. "I don't have to worry about you; you can take care of yourself."

Stella was small, quiet, observant in a crowd, but what spiraled inside was much different. A powerful energy inside her consistently turned for the unjust. She had a passion to make things different, and the desire to speak her truth propelled Stella every day to seek her purpose and put it into use to serve others.

Stella had a session with Rachel later that afternoon after she went to Robert's house.

"How did things go with your dad and Susan?" Rachel asked.

"I have been picking up the pieces for my dad as long as I can remember," Stella replied. "I feel really bad for him—the way he is dying."

"What do you mean, Stella?" Rachel asked.

"It's just really hard for me to see him like this, dealing with the cancer, and also how Susan has to deal with this issue with Spring. They should be saying their goodbyes, not having conflict now."

"This is your dad's journey. You've been right there the whole time, and you should be very proud of yourself for the way you're handling this situation, being that your dad is dying."

Stella sat for a while, letting Rachel's words soak into her being. She was right. Stella had been present and her ability to stay grounded and clear with her emotions had made that journey with her dad all the better. She was healing what she didn't get from him by being able to walk with him through the dying process.

12

"Integrity is telling myself the truth.
And honesty is telling the truth to other people."

— Spencer Johnson

Stella arrived the next day to sit with Robert and go over his eulogy and burial wishes. He wanted to be buried back in Massachusetts with his parents and Michael, so they started the conversation with what that would look like. Because Shirley had no say in the matter, Robert wanted to be buried with Michael; he had already asked Stella to go to the cemetery to retrieve Michael's ashes and place them in an urn, which had been on the fireplace mantel ever since. Robert had researched earlier whether he could possibly be placed where his parents resided, and the cemetery sexton had confirmed that Robert and Michael could share the same plot. They were to be buried at the far end of Robert's Dad and Mom's gravesite.

"Dad," said Stella, during their review of the burial plans, "it's apparent to me the grief that you experienced all these years with Michael's death."

"Honey, do you think it's weird that I want to be buried with Michael?"

"Dad, Mom never thought Michael was in the mausoleum at the cemetery. You were the one in the family who visited him the most. You know, Dad, it's very touching that you want to be close to Michael in death because you didn't get much time with him in life, only eighteen years."

Robert started to cry, so Stella put the pen and pad on the couch and went over to give him a hug.

"You know, Dad, I always felt bad for you about the divorce and Michael's death. I watched you try to drink away your pain, eat away your pain, and now, as you sit here at the end of your life, I see peace and acceptance. I am profoundly moved by your grace in your commitment to make his burial right."

Stella went back to her chair and continued to write down Robert's wishes. Because Robert knew about Stella's previous fear of flying and that she would have to get on an airplane to travel back East, he then said, "Honey, why don't you have your cousin David read the eulogy?"

A part of Stella was relieved, but she replied, "No, Dad, I really want to do this for you, and you can count on me to be the person who will transport the ashes back East. Gabrielle will be going with me, so I'll be fine." It would take a lot of courage to board that plane, but she really wanted to go back and honor her father with all her cousins and his friends and siblings.

■ ■ ■

A few weeks later, Stella arrived at Robert's house on New Year's Day 2010. Once she entered the back room, she knew something was wrong. Robert was sitting up in his bed with an oxygen mask on, wheezing uncontrollably. Susan stood up and said, "We need to take your dad to urgent care."

Stella wasn't too worried; she had seen her father like this a few weeks earlier and the situation had passed with medication. "Okay," she replied. "Do we need to call the ambulance, or are we taking him in the car?"

Susan looked concerned. "I don't think we can wait, so we better take him ourselves."

Robert had no muscle mass to lift himself, so they had to wheel him outside to the car and carefully place him in the passenger front seat. He was so heavy, not that he was overweight, but because he had no strength to pull himself into the car, Stella had to pick him up. It took her a few attempts. It was so hard to see him like that, all of his internal functions gone and depending solely on diapers and a wheelchair.

Stella straightened Robert's robe and positioned his shoes on the correct feet. She fastened his seatbelt, and then she hopped in the backseat directly behind Robert. While Susan sped away, Stella was rubbing Robert's back. "Dad, how are you doing?"

"It's really hard for me to breathe."

They arrived at the clinic's urgent care entrance. Susan pulled up to the emergency door while Stella went inside to ask for assistance. A minute later, Stella came out with a wheelchair and a nurse and they wheeled Robert into the building. Susan parked the car and joined them a few minutes later.

They were led into an examining room where the nurse hooked Robert up to oxygen. "This will ease the panic of not being able to breathe and provide some medicine to open up the airways to your lungs," the nurse told Robert.

"Much better," Robert muffled through the mask as he sat there in his white cotton robe, sweat pants with food stains, and old slip-on garden shoes.

Robert's usual hospice nurse had the day off. The urgent care nurse didn't ask Robert to undress and put on a cotton hospital smock. Stella thought this would be an in-and-out examination—the nurse would give him some oxygen and antibiotics and drain his lungs. They had only been there once before when he had passed out while playing tennis a few months ago.

"Why don't you make yourself comfortable? The doctor won't be able to meet with you for a while," the nurse said.

Susan was holding Robert's hand, crying while she stroked his arm. "Everything is going to be all right."

Stella was starving. "I'm going to walk over to the market across the street to get some soup. Can I get anyone something?"

"If you could get me some soup too, that would be great," Susan said.

"Dad, I'm going. I'll be back soon," Stella said. Robert shook his head in acknowledgment.

While Stella walked over to the market, she thought about her relationship with her father:

> *We weren't very close, my dad and I. He really didn't know what to do with a daughter, how to cultivate a relationship with me. I tried my best to make him proud, playing sports and agreeing with his Republican views, but he was a man's man, all about sports, and didn't communicate his dreams or what his expectations were for me. The few memories I do have as a child are from when we lived on the East Coast and he played on a rugby team; he used to take me to the matches in Washington D.C., the bright lights and cold nights. He would wrap my hands in his to keep me warm when he was on the sidelines, so I did see the nurturing side of him. My other memory of us being close was when my mom was leaving the marriage; he showed up in my bedroom early one morning, sat in my wicker chair...and proceeded to cry, asking me*

why my mom was leaving him. I know he loved her very much and it was hard for him to accept the failure of a marriage. Other than that, our conversations were minimal and about who was winning in the sports series or how pissed off he was when any Democrat was in public office. Our visits were generally sitting in front of a TV watching sports or the news.

Just a minute after Stella got back to the room, the doctor arrived with the nurse. "Good morning," he said and proceeded to pull out his stethoscope to listen to Robert's lungs. Stella focused on eating her soup while the doctor explained, "We could drain the lungs and pre-scribe some antibiotics, but the fluid would come back in a few days. We would have to continue with this procedure every few days…or the other option would be to make you comfortable with a morphine drip."

Stella was thinking that would be good so her father could regain his normal breathing and then they could go home. Robert looked over at Susan and said, "What should I do?" Susan put her head down on the bed while rubbing Robert's arm. "Sweetie, what do you want to do?"

Stella had never read the literature that hospice gives family mem-bers to explain the process of dying, so she just thought that a morphine drip meant taking away the pain. The hospital term of administering a morphine drip to make you "comfortable" means you are deciding to end the battle. It took her a moment to understand…. Then she lost her appetite quickly, threw her soup into the garbage can, and stepped out into the hall. She couldn't comprehend what was going on. She wasn't ready to lose her dad.

A few minutes after the doctor and nurse left, Susan stepped out into the hall and motioned to Stella that Robert wanted to talk to her. Stella stood up, walked over to her, and placed her hand lightly on Susan's arm.

"Susan, what if my dad asks for the morphine drip? Are you ready to say goodbye?" she whispered softly with confidence.

"No, I can't say goodbye just yet," she replied with tears in her eyes.

Stella waited outside the curtain for a moment, preparing herself for what was about to occur. She knew he would ask her to make this decision for him. She opened the curtain and walked up to the bed. She placed her hand into his, holding it tightly.

"Honey, I want to let go…. I'm ready." His voice was weak.

Stella was surprised by her dad's strength and quick decision to opt for the morphine drip. They had had countless conversations leading up to this moment, in which he had said he was going to beat the cancer.

He looked into Stella's eyes. "Do you give me permission to let go?"

Time seemed to slow down…. She had seen that look in his blue eyes twice before: once when her mom left the marriage, and later when her brother had died. Daughters always look at their dads as a source of strength and love. She had not experienced that feeling until now and didn't have time to think.

"Yes, Dad, I give you permission to let go." She didn't know how to cry—her tears had been all about what she didn't get from her dad and having to deal with his craziness. What came next brought Stella back to the last time she was in urgent care with him.

"Honey, would you call Spring for me? I want to say goodbye to her." His eyes shifted from the curtain to Stella.

■ ■ ■

They had been at the clinic in urgent care all day and night. The hospital didn't have a hospice room available for Robert, so Susan and Stella went downstairs to eat something while the nurses wheeled him over to his room at the hospital. The conversation was silent; neither of them had any more energy to talk. Stella wanted to know what to expect, so she asked Susan how long it took for someone to die once the morphine drip was administered.

Susan lifted her head and said, "It depends on when the body dies."

"What do you mean, 'when the body dies'?"

Susan wiped her mouth with a napkin. "Well, morphine is administered as the last medication to help your dad be comfortable before the death naturally occurs."

"So how can you tell if my dad is ready to die?" Stella asked, taking a drink of water.

"Well, you can tell in the person's breathing pattern. It becomes irregular with pauses. Then it is often followed by a few fast deep breaths. Then you know—when he doesn't draw a breath again after the pause."

Stella wasn't sure whether she wanted to be in the room when her dad passed away, and it weighed heavily on her mind.

■　■　■

When Susan and Stella returned from eating, Susan sat down. Stella stood in the room for a while watching the nurse plump the pillows and check Robert's vital signs. Stella started to cry so she stepped out of the room, explaining that she had to use the restroom. The only room available that evening was on the floor for burn victims, so that was where Robert was going to take his last breath.

It was hard for Stella to fathom that her father was dying; watching other families deal with their loved ones allowed her to deny what was going on in his room, watching the morphine drip take his life. She thought how much courage it took to decide to end one's life—it wasn't like he was taking his own life or participating in any form of euthanasia. It was explained to Stella that morphine is a way to assist in the process of dying by easing the feeling of shortness of breath and reducing any pain. The dose increases until the body shuts down. Her dad's fear of dying was amplified. After all the decades of his heavy drinking, his heart attacks, and his two triple bypass surgeries, she thought his heart would suddenly take him, but instead, it was cancer, and he'd had to decide to let go.

When Stella came back to the room, she asked Susan whether she would step out into the hall so she could talk to Robert. Soon, she was alone with him and the beep of his heartbeat on the monitor. Stella stood over his body for a minute, stroking his arm, and then she bent down to his left ear to talk to him.

"Dad, I love you. You have been good to me."

She thought about what he said to her earlier in urgent care, just before they gave him the morphine drip.

He replied, "If I hurt you in any way, I apologize," and he stared into Stella's eyes with conviction.

"You were a good dad to me, and I love you." She didn't really know what else to say in that moment; she felt he was the best dad in the world; the closeness they had experienced in the past year was a miracle.

Stella wasn't crying, but she felt compelled to say, "Dad, when you see the light, go toward it." She didn't know what prompted her to say that, but when she moved away from his ear and looked at his closed eyes, she saw a tear running down his left cheek. She wanted to think that he had heard her and that was his way of saying goodbye. While she was holding on to him, she thought of all the times throughout her life whenever they had said goodbye that he would hug her tight and not let go. She was always the first person to let go. Now, she wanted him to hug her tight and not let go because, this time, she didn't want to let go.

■ ■ ■

Stella cried all the way home. It was late, so none of the lights in the house were on. She didn't feel like turning on any lights, so she navigated in the dark to her bedroom and collapsed on the bed.

Earlier, she had asked Susan to phone her when Robert was near the end. The phone rang at two in the morning; it was Susan saying that Robert was drawing near to his last breath. Stella had thought about that all the way home and wasn't sure what her decision would be about going back to the hospital to witness his death. The only other time she had been in a room with a person who had just died was with her brother. It was different this time, however, since she had developed a solid belief around the body and soul. Rachel, especially, had helped her understand death and not to fear it—that the body dies but the soul has energy and cannot be destroyed.

Stella hesitated for a brief moment and then told Susan that she wasn't going back to the hospital; she had already said her goodbyes. She lay awake most of the night running over the day and how unexpected all the events were. She hadn't expected her dad to die that day. She had thought he would be in urgent care for a few hours and then they would bring him back home. It was funny how life could twist and turn. Leaving her house that morning, she had never imagined she would be saying goodbye to her dad.

In the morning, she called Susan and learned that her dad had died just ten minutes after Susan had called her. Even if Stella had headed back to the hospital, her father would have died before she could get there. With Robert's passing, Stella felt like an orphan. She didn't have a relationship with Shirley, and Lynn had never been around for support since she had moved out of the family home when Stella was sixteen. Now Stella felt like she didn't have a place to go if she were scared or lonely. Robert stayed home a lot, so he had always been available to Stella through the years when Gabrielle went to her dad's house. Robert's house was the place Stella could go for holidays so she didn't have to spend them by herself. It was going to be really weird for a while, not being able to call her dad when she felt like an orphan. But she did feel good that her dad was finally at peace. He had believed he would be with her brother now. Stella respected that way of thinking because it definitely gave him a place to land and rest. That helped her to feel at peace and complete.

13

"Forgiveness is giving up the hope that the past could have been different. Let go of what wasn't, could have been, and what was lost."

— Author Unknown

Susan took care of the cremation specifics the next day. Stella and Gabrielle had cleaned out Robert's files and drawers a few months prior. Gabrielle requested that Stella keep the files about Michael's death and her grandparents' divorce because she wanted to know more about them. Stella didn't talk much about either one of them to Gabrielle, but with reservations, Stella agreed. Robert had kept all of Michael's car accident clippings and the police report in a large drawer near his office desk. In another desk drawer were the divorce papers from Shirley. Stella was shocked that he still had the past tucked away in drawers for no one to see. She went through each paper in disbelief, not knowing what to do with all the emotions that were surfacing. She felt bad for him that he had felt he needed to hang on to those memories. It really gave her an insight into her dad's heart. It was hard for him to put the past behind and savor the now. It explained a lot to her about his behavior and how he always wanted to talk about the past. He used to get so upset with her that she didn't remember anything. It was like she insulted him because she didn't recall all the times they, as a family, went on trips and she didn't have fond memories of those times. Most of her childhood memories were about pain, anxiety, and being scared.

While they were shuffling through the papers, Stella got an idea about what to do with all of them. She had already put aside some special items to be burned with Robert when he was cremated in his favorite football team's cap that he wore every time they played. He had bought that for himself when they lived in Washington D.C. back in the '60s. It was old and smelly, but every time his team played a football game, he wore the cap. She also kept his army uniform and a silver necklace his mother gave him that he always wore around his neck. When Robert's doctor stopped chemotherapy, Robert and she had a conversation about how he was unable to let go of her brother's death and his divorce from Shirley. He explained how much of a heartbreak that was. It was something she had already known about him because she had witnessed his grief for so many years through his drinking. She told him that he had done a really good job with his life after those two tragedies, so he should be very proud of himself for the life he had built and lived. It would be hard for anyone to have had those happen simultaneously, let alone having to deal with major heart surgery.

It didn't take long for Stella to gather up all the papers and transport the items to the crematory to have them cremated with Robert. It was a way for her to honor her dad and burn the past for him so his soul could be set free. It was the least she could do for him.

Susan had planned a small gathering at their house for Robert's friends. Stella called Lynn to invite her.

"Hi, Lynn. How are things going?"

"Work is going good, and it's keeping me busy."

"Dad's funeral is on Sunday; so will you be there?"

"I'm really busy with work and I don't really like funerals, so no I won't be there. Stella, I have already let go of Dad."

"Well, if you change your mind, it starts at one, and it would be good to see you there," Stella said, and she hung up the phone.

■　■　■

When Stella and Gabrielle arrived for the memorial service at her father and Susan's house, Susan asked Stella and Gabrielle to keep an eye on the guests in the family room so anyone who wanted to share memories or stories could. It didn't surprise Stella to be pushed into the back room and not be a part of the gathering. All the holidays that she and Gabrielle attended through the years at her dad's house were always in the family room, and Susan and her kids were all in the living room. It was so weird and awkward for all Stella's dad's friends to be gathered in the family room and all Susan's kids and friends to be gathered in the living room. It really showed the separation in her dad's marriage to Susan. It had always felt that way—like their families were separate, especially during the holidays.

As Stella stood in the family room, watching Robert's friends look at his pictures and tell stories about him, Michael's urn was still on the hearth above the fireplace. Stella kept the urn there until she was ready to mail Robert and Michael's ashes back East. Earlier that day, Stella had sent Shirley an email telling her that Robert had passed away. Shirley had responded, "Thank you for letting me know. I'm sorry for your loss."

Finally, everyone left, except for Susan's kids. Stella talked with them for a while; then she helped Susan clean up a bit and said her goodbyes.

As Stella walked to the car with Gabrielle, she felt relieved that it was over. It had felt fake to her; however, her dad would've been pleased to see that his very good friends had shown up and spent a great deal of time in the family room reminiscing about their relationship with him. Stella really enjoyed talking with them about her dad and how much they would miss him. A few friends had commented on the awkwardness, but Stella had just kept quiet and greeted everyone with kindness. Once Stella and Gabrielle were in the car, Stella asked, "Well, what did you think about the funeral?"

"It was nice to see all of Grandpa's friends and listen to the stories about him," Gabrielle said.

"How are you feeling about Grandpa being gone?" Stella asked as she merged onto the freeway.

"I miss him, but I said my goodbyes to him the last time I saw him. I know he's in a good place," she said, cracking the window for air.

When they finally pulled into the garage, Stella hugged Gabrielle, and then she went into her bedroom and collapsed on her bed in exhaustion. She had a session scheduled with Rachel the next day so she went to sleep early.

■ ■ ■

Stella arrived at Rachel's early, so she had some time to gather her thoughts about Robert's funeral. Rachel came in, gave Stella a big long hug, and sat down in her chair.

"How did everything go yesterday at your dad's funeral?" Rachel asked while drinking her tea.

"It was good to see all my dad's friends there and listen to the stories and memories they had of him."

Stella's thoughts switched to eleven months ago, so she said, "What's coming up in my mind is when I went to the cemetery and picked up my brother's ashes to bring to my dad's house."

"I only visited my brother a few times. It was weird to stand in front of the niche and read his name. I hadn't been back there for over twenty years, so I remember how apprehensive I was about the whole thing," Stella said, pulling a blanket over her for comfort.

"What made you think of that time?"

"I don't know. I think the death of my dad and having to bring my brother's ashes back East just made me think of that day I went to pick them up. I remember sitting on the floor looking up for some time at my brother's niche. I was the only one there and it was so quiet. The last time I was there was twenty-nine years ago when Michael died. I'm glad that my dad wants to be buried with Michael back East because the only person who ever visited him was my dad."

"Your mom never went to visit Michael?"

"No, she didn't want him buried there. When Michael died, my mom and dad couldn't agree on a place for his ashes. My mom wanted to spread them over the water, but my dad wanted them to be placed in the cemetery. Both hired a lawyer and fought in the courts for several months until the judge awarded my dad's wishes and my brother was placed in the columbarium."

"Wow, they fought over Michael's ashes?"

"Yes, that was a really messed up time." Stella looked down, adjusting the blanket. "It was really weird to go pick up Michael's urn. The guy who worked at the columbarium who handed me the urn was really nice. It was so heavy, felt like twenty pounds of bronze. I carried it to my car and placed it meticulously in the backseat on the floor so it wouldn't tip over. The feeling was so surreal for me, driving in my car with my brother's ashes in the backseat. I don't do well with death, so it kind of freaked me out. I turned on the radio to drown out my thoughts."

"Well, you handled your dad's death very well, Stella. I know it is unusual to pull someone's urn out of a niche so it can be buried somewhere else. It does happen, though. I am proud of you." Rachel reached over and rubbed Stella's foot.

"Thank you. At least I didn't have to worry about how my mom would feel in the matter. When my dad told my mom he wanted to move Michael's ashes, she told him he could have full rights to them and do what he wanted with them. When I asked my dad why she gave him full rights, he said she had never felt Michael's soul was there at the cemetery. That's why she never visited him."

Rachel leaned toward Stella and said, "Your mom has the right to feel how she feels."

Stella looked at Rachel and nodded her head. "I know."

■ ■ ■

The next week, Stella arrived a bit early for her appointment with Rachel. She did the usual ritual for entering into Rachel's space. She lay down on the futon mattress, placed her head on the white pillow that hugged her so softly, and wrapped a plushy white blanket around her delicate body. She felt safe and warm.

Then Rachel came in and, as always, she gave Stella a long hug, wrapping her arms completely around Stella's body and holding her tight. Rachel always waited till Stella let go first; then she squeezed her a few more times.

In Stella's family, hugs were not given at all until she was an adult. She would always let go first with her mom and dad. With Gabrielle, she hung on for dear life! Stella had brought along her pink cord so she and Rachel could do some womb work.

After their usual greetings, Rachel said, "Stella, pull out your pink cord so we can do some work around anxiety."

Stella pulled the cord out of her purse and unwrapped it from the white lace handkerchief she kept it in. Then she handed one end to Rachel and held the other end herself. Because the cord was long, Stella wrapped it around her hand several times and Rachel did the same so that the cord was taut.

"How are you feeling about the loss of your dad?" Rachel asked.

"I feel grateful for the last year," said Stella, "because my dad and I were able to heal a lot of our relationship. I really felt for the first time that my dad really loved me the best way he knew how." Rachel toyed with the end of the cord to make sure it was secure while Stella shared her feelings. "I felt a sense of relief," Stella continued, "that he didn't have to suffer anymore, and that I no longer had to feel responsible for his happiness." As Stella started to cry, Rachel got up out of her bean bag chair and sat down next to Stella, gesturing for her to lay her head on her lap. She stroked her hair and rubbed her back as she always did when Stella had a major epiphany around her wounding. Stella was thinking about the first time Rachel had asked her to lay her head on her lap; how it had felt so weird. She said to Rachel, "You know I don't freeze up like I used to when I lay my head on your lap."

"You have done lots of thawing out over the years," Rachel said while she rubbed Stella's back.

"You always use that term, 'thawing out,'" Stella said with a smile.

"Do you remember when we first started working together," asked Rachel, "how you described yourself as having a block of cement around your heart?" You would draw me a picture in your mind, of you as a stick figure with a big block of gray cement encased around your body, and the only things sticking out were your head, arms, and legs."

"Yeah, that's right. My whole body felt so heavy, like I was carrying around a big block of rock," said Stella while sitting up. "Now I am able to receive the love you give me."

"Are you ready to go outside and do a ritual?" Rachel asked, getting up off the futon.

"Yes, let's do it," Stella replied as she put her shoes on.

They both went outside to Rachel's firepit and gathered some sticks and paper to start a fire.

"It's a traditional Native American ceremony around smudging with sage," Rachel said. She lit the sage and swished the smoke from her head to her toes to cleanse herself; then she cleansed Stella.

"Smudging ceremonies are often carried out for the purpose of clearing any energy, and when performing this ritual, it's important to be clear about your intent and focus on what you are trying to accomplish," Rachel explained.

"I want to let go. I have come to a place with my dad of peace, acceptance, and love. It's important for me to let go," Stella said, while breathing in the smell of sage.

"Stella, you have done so much healing around your relationship with your dad, and it's wonderful that you want to honor your relationship and give it a proper burial so you can move forward," Rachel said while stoking the fire.

"I remember the choice I made not to go to the hospital when my dad was in his last stage of life. I said goodbye to him earlier. I do feel there is some residue from this experience so I really want to work on releasing anything that I may be holding on to," Stella said while staring at the fire.

There was no drumming—just the silent wind rustling through the trees. Rachel and Stella stood there for a bit in silence.

"I really want to make this count," Stella said.

"Are there any images or thoughts coming up?" Rachel asked.

"Yeah, I'm thinking about the time when I was young and my dad and I were standing on the sidelines watching the rugby match back in D.C. It was so cold that night, so my dad picked me up and held me tight, and he wrapped his hands in mine to keep them warm 'cause they were so cold," Stella said, crying. "This is the only memory I have as a small child about my dad's love toward me."

"What a beautiful memory you are experiencing of your dad's love," Rachel replied. "Is there anything else showing up for you?"

Stella stood there for a minute, watching the flames dance slowly. "The other image that popped up was when my dad was sitting in his leather chair talking to me about how he wanted to be buried. I remember how we both cried during this exchange; the only other time I ever saw my dad cry was when he sat on my wicker chair in my bedroom when I was eighteen years old and asked me why my mom was leaving him. You know, Rachel, I never saw him cry when my brother died."

"Your dad was in a lot of pain back then, just coming out of his surgery and then losing Michael."

Rachel moved around the remaining logs to finish out the fire. "Anything else you need to let go of, Stella?"

"Yeah, the last image that appeared is when my dad asked for my forgiveness just before the morphine drip was administered to him." Stella started to cry. Tears poured down her cheeks as if a dam had finally broken inside her. Stella wasn't going to stop them; she knew that she had to let them flow in order for her to move on. All the years of pain accumulated in the salt of the tears. Stella was cleansing her soul of any leftover residue with her dad.

Rachel eventually wrapped her arms around Stella, holding her as she cried, and she stood there for a bit longer, watching the fire burn out till only ashes were left. Stella thought about how what she loved and appreciated about Rachel was her heart. She felt so much love from her, and she was grateful to have her in her life to show her a better way of living.

14

"Nothing ever goes away until it has taught us
what we need to know."

— Pema Chodron

Stella toyed with the notion of flying Michael and Robert's ashes to the funeral with Gabrielle, but she couldn't get up the courage to fly, so she decided to send the ashes by mail. She contacted the funeral home in Massachusetts to let it know she was mailing the ashes and asked the director to call her when they arrived so she could give them instructions. Stella's cousins and aunt were really looking forward to her visit with Gabrielle; most of them hadn't met her yet, so they were really disappointed when Stella said that they weren't coming. Stella used the excuse that she didn't have any money to fly her and Gabrielle out.

Stella's anxiety was much greater than her concern over whether anyone was disappointed. She felt bad for mailing the ashes—it seemed so impersonal, but she just couldn't get up the courage to fly. She had promised her dad she would get his ashes back East, so she hadn't gone back on her promise; it just wasn't her taking them back.

When Stella left the local post office after mailing the boxed up ashes, she felt awkward because the person behind the counter knew they were cremated remains. She felt ashamed that she couldn't muster up the courage to fly. The fear encapsulated her so much that it felt suffocating and she started to hyperventilate. Stella ran back to her car where she knew no one would be watching her anxiety attack. She practiced the mantra that had helped her in the past, *I'm OK, I'm OK!* She tried to slow her breathing down, but it wasn't working, so she called Rachel to leave her a message. Usually, just hearing Rachel's voice on the message recorder helped Stella calm down. After leaving the message, in which she told Rachel she had mailed the ashes, she started the car and drove home where she felt safe. Rachel had always been a light for Stella to focus on when she had panic; it reminded her that she wasn't alone. *I couldn't help thinking that I did it—that I mailed the ashes despite my feelings of being ashamed that I wasn't able to fly on an airplane.*

Once home, while Stella waited for Rachel to return her call, she grabbed something to eat even though she wasn't hungry. From her work with Rachel, Stella now understood how important it was to have some protein to reduce her anxiety. In the past when Stella became anxious for long periods of time, a month or so, she would lose her appetite. Starving herself was not a form of anorexia; it came from being starved when Stella was young. Not being nurtured by her parents had taught her not to take care of herself by eating properly. She had not learned to stay healthy and give energy to her body so she could move about life with assurance. When Stella was anxious, food was the last thing on her mind; it was like her digestive system shut down, not allowing any bodily sensations, including a desire for food. Depending on how long the apprehension would last, Stella could lose up to ten pounds in a month. Sometimes that was detrimental because she was already small and didn't have much weight on her at the best of times. But during these times, she literally couldn't put food in her mouth or even drink water; it was like her taste buds had become extinct, so Stella would become dehydrated and weak. The only thing she could concentrate on was her fear that she would never recover from this deprivation—never pull out of this impoverished state of being. Her soul yearned to feed itself, but she didn't have the tools to accomplish the task.

When Stella had started her work with Rachel, Rachel had immediately recognized the symptom and made it a top priority to dissolve that form of thinking in Stella's mind. Every time Stella had a session, Rachel would wrap her in a white blanket and hold on to her foot. It didn't matter which one—she just had to connect with Stella, and most times when Stella started crying, Rachel would move closer to her so Stella could place her head on Rachel's lap while Rachel stroked Stella's hair.

What Stella learned from working with Rachel and also a naturopath whom Rachel recommended was that nutrition plays an important role in anxiety, and specific foods and nutrients feed the body so anxiety will stay at bay under stressful situations. Omega-3 fatty acids are found in fish, so Stella started to incorporate salmon into her diet and took a fish oil supplement at night to help with insomnia. Along with the fish oil, she would drink a cup of hot water with magnesium powder, which has a calming effect on the nervous system. Stella's naturopath prescribed a Tryptophan, L-theanine, and melatonin supplement for Stella to take at night with the magnesium to give her a full night's sleep. Stella used to wake at 3 a.m. and was unable to fall back to sleep, so this regimen helped her feel rested the next day, which helped her to tackle any undue stress.

Rachel's work also honed in on Stella's cells where her emotions were lodged and suppressed in fear. Because Stella had been beaten as a child, she continually feared being hurt, and she dreaded being abandoned entirely if she were to express her emotions or react to the pain. Stella had been trapped in a world of mental illusions of not being worthy or loved that didn't fit within her present environment as an adult. The illusions were so automatic and easily triggered because they had provided Stella with comfort—the only way she could survive as a child.

Rachel knew how to comfort the small, un-integrated child living within Stella, whose fear and panic had been a part of her since the beginning. Anxiety and panic can suddenly attack without warning, and the unconscious fear brought about in childhood can last for many decades, even a lifetime, if you have no one to help you let go of the demons. Stella was grateful that she finally had someone to help her let go of them.

Rachel called Stella back right after she had finished eating. They scheduled a time for Stella to come in and work on some more things that might be causing her anxiety and lack of appetite. Stella had been feeling anxious, unable to sleep, and revved up for the last few days. She thought it had to do with her guilt about not going back East for Robert's funeral.

■ ■ ■

At Stella's next meeting with Rachel, Rachel did some probing into Stella's energy field. Through the work, Rachel uncovered the core of Stella's apprehension. Most of Rachel's work with Stella was tapping into Stella's energy field and locating the block. Images would appear in Rachel's mind to help her navigate through Stella's body, and because they had been working together for nine years now, Rachel really had a sense of Stella's energy blocks. Stella had not fully dealt with Michael's loss, so Robert's death had stirred up some of Stella's old energy about Michael.

Stella had felt the same sense of responsibility for Michael that she had for her dad, plus she felt guilt over not being able to get on the plane, and she felt guilt over being alive when her brother, the beloved one in the family, had died.

Stella thought she had dealt with all her emotions around Michael, but the work she had been doing with Rachel had gone much deeper in her psyche than any other therapy. She felt safe with Rachel, so she was able to shed those barriers that had prevented her from deeply feeling her emotions. Rachel motioned her to get on the massage table so she could do some cranial work. Rachel had many certifications for this level of work and had spent several years living on a Lakota tribe reservation studying with the medicine people. She told Stella that this work would be much gentler, but it would have the same effect as working through the pink cord. Rachel had such soft, warm hands. Stella felt so good when Rachel cradled her head while she worked on her nervous system. Rachel tapped into Stella's cerebrospinal fluid to increase her oxygen and alter her brain chemistry, which could benefit her mood and emotions. Rachel worked with Stella's spine, sacrum, and the bones of her cranium to reset her nervous system by bringing the craniosacral rhythm to a "stillpoint." Then Rachel tapped into the rhythm of the craniosacral cycle, with her hands cradling Stella's neck and skull, to fill and empty the cerebrospinal fluid along her cranium and spinal cord all the way down to the sacrum. This process would give Stella's nervous system the ability to rest and correct. Stella felt the shift and immediately went into a calm and peaceful state known as the Parasympathetic Shift. All Stella's tension, depression, and anxiety shifted, and she felt more positive and balanced. Rachel explained to Stella that the craniosacral cycle was also where the unconscious mind went from Fight or Flight mode into a balanced mode. Stella felt her anxiety release.

After the session, Stella felt relaxed and connected to herself again.

She got up off the table and went back over to the futon to lie down. When Stella started to cry, Rachel sat next to her. Stella hadn't realized she was still hanging on to her grief over her brother. It had been nearly thirty years since his death. Stella understood that it wasn't her fault that Michael had died, nor had it been her responsibility to save Michael or Robert. Rachel got up and walked to the side table by the chair in the corner to light a candle to represent a sense of purity in the room. She sat back down next to Stella and asked her what she would like to say to Michael. Stella thought about it for a minute. It was weird to talk to someone who hadn't been in existence for a long time. What could she say to him?

Stella looked at Rachel. "I'm really sorry that Michael's life ended the way it did and so young."

"Tell him why you felt responsible for him and his death."

"Michael," began Stella, "Mom and Dad loved you so much, more than Lynn or me. Our family was so fucked up, so dysfunctional, and I don't know if you saw that. You were so young at the time and so protected by Mom. I hated you so much when you were born. I used to come into your room and rattle your crib to wake you up so you would cry; I thought maybe then they wouldn't like you so much."

Stella started to cry again and wiped her nose. "I used to be so mean to you. I was only jealous that you received so much attention, and me, none. I understand why it was you that died and not me or Lynn. If it were me or Lynn, I don't believe Mom or Dad would've been very upset. But you, you dying would make an impression on our family in hopes that we all could heal. It was a much bigger impact that you left instead of me."

Rachel grabbed another tissue for Stella. "The work you have done here with me, Stella, has healed that part of you that felt you were unwanted or not deserving enough to be loved by your parents."

Stella rested her head on Rachel's leg for a while. Tears rolled down her cheeks, but she wasn't sobbing. The tears were indicators of her soul cleansing itself of grief. She didn't grieve the loss of Michael; she grieved the loss of herself. She felt stronger, yet lighter in her energy. Stella took a deep breath and blew it out to release anything else she may have held on to. Rachel had fed her with love and affection and allowed her to express her deepest fears and emotions in a safe environment where she was heard, understood, and taken seriously, rather than having to hide her feelings. That was the nourishment Stella had been searching for all her life.

■ ■ ■

Stella was coming down off the death of Robert and the letting go of pieces from her past. She hadn't heard from Lynn since Robert's diagnosis. Lynn had made it perfectly clear that she didn't want any part of their dad's death and funeral. Stella thought about Shirley and what she was up to. It had been many years since she had sent the email, refusing contact with her. She felt stronger since she had dissolved the relationship with her mom. But she also felt alone, especially since Gabrielle was gone. She spent most of her time working in sales and visiting with her friends Stacy, Maggie, and Jeff. Stacy lived close to Stella and had been her friend since high school. Maggie was Gabrielle's kindergarten teacher so they had been friends at least fifteen years. Jeff and Stella had become good friends after meeting through mutual friends over twenty years ago.

And Stella also had Tiger, although he was fourteen years old and starting to slow down. He meant so much to Stella, being her confidant and companion who helped her feel safe and secure. She loved him so much. Stella walked him every day to help his arthritis, and she frequently took him to the vet to make sure he was healthy. Then Gabrielle came home one weekend and mentioned to Stella that Tiger didn't look good.

"Mom, is Tiger feeling okay?" she asked.

"Yeah, he's okay, just a little arthritis."

"You know he's getting old and not able to walk around that much anymore."

"I walk him every day; he seems to be all right. He may take a bit longer to walk around the block, but he does it."

But Stella knew Gabrielle was right; Tiger wasn't doing very well. She just couldn't bear to think about losing Tiger. She had just lost her dad and she didn't have any relationship with Lynn or Shirley. It was too hard to grasp that she would one day have to let go of Tiger. It was up to him to decide when he wanted to go. She didn't want to have to make that decision ever.

One day while Stella was taking Tiger for just a short jaunt around the block, he fell down and wasn't able to get himself back up. He was a big dog, but he had lost some weight—down to seventy pounds from one hundred pounds most of his adult life. Stella sat down with him on the side of the road and waited for him to get his strength to stand up again so they could walk back home. He just looked at her with those brown eyes. She could see that he loved her so much. Besides Gabrielle,

Stella had never experienced any kind of love so deep. "Please don't leave me," she said to him. After a while, Stella helped him up and they slowly walked back home, taking breaks along the way. Stella didn't want to face the truth that Tiger was deteriorating and she had no control over his condition.

Stella called Jennifer, Tiger's vet, when she got home and scheduled an appointment for Tiger. Jennifer was able to see Tiger the next morning, so Stella rearranged her work schedule to take him in. Tiger didn't like the vet clinic, and he was always anxious about going. It seemed that the older he got, the worse his condition was. Stella petted him and he sat close to her during the wait, shaking and panting. When Jennifer weighed Tiger, he had lost another five pounds in a month. She checked his vitals and found a large mass just under his left front leg attached to his ribcage. It had been there for a while, Stella said, but she noticed it had grown significantly since their last visit.

"We could do a biopsy to see if it's cancer," said Jennifer. "I wouldn't recommend it, though; it's too much money and Tiger is old. My guess would be that it is cancer."

Stella just sat there listening. "I can't make the decision to put him down," she said, crying. Jennifer looked at Stella and told her that she didn't have to. Hopefully, Tiger would go on his own; she had seen that happen before. She gave Stella some pain medicine to make him comfortable and told her to keep them updated on his progress.

Stella took the medication and she and Tiger went home. She spent the rest of the day lying next to him while he slept. The medicine seemed to help make him comfortable. She didn't realize how much pain he was in. The doctor had told her during their visit that dogs mask their pain so their owners won't worry about them. It's all about them making sure their master is protected. Lots of thoughts went through Stella while she lay there stroking Tiger's fur. She eventually fell asleep on the floor next to him. She didn't want him to be alone. Later that night, Gabrielle called.

"Mom, what did the vet say?" she asked.

"Well, the doctor checked that mass by his ribcage and it has grown. She thinks it's cancer."

"Oh, are they going to put him down?" asked Gabrielle.

"No, they gave him some pain meds and said to keep an eye on him."

"Mom, he's old and sick; why don't you put him out of his misery?"

"Gabrielle, do you want to go with me to have him put to sleep? He is your dog," she said, angrily.

"No, I don't want to go."

"Well, then don't tell me what to do. Since it's my decision, let me have some time with it. He isn't in pain according to the doctor."

"Okay, Mom. I need to go study."

"Okay, have a good rest of your day," Stella said as Gabrielle hung up the phone.

Stella started to cry. She didn't want to be alone with this decision.

15

"Until one has loved an animal,
a part of one's soul remains unawakened."

— Anatole France

Robert had been dead for six months and it was coming up on Tiger's fifteenth birthday. Gabrielle had picked him out in the litter when he was just six weeks old, so his birthday was July 25th. Stella knew it was time to let him go, but she just couldn't.

Gabrielle, Stella, and Tiger celebrated his birthday together. It was hard for him to walk and eat so Stella got some natural freeze-dried dog food and mixed it with some water and sat next to him while he ate. Stella would get him up in the morning, wrap a towel around his mid-section, and help him outside to go to the bathroom. She would then make sure he had enough water and sit with him for a while. One morning,

Tiger had his head on her lap and was looking into Stella's eyes. The vet had told her that Tiger would let her know when he was ready to go. He looked at her and said, "I am ready to go."

The next morning, Jeff called Stella to see how Tiger was. She started sobbing into the phone.

"I can't put him down. I love him so much." Jeff had just recently had to put his dog down, so he talked with Stella about how when pets are ready to go, the best way to show your love is to honor their situation and bring them peace.

"I know, but it's so hard to let go of him," she replied. "He has been so good to me, loving me unconditionally and being my companion for all these years, helping with my loneliness and anxiety. How am I going to live my life without Tiger?"

"You will," said Jeff. "Tiger wouldn't want you to do otherwise."

Stella hung up the phone, went over to Tiger, and lay down next to him so she could hold him. Except for Gabrielle, she didn't think she could love anyone as much as Tiger, ever. The thought of putting Tiger to sleep stirred up Stella's anxiety, so she called Rachel to schedule an appointment. Rachel was able to fit her in the next day.

. . .

Stella had almost always brought Tiger to her appointments with Rachel. He would sit in the car waiting for Stella to come out, and he would be so excited when she did. He loved riding in the car with the window down. Most of the time when Stella would leave the house, Tiger wanted to go with her, so he would sit patiently by the door, looking at her with those beautiful brown eyes. It didn't matter where she was going, he wanted to go. One of his favorite places was the bank because they gave him dog treats. The other place was around water—well, in the water; he loved to swim.

But today, Stella left Tiger at home when she went to visit Rachel. He wasn't able to walk very far and it was hard for her to pick him up, so she thought he'd be more comfortable at home.

Rachel and Stella talked about how hard it was to put Tiger down and how alone Stella felt in the process.

"I get all this advice, but most of the people giving me the advice haven't had to put down their beloved dog before," Stella said, crying. She talked about how much Tiger had been there for her during all the lonely times when Gabrielle had gone to her dad's. Tiger really had become Stella's dog—her companion during all the years of her healing with Rachel.

"It's so hard to let go of someone you really love," she wailed. "I really felt his love for me too; I can't bear this feeling." Rachel wrapped her arms around Stella to comfort her. She knew how much Tiger meant to her and how he had aided in working toward healing Stella's anxiety.

When Stella got home, she lay down next to Tiger and stroked his face and rubbed his ears. She slept by his side all night long.

■ ■ ■

Early the next morning, Stella woke to Tiger crying. She hadn't heard him cry like that before, so she became really concerned and called the vet. Dr. Jennifer had said Stella could call anytime and they would make room for Tiger to come in and be put to sleep. The vet now told Stella that it sounded like it was time and to bring him in. In a few hours, they would be ready. Stella hung up the phone and got dressed; then she sat down and put Tiger's head in her lap. She kissed him, stroked his face, and talked to him.

"Tiger, Mama loves you so much," she said. "You don't know how much you changed my life, loving me the way you did."

Stella sat there for at least an hour with tears running down her cheeks, thinking about all the good times they'd had and how much he would be missed. She thought of all the times she'd had anxiety and felt really lonely when Gabrielle wasn't home; Tiger was always there, wagging his tail, ready to comfort her. She didn't know what she'd do without him. She was scared. She wouldn't be the same. The time was coming near, and so she got up and gathered all the items she would like for him to be cremated with. His blanket, his old man sweater, and his purebred papers, as well as his parents' papers. Then she called Jeff, who lived nearby, and asked him to help her carry Tiger to the car and get him out again once they reached the vet's office. The clinic was only five minutes away, and the car ride was very quiet.

When they arrived, the vet already had a room set up for Tiger. Jeff carried Tiger into the special room and then went to wait in the waiting room. Stella entered the special room for Tiger and laid his blanket down on the rug, which was nicely placed next to a bunch of stuffed animals. Tiger's blanket was a jaguar print that Stella had received from a friend, but she thought it belonged to Tiger, so he adopted it and slept on the blanket for years. It had his scent on it to remind him of home. The doctor came in and talked with Stella for a while, explaining the procedure.

"The first thing we will do is give him a shot to relax him; then I'll administer a shot to end his life," she said. Stella didn't say anything; she was crying and rubbing Tiger's face.

"I love you so much," she told Tiger. "It's going to be all right." Stella knelt on the ground next to him, bent over, gave him a kiss, and whispered in his ear, "Thank you for loving me." Stella looked into Tiger's eyes, but it didn't seem that he was there. He was breathing, but she could tell that his spirit wasn't there. He had a big smile, but his eyes were blank. Stella looked over at the doctor and saw that she was just putting the second injection in. Tiger's spirit had already left his body before the second shot. It just took a few minutes before his heart stopped. Stella bent over and held on to Tiger tightly. She didn't want to let go of him.

"Stella, he has passed on," said the vet. "You stay as long as you want and let me know when you are ready to leave." Stella stayed a bit longer going over their life together. He was such a good dog. She had had many dogs in her life, but she had never attached herself to any of them like she had with Tiger. Finally, Stella got up and went outside to find the doctor to give her some of Tiger's belongings.

"I would like to have these items cremated with him," she said, handing them to her. Stella walked out to the front desk where the receptionist was waiting for her.

"We will have the urn ready to pick up in three weeks along with his paw print," she said.

Stella thanked them and walked out to the waiting room where Jeff was waiting for her. Jeff gave Stella a big hug, and then they both got in the car and drove back to Stella's house. Stella thanked Jeff again and then he headed home. When Stella went inside, there was a message on her phone from Gabrielle, so she called her back. She got her voicemail, so she let her know Tiger was now gone and to give her a call if she needed too. Gabrielle called a few hours later.

■ ■ ■

For the next several weeks, the house felt so empty. Stella kept Tiger's bed in the same place with his stuffed monkey and his leash. The vet clinic had called and said that the urn of Tiger's ashes was ready to be picked up. Stella put the urn on the ledge above her fireplace along with a picture of him and his paw print in plaster. It was completely outside her nature to keep cremated remains in her house and an altar too. But Stella had thought about how she wanted to honor Tiger when he was starting to get sick. She thought of all the places she and Tiger had been, mainly around water, so she wanted to take the whole year and go to those places to spread some of his ashes.

When Gabrielle came home one weekend, she mentioned how empty the house felt and how much she really missed Tiger. "Well, he was your dog, so this must be hard for you," Stella said.

"Yeah, I haven't been around much for the last few years; it just seems really weird not to have him here," she said, crying.

"Oh, sweetie, it is hard not to have Tiger here anymore," Stella said, as she wrapped her arms around Gabrielle and told her how much she loved her.

Gabrielle wiped her tears and said, "Do you remember the times we took Tiger to the beach and he would never get out of the water?"

Stella laughed. "Yeah, either you or I would have to go in the freezing cold water and fetch him out."

Gabrielle started laughing too. "And how he always wanted to ride in the car—didn't matter if we were just going to the store, he wanted to go."

They cried, laughed, and hugged each other till Gabrielle had to go back to school. Just before she had to leave, Stella talked about what she wanted to do with Tiger's ashes.

"Gabrielle, what would you think about spreading his ashes throughout the year at all the beaches he went to?"

"Yeah, that would be cool, but you can do that; I don't want to," said Gabrielle, as she put her coat on.

They said their goodbyes, and then Stella stood at the front door and watched Gabrielle drive away, waving and blowing kisses.

■ ■ ■

Over the course of the next year, Stella traveled to the different beaches Tiger enjoyed, like Ebey Landing on Whidbey Island, Alki Beach in West Seattle and Edmonds Beach and took some ashes along with her in a plastic bag. It was coming up on Tiger's birthday July 25th, and a year since he was cremated, so Stella had a considerable amount of ashes left in the urn and wasn't sure where she wanted to spread the rest. She was looking at some photos on her phone one day when she came across a place around Leavenworth, east of Seattle; she had been there a few times when she needed some time to relax. It had been a very healing and sacred place for her. This would be a great resting place for Tiger and a way to honor him too. Stella had picked a date just after his birthday to drive east over the Cascade Mountains to this special spot. She wanted to take the trip alone because she couldn't think of anyone else besides Gabrielle to have this experience with, and Stella needed to practice driving for long distances so she could continue to face her anxiety issues around driving.

She had done a great job eliminating most of the symptoms with driving in traffic and crossing bridges, and since it was summer, she wouldn't have to worry about any snow when she crossed over the pass.

The day of the outing, Stella got up early, packed some food, and carefully placed Tiger's urn in the car, wedging it between her purse and a huge bottle of water. She brought along the paw print and his picture. She and Tiger traveled along the road quietly. Stella didn't feel like listening to any music because she wanted to be in her thoughts. She stopped a few times, but she eventually got to the destination just as it got too hot. Eastern Washington that July was one of the hottest months with record highs in the nineties. The threat of forest fires was really high because the heat and a lack of rain had made everything so dry that it would easily burn. The place was hard to find. It was just off Highway Two, east of Lake Wenatchee. Stella drove a little under the speed limit so she wouldn't miss it. As she pulled in, she recognized the wooden sign placed at the edge of the parking lot overlooking the river. Skookum La Metsin sat in the Wenatchee National Forest along the Wenatchee River. The name came from the Chinook Indians and meant "Strong Medicine." Stella loved the place. During difficult times in her life, the soothing sounds of the river flowing and the warmth of the sun had been very healing for her. Stella stepped out of the car and stood on the bank to see where she would like to do the ceremony. A few patrons were lingering, so she waited till they were gone. Then she went to the car to get Tiger's urn and trinkets, and the sage and sweet grass wrapped in a cloth to cleanse the area and honor the space where she was going to lay Tiger to rest. Rachel had taught her the ritual.

Stella hiked down to the river edge with Tiger's urn under one arm and the other items in her other hand. She found a spot just east of the parking lot where if people drove up, they wouldn't be able to see her. It was a beautiful summer morning just before noon, around eighty-five degrees. A light wind came from the west, and the sounds of the river were very calming. Stella stuck her foot in the icy water. She could see the rocks that lay solid beneath the green blue water, and she could feel the sun on her face. Stella thought of how final it all was. It took her a while before she got up and started the ceremony. First, she lit the sage and sweet grass to purify the area; then she said a prayer of gratitude for Tiger coming into her life so she could feel his love, which helped allow her to heal her heart. Stella threw the paw print casting into the flowing river and then opened up the urn and took out the plastic bag of the remaining ashes. She stood there crying as she turned the bag upside down and allowed the wind to carry the ashes down the river. Some stayed by her feet, but most of them moved along with the waters. She threw the urn into the middle of the river and watched it and the ashes travel down the river until they disappeared. Stella studied Tiger's picture. Then she placed it carefully in the river and watched it float away.

When Stella left Skookum La Metsin, she cried until she reached Stevens Pass summit. It felt like the day she put Tiger down at the vet; then once she descended the mountain, the tears stopped and she felt energized by the way she had honored Tiger. When she got home, she felt a lot calmer and grounded. She went over to the fireplace ledge where Tiger's urn had been for a year and placed some rocks there that she had picked up at the river. She was very tired and went to bed early, sleeping peacefully.

■ ■ ■

The next morning, Stella called Gabrielle and told her about the ceremony. "It was beautiful, honey; you should have been there."

Gabrielle was quiet for a minute; Stella could hear her texting on her phone. "Mom, that's great! Did it make you feel better?"

"Well, yeah, it needed to be done. Don't you think?"

"Mom, this was your thing; you needed to do the ritual." Gabrielle accepted her mom's fascination with rituals. Stella hung up the phone laughing because she could imagine Gabrielle's twenty-two year old millennial facial expressions during their conversation: the eye rolls and smirks she had witnessed throughout her life whenever she had told her daughter about one of her quests for healing and completion.

■ ■ ■

After several months went by, Stella got used to Tiger's absence. She missed him a lot, but she kept her mind preoccupied with work. The loneliest times were in the evening when she used to curl up next to him and watch television or read a book. She replaced that time with working in the yard or visiting with friends for dinner. Changing her routine seemed to help her cope better.

One day, her friend Stacy called. "Hi, Stella. How are you?"

"Hi, Stacy. I'm okay. It's just really lonely here without Tiger," Stella said while pulling laundry out of the washer.

"Hey, do you want to meet for tea today?"

"Sure, I could use some company. Where do you want to meet?"

"Let's meet at Third Street Coffee."

"Sounds great; let's meet in an hour, if that works."

"Sure, I'll see you then," Stacy said, and hung up.

They hadn't seen each other in a few months and wanted to catch up on each other's lives. Stacy had recently gotten married in Barbados, but Stella hadn't been able to go to the wedding because she would have to get on a plane.

At the coffee shop, they hugged and sat down on two comfy leather chairs. They talked for hours about Tiger and then about Stacy's wedding.

"Hey, come over next week and I'll show you my wedding pictures," Stacy suggested when she stood up to leave.

"I'm sorry I wasn't able to go—work stuff," Stella said as they walked out the door. They agreed on a day and time to meet again and said their goodbyes. Stella drove home thinking about how she hadn't been able to tell Stacy she had flight anxiety. She didn't like lying, but she felt so ashamed of the fear. Hardly anyone knew because she was afraid of people judging her or looking at her differently.

16

"We have it in our power to begin the world over again."

— Thomas Paine

S tella couldn't imagine in a million years that she would be doing what she did—to have this opportunity presented in her life. It had all begun a few months earlier when she had gone to Stacy's to see the wedding pictures. She and Stacy had been sitting in the living room talking about her wedding when Stacy said, "You wouldn't believe where I was yesterday." Stacy then told Stella about how her maid of honor had just bought a house and she wouldn't believe whose house it was. Somehow, Stella had known what Stacy was going to say. "Your old house you grew up in. You wouldn't believe that nothing has changed. Do you remember the place where you used to sit in the kitchen? It's the same. Nothing has changed."

It felt so surreal that Stella couldn't say anything.

"Do you want to go see it?" Stacy then asked.

Stella didn't say anything for a while. She was thinking how much healing work she had done about her childhood, especially the time she was living in that house.

"Maybe," she said. "Let me think about it." She needed to think about whether she really wanted to go see the house or just keep her memories of the time she had lived there as it had been. Stella texted Stacy a few days later to say she wanted to see the house, and after putting much thought into the opportunity, she said she wanted to see it on the next new moon. The new moon, according to myth, is a time of growing energy, newness, growth, renewal, and hope. It is a good time for making changes in one's life, such as ending bad habits or relationships.

Stella called Rachel to tell her about the situation, and they scheduled a session to help Stella create some clarity about how she wanted to handle going to her childhood home.

At the appointment, Rachel asked Stella what her thoughts were.

"I have done so much healing work around my childhood and specifically around the time of my life in that house."

"Yes, you've done a lot of work with your childhood."

"I was thirteen when we moved into that house. A lot happened there that took many years for me to heal. There is obviously something presenting itself for me to heal and let go."

Rachel sat for a minute shaking her head. "Yeah, this is good, so let's figure out what you need with this situation."

Stella told Rachel about an image that kept coming up in her mind. "It was the white balloon incident at my brother's funeral. The balloon never flew away."

Rachel shifted in her chair and took a drink of tea. "What do you need to do in order to let go?"

Stella looked up. "I'm going to buy a white balloon and release it at the house."

Rachel smiled. "Okay. When you get ready to go, hold the balloon and sit for a while. See what you remember about living in the house. Ask yourself whether you're holding on to anything you're not conscious of, and say, 'Please help me to let go.'"

Stella sat up and looked at Rachel. "I remember I lived in that house from the age of thirteen to eighteen. Then I moved out, but I moved back in till the age of twenty-four. When I lived there, I felt lots of fear of being alone, not loved, and beaten. My mom was so abusive and my sister always hit me; we got into many fights. My mom always ridiculed me and was not available emotionally. My parents got a divorce in that house. My beloved dog ran away. My sister moved out before I graduated from high school, and my brother died a tragic death."

"That's good information to work with when you sit with the balloon," Rachel said, and then they said goodbye.

■ ■ ■

Stella prepared for that day. She got up early and went down to the local grocery store to buy a white balloon. She also got a light blue and a dark blue ribbon to symbolize a baby and a young adult. She bought her friend Stacy and herself Gerbera daisies. At home, before meeting with Stacy, Stella looked at the balloon tied to the dining room table. It was a typical Seattle day, cloudy and raining.

Stella had an hour before she needed to leave to meet Stacy at the house. Stella burned some sage and used her eagle feather to direct the cleansing smoke all over her body, which she had learned from Rachel. "God help me to stay grounded in my body so I can embrace anything that comes up so I can heal and let go," she prayed. She gathered some cedar, sage, sweet grass, and a piece of bark off the birch tree in her yard; then she bundled everything inside the birch tree bark and wrapped the blue strings around it to make a bundle. As Stella waited in the house's driveway, Stacy and Laurie, the owner of the house, drove into the driveway. Stella gave Stacy the flowers and gave her a hug; then she shook Laurie's hand and chatted for a bit before Laurie unlocked the door to let them in. While Laurie opened the drapes in the living room, family room, and dining room, Stella couldn't get over the stale, old smell of the house.

"No one had lived in the house for over two years," Laurie said.

Stella walked into the foyer, holding the balloon in her right hand.

Laurie asked, "Why do you have the white balloon?"

Stella looked at Stacy. "Were you at my brother's funeral?"

"Yes," Stacy said.

Stella smiled. "Do you remember the white balloons we released that day?"

"Yes, why?"

"Well, that day my balloon didn't release like everyone else's did," Stella said. "So while I felt like everyone else let go of Michael, I never did. Now I'm ready to do so."

"Wow, you never told me that story," Stacy said.

Stacy looked at Laurie. "Let's go outside so Stella can have some time alone."

They both left to sit in Laurie's car. Stella stood in the foyer for a bit, and then her tears started up as she walked into the kitchen. The tears weren't of loss; they were about the experience of coming into her childhood home after thirty years; she had never thought this would happen in her life. She took her time in the kitchen, mainly staring at the view. What a remarkable view the house had of the Olympic Mountains. She missed it so much. She went to her parents' bedroom. She suddenly had a memory from right after her brother died. She had crawled into her mom's bed one night to sleep with her. She wasn't sure who needed whom that night, but it had been a painful time for both, and she hadn't known how to comfort her mom or how to feel about her brother's death.

Stella went into the master bathroom. She remembered the pink porcelain tiles all over the walls and floor. Even the sink and tub were pink. She went to the mirror and pulled the steel ring that fit so nicely onto one of the lights and remembered when her mom told her that just after Michael died, the steel ring had lifted up and dropped on the floor one morning when she was putting on her makeup. Stella had told her mom that it was Michael telling her that he was in the bathroom with her.

Stella went down the hall to the room next to the garage. She wanted to go into the garage, but there was an alarm system, so she wasn't sure whether she would set it off. The room had rocking horses painted all around the upper part of the wall. This must have been a baby's room. When Stella had lived there, it had been her dad's office, and he had spent more of his time there than anywhere in the house.

Then she went into Michael's bedroom. It was the best room in the house for the view of the Olympic Mountains. Stella spent the most time in that room. She remembered when her sister had called her to find the pot and money, and then the day after her brother had died when her mom went into his room and packed up all his clothes. And she remembered that night just after he died, when he came into her dreams and told her he was okay and rubbed her back—how it had all felt so real and how he had told her he was at peace. Stella thanked the heavens for that experience.

Stella walked downstairs where her and Lynn's bedrooms had

been. She turned to the right just at the bottom of the stairs into the furnace room. She had always been scared of that room. Dark and dingy always gave her the creeps. Stella turned to the left and stepped down onto the carpeted floor where the family room was. Right away, she thought of her dad sitting in one of the chairs. Robert was always in front of the TV on Sundays watching sports. Stella would lay on the floor with a pillow and fall asleep. Mainly, Stella was usually hung over from drinking too much the night before. The only window was below ground. The whole downstairs was three-quarters underground, so the only light that came in was close to the ceiling. It hadn't changed a bit, although the bar was gone and the door to the laundry room was replaced with one that didn't have a window, so it was very dark.

Stella went into Lynn's bedroom. When Lynn had moved out, Stella had made it into her bedroom. Suddenly, she remembered when her father had sat in the wicker chair and cried, asking her why her mother was divorcing him. Stella had felt so responsible for her dad's wellbeing. It was amazing that she had taken that on at such an early age.

Next, Stella remembered her boyfriends crawling into the window late at night after partying. She'd have sex with them while her parents were sleeping upstairs. Stella shook her head as she entered her old bedroom. The walls were as blue as Lynn's room was pink. She imagined the twin beds snuggled up against the north wall under the window and how dark the room was compared to Lynn's. The room had the energy of a dungeon, and it smelled and tasted musty. She went over to the window and could barely touch the bottom of the windowsill. No wonder she had felt closed in there as a teenager. Stella remembered how lonely, fearful, and anxious she had felt in that room. Stella could now feel some of the claustrophobia symptoms she'd felt in the room as a teenager, so she left the room and walked into the bathroom that Lynn and she had shared. The owners hadn't changed a thing; it was still forest green and had a bathtub/shower combination. Stella remembered sitting on the toilet, crying that day when Shirley came home to find out that Michael had died. Stella had held on to her stomach and thought it should have been her. Immediately, her thoughts changed to how she no longer held that feeling about herself. All the work Stella had done with Rachel had given her the healing she needed to feel wanted and worthy to be alive.

Stella walked back upstairs and into the sunken living room. She remembered family holidays and hanging out with her friends, pretending they were in a band. Robert had hated when Stella used his record player. He would always tell her not to use his stuff. He used to come home drunk after work. One night, Shirley was gone somewhere, and Stella, Lynn, and Stella's friend Stacy were home alone. Her dad came home very drunk, walked in, and fell down the living room steps where her friend and she were sitting. His glasses flew off. Stella thought it was funny when her parents got drunk. They both entertained and drank a lot in that house. So did Stella.

The last room Stella went into was the family room, just off the living room. Even though it was a family room, she remembered it being a lonely place. None of the family ever spent any time together in this room.

As she walked through the house, Stella had been putting all the memories into the balloon for her ritual. Despite all the pain, abuse, and craziness that had gone on in the house, she felt grateful that it was such a lovely place to live. Stella walked back into the kitchen and had some sage left over so she placed it on the kitchen counter in gratitude to Laurie, Stacy, and this opportunity to heal any last thing Stella needed to let go of.

Then Stella walked outside to meet up with Laurie and Stacy.

"Nothing has changed in the house since I lived there," Stella said.

"Did you see the cross from the church that your brother's funeral was in?" Stacy asked.

"No, I didn't know you could see a cross. Show me," Stella said.

They all walked into the backyard as Laurie talked about how she was going to change the yard. They stepped up onto the back patio just off the kitchen. This was one of Stella's favorite spots in the whole house. Her friend Claire and she used to sleep outside on the patio.

"The whole eleven years I lived in this house, I never knew there was a cross you could see from the patio," Stella said, looking out to see the cross.

Stella had one more thing to do. "Laurie, would it be okay if I stayed a bit longer?"

"Yes, of course," Laurie said as she and Stacy walked out to the car in the driveway and drove away.

Stella stood on the patio for a while soaking up the view and thinking about the day of Michael's funeral.

She walked down the cement steps to the lower yard as she had many years before, many times. She stood in the place where she had stood thirty-one years before with the white balloon, and she recalled all the times she was scared, lonely, and anxious. The wind was blowing the broken clouds. A slight sprinkle splattered Stella as she thought about that day and remembered that white balloon.

She was not in a hurry, and she wanted to make the most of her experience. She let the breeze caress her and the sprinkles cleanse her. The wind came in with a force and whipped the balloon, so she tightened her grip. She wasn't ready to let go yet. She asked herself whether there was anything she needed to let go of that she wasn't conscious of. She thought about how unworthy she felt in her family, how insecure, afraid of herself, of being alone, and not being worthy of love. Desperate for love, she took any abuse just as long as she felt loved and not alone. She put all these emotions in the balloon.

"I am not this person anymore," she said, over and over.

She gradually eased up on the string, feeling ready to let go. She faced west looking at the beautiful view and knew it was time to let go. She released the balloon. It flew up to the right, heading north, carried away quickly. She watched it till she couldn't see it anymore.

As Stella walked back to her car, she felt so grateful for the experience and the opportunity to walk through the house thirty years after she had been a pain-filled teenager and to come back full circle to let go.

Stella got into her car and yelled, "I am grateful. Thank you!"

17

"Be the love you never received."

— Rum Lazuli

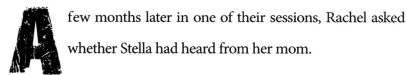 few months later in one of their sessions, Rachel asked whether Stella had heard from her mom.

Stella looked at Rachel with confusion. "No, why would I hear from her?"

"Well, a few months ago, you had the opportunity to visit your family home. Do you see that as a sign that maybe it's time to reach out to your mom?" she asked.

Shirley had been sending cards and emails to Stella for the past five years, but Stella had never replied to her or written other than when her dad had died. Often she had been tempted to, but she had told herself she just wasn't ready. Now she realized she felt differently.

"I do think about her more now than ever," Stella said, "but I don't know whether she has changed. That said, I feel much stronger and pretty much all of my anxiety has been nonexistent for many months, so maybe I could deal better with her now."

Rachel looked up at Stella. "Just think about how it would be for you to reach out to your mom. See how that would feel in your body."

Stella had never had this conversation with Rachel before. "It was in my mind that I would never see my mom again. I was okay with that."

"I know you're okay with that, but I also think that one day you will reach out to your mom," Rachel said.

Stella looked at Rachel. "You always knew that I would come to this place with my mom?"

"Yes. It's natural when you go through this healing process that you will want to reconnect with your mom."

■ ■ ■

That night, Stella thought about how she would reach out to Shirley after all those years—email, letter, phone call? *How do I write a letter to my mom? I haven't spoken to her in over five years. What do I say to her? I can start the letter by saying, "I've been thinking about you. I know I have hurt you by not talking with you for some time. I needed space because I felt very hurt by you. You have hurt me, and I felt I needed to step away from the relationship."* Thoughts swirled in Stella's mind.

Stella could not deny her connection with her mom, despite all the pain from her past. She'd had to put up a steel wall between Shirley and herself so she could heal her anxiety with Rachel. Now the wall of disconnection was opening, and Stella couldn't ignore that she was walking through the door to contact Shirley. Stella had never thought the day would come for her to want Shirley in her life. She wrote in her journal:

> I am a different person since the last time I saw her. I have done so much work with Rachel in healing myself. Rachel reminded me of the big pond visualization in our last session— to visualize a strong white light beam in the center of my being, expanding with each breath until it encompassed the whole planet. A large rock can be thrown in the middle with ripples, but my being doesn't change shape. I see the ripples, but I am not moved by them. The ripples are anything that occurs in my

life. What fantasy do I have regarding the relationship that my mother and I have?

.   .   .

A month later, Stella met with Rachel and they talked about her reconciling with her mom, which Rachel encouraged her to do.

That night, Stella sat down at her desk and looked up Shirley's email address. She sat there for a minute and then she composed an email. "Hi, Mom. You have been on my mind lately. I would like to know if we can meet for coffee soon. I miss you. Stella."

Stella received an email the next morning. "Hi, Stella. I've been waiting for you to reach out to me, and I would love to meet with you. I will be out of town until next Wednesday, but when I get back, let's plan on you coming down here to my house if you're comfortable with that. It would give us more privacy than a coffee shop."

Stella replied, "Hi, Mom. That's fine. I'll come to your house next Thursday around 2 p.m."

Shirley responded, "That would be great! I love you."

"I love you too," Stella wrote back.

Stella phoned Rachel to let her know when she and her mom would be meeting. "Do you need to see me before you go?" Rachel said.

"No, I feel good about the meeting, but I'll let you know how it goes."

"Okay. If you change your mind, let me know and I'll fit you into my schedule. You've a few days before the meeting with your mom."

"Thank you, Rachel. If I feel that I need to see you, I'll call you by the end of the week to schedule."

"Okay, dear. This is big."

"I know. I have my pink cord to wear if I need to, and I know you'll be there in spirit too," Stella said as she hung up.

■ ■ ■

The next Thursday afternoon, Stella drove down to Seattle and pulled into her mother's driveway. She knew her mother and her husband had moved from an email Shirley had sent her prior to their reconnecting. The house sat on a cliff overlooking downtown Seattle, in an affluent neighborhood. She started feeling nervous, not anxious, but excited to see her mom. The emails back and forth had been positive so she was optimistic.

Stella knocked on the door and heard a dog bark. *Am I at the right house?* she wondered. Her mother had never had a dog before.

The door opened and Stella looked into a familiar face. Then she looked down and said, "You have a dog?"

Shirley smiled and said, "Yes, her name is Taby."

They looked into each other's eyes, embraced, and hung onto each other for a while; Shirley looked really good and happy. Stella wasn't feeling so nervous; she was relieved to have finally reached this point of connection with her mom.

Stella snuggled into Shirley's shoulder and started to cry. "I really miss you."

"I missed you too, honey. Can I take your purse and coat?"

Shirley hung up her jacket and placed her purse on the table next to the front door. "Is there a special place you want to sit?"

"No, this will do." Stella sat down in the living room and looked at the view of the Space Needle and Mount Rainier. She stared out the window for a bit. Then Shirley asked her what she had been up to—whether she was dating and where she was working.

"I'm not dating anyone serious, and I'm working in sales still."

"Oh, that's good. How's Gabrielle?"

"She is doing great. She moved home right after she graduated from college, and she has a job; she's thinking about getting her master's degree."

Stella wanted to change the subject from Gabrielle because of her last episode with her mother during Gabrielle's high school graduation party. "How's everyone in Georgia?"

"My brother died a year ago from a heart attack," Shirley said.

"Oh, wow. I'm sorry to hear that. I know you two were close."

Taby had been sitting by Stella all this time. Now she started to paw the air like she wanted to be petted.

"Where you're sitting is Taby's favorite place to sit, so if you want her to sit on your lap while you pet her, she would love that."

"I had to put Tiger down last year. It was one of the hardest things I had to do. I really miss him," Stella said while she petted Taby.

Shirley looked out the window. "Why did you reach out to me now?"

"I have done a lot of healing, and I have forgiven you," said Stella. "You're my mom and I love and miss you very much. I want to have a relationship with you."

Shirley looked at Stella, "I'm not sure what the forgiveness is about, but I guess you'll tell me if you want me to know."

Stella thought about what Shirley had just said. She felt she had done so much healing around her issues with Shirley that she was grateful she had come to this place with Shirley of reconnecting.

After a minute, Shirley said, "Let's have lunch."

They went into the kitchen and Shirley pulled some chicken salad out of the fridge. Stella retrieved some crackers from the cupboard. Then they poured themselves some iced tea and sat down at the kitchen table.

"How are you feeling about your dad's death?" Shirley asked.

"I was able to be with him during the dying process for the eleven months."

"Was Lynn with your dad too?" Shirley asked before taking a sip of her iced tea.

"No, she didn't want to have anything to do with him. She told me that she didn't like being around death."

Shirley simply nodded her head.

"Where is your dad buried?" asked Shirley.

Stella looked up at Shirley. "His wishes were to be buried in Massachusetts with his mom and dad, and Michael."

Shirley and Stella stared at their food. Then Shirley said, "Why would he do that?"

"He just wanted to."

Shirley stared out the kitchen window. "I don't think I will ever see Lynn again. I have done so much healing around that relationship, and I feel completed and done with Lynn."

"You never know, Mom," said Stella. "Things happen in weird ways, and I believe in miracles, so you don't know what is planned."

"No, I know I won't see her again," Shirley replied.

They decided to take Taby for a walk so they went down to the marina just below the house. It was sunny and they walked along the boardwalk, looking at all the boats moored in the marina.

Shirley stopped walking while Taby sniffed around. "Do you still do energy healing?" she asked Stella.

Stella pulled her hair away from her face as the wind picked up. "Yes, I have done some chakra work for many years. It has really helped with my healing journey."

"Yeah, I did some chakra work a long time ago; it really helped me too."

They came to a bench just across from the marina and sat down. "How was it for you when your dad died?"

"You know, Mom, I had done so much healing work with this gal named Rachel that it really helped me to come to terms with him dying, so I was able to go through the process with him."

Shirley patted Taby while she lay on the ground. "Your dad was hard to love. He had affairs with other women while married to me, and I remember how angry I was in the marriage. At times, I took it out on you kids."

Stella was looking out at the boats, thinking how much Shirley had changed. Before the five-year separation, she never would have admitted anything about abuse with her kids.

"I never did love your dad. I married him because I felt so alone and wanted companionship. Actually, I felt alone most of my life. That's part of the reason for Taby," Shirley said. Stella really related to her mother concerning the loneliness. She had always felt alone, even when she was in a relationship.

"Does this loneliness get passed on from generation to generation?" Stella asked.

"I'm sure it does!"

Stella stayed for about six hours. While Shirley's husband was downstairs watching a movie, she and Shirley laughed, cried, and talked very spiritually with each other, never having had deep conversations in the past. Stella realized how much she missed her mother and how much she really wanted her in her life. One of the nicest things Shirley said to Stella, besides that she missed her and loved her, was that she hoped Stella would find someone—a special man she could share her life with, who would love, respect, and adore her.

■ ■ ■

After that meeting, it felt like Stella and Shirley had never lost contact with each other. The phone calls came every other day, and they visited each other often. About three months later, Shirley phoned Stella and said that she needed to talk with her about something. They agreed Shirley would come over to Stella's house and have a cup of tea.

When Shirley showed up the next day, Stella looked into Shirley's eyes and saw a familiar look. She'd seen that gaze before and felt that energy. It felt very old. Stella asked Shirley whether she wanted some tea, but Shirley declined. They went into the back room and sat down on the couch. Shirley didn't waste a minute and got straight to the point.

"Stella, I just need to let you know that I'm going to give Gabrielle some money and stocks so she can have a secure future, and I want to meet with her and discuss what my plan is for her," Shirley said with confidence.

"Why do you feel you need to give Gabrielle money?" Stella asked.

"Because I want to have a relationship with her and help her to succeed financially," Shirley said.

"Don't you think she is capable of building her own life?" Stella asked.

"That's not what this is about. I just want to give her money, that's all," Shirley replied.

"Mom, you manipulated and controlled me as a child and I won't have you do the same thing to Gabrielle," Stella said with conviction.

Shirley shifted and said, "You're the one who is manipulating."

"Don't you think it's manipulating for you to come over here and tell me these things?" Stella asked. She couldn't believe what she had just said. She had never, ever stood up to her mom. In the past when Shirley had said, "Jump," Stella had asked, "How high?" Shirley leaned back as if she were shocked by Stella's newfound assertiveness.

"No," said Shirley. "I'm trying to be a good grandmother. I have no other intentions. I just want to give Gabrielle something for her future."

"I have been protecting her from you because everything you give has some kind of motive. I don't trust you with her or me," she said with a calm, cool tone.

Shirley sat there for a minute, and then she got up and said, "I'm done with this conversation. I'm leaving and I need a break. I'll contact you when I'm ready to talk again," she said, walking to the door.

Stella got up and started to cry, but it was different from all the other cries she'd had with Shirley. "Mom, all I have ever wanted from you is for you just to love me; that's all," she said, hugging Shirley before she walked out the door.

Stella shut the door. She was shaking so much, not from being scared, but from standing up to Shirley. "No wonder I was so fucked up with low self-esteem and anxiety," she told herself and began to cry again. She called Rachel and left her a message because she had not expected the conversation with Shirley to end with Shirley not wanting to see her. She went into the bathroom to take an Epsom salt bath, which always helped her to calm down. She was surprised by how calm she actually was. She had done so much healing with Rachel that she had been able to stand up to Shirley.

Since their reconciliation, Stella had thought Shirley understood her now. It had given Stella hope that perhaps Shirley could love her unconditionally. She took out her journal and wrote:

> All I ever wanted was contact and love from my mother. No wonder I always felt hopeless; that came from my mother's refusal to connect with me, to nurture me and accept me. I now realize I don't need that connection from her; she isn't capable, has never been capable. This has nothing to do with me and who I am. I am worthy. I am lovable. Rachel has revived that hope in me through her love. I know Rachel loves me. I know.

As Stella finished writing, the phone rang. It was Rachel.

"Hi, Rachel. Is it possible that you have any openings this week so I can come see you?" Stella asked.

"What's up?" Rachel said.

"Well, my mom and I had a conversation earlier today, and it didn't end well, so she told me that she needs a break from the relationship."

"Oh, no, Shirley…I wanted more from you than that," Rachel said. "I might have a client who can see me earlier; if so I can schedule you on Wednesday at noon."

"That would be great," said Stella.

"Okay. If I don't call you back, then it's a go," said Rachel before hanging up.

■ ■ ■

That same night, Stella had a dream that was so real she woke up weeping. In the dream, Shirley was having a conversation with Stella about how she felt about her.

Stella talked with Rachel about the dream in their session together. "I dreamt that my mom was telling me that she didn't love me, never has loved me, and never will love me."

"What happened with the visit with your mom?" Rachel asked.

"She went on about how much she wanted to give Gabrielle stocks, and provide for her future."

Rachel sat in her chair for a moment, processing what Stella had said. "I'm disappointed in your mom," she finally said. "It's obvious she still hangs on to some resentment with you and to her controlling nature. The most amazing thing about this situation is your dream. When you dream like that, as if you are actually having the conversation with the person, it's your souls that are speaking together, working something out."

"Yeah, I have had a handful of dreams like that where they felt so real," said Stella.

When Stella had finished telling Rachel all the details about the incident with Shirley and the dream, she cried like a little child. "I get that my mom doesn't have the capacity to love me like I need or needed to be loved."

Rachel sat in her chair and let Stella cry for a minute. Then she got up and sat next to her. "Here, dear; let me hold you."

"Your mom does love you, Stella," Rachel confirmed, "but not in the way you need. You were looking for some resolution and wanting to fill a childhood wound."

"Well, Rachel, you've filled and salved that wound by our connection," Stella said, as she sat up.

"It has been our work together that has healed and filled this void with your mom," Rachel concluded.

■ ■ ■

Stella went back to not wanting to have anything to do with Shirley. Even though she had healed that little child within her, she knew Shirley had some old resentments, and Stella didn't want to be bothered with them.

A few weeks later, Stella received a letter in the mail from Shirley. She instantly suspected that Shirley was writing to dissolve the relationship. Stella called Rachel and told her about the letter. She said that she wasn't going to read it.

"Do you want me to read the letter?" Rachel asked.

"No, I don't care what is in it."

A few weeks later, Shirley reached out to Stella in an email and said that she really wanted to talk about the situation. Stella replied by saying that she hadn't read the letter yet, but she would reach out to her when she did. However, Stella shoved the letter in her desk drawer with the intent never to read it. She knew Shirley would not change.

18

"The human heart, at whatever age, opens to the
heart that opens in return."

— Maria Edgeworth

Several months went by and Stella still hadn't reached out to Shirley. Finally, she decided to give Shirley's letter to Rachel to read. The next day, Rachel called Stella and told her that her mother had apologized in the letter, telling her that what she did and said that day was old stuff. Shirley continued to say that she wanted to have a relationship with her and to let her know when they could start talking again.

"Are you going to reach out to her?" Rachel asked.

"I don't know, Rachel. I don't trust her, and I don't think I'll be able to trust her ever."

"If you decide to reach out to Shirley, I will be there to support you," Rachel confirmed.

"My mom has never apologized to me before," Stella said. "That's a first. I'm surprised by the letter's contents. It does give me hope."

A few days later, Shirley called Stella and left a voicemail. Stella was reluctant to listen because she wasn't ready to make contact with Shirley. But when she listened to the voicemail, she was taken aback.

"Stella, I received a call from Lynn's boyfriend. She's in the hospital with head injuries from a car accident. They operated yesterday, but they aren't sure what the impact will be and whether she will come out of her coma."

Stella couldn't believe what she was hearing—another tragedy in her family. How could that be? Stella immediately called the hospital to see what room Lynn was in and to get an update on her progress. The doctor told her Lynn was still in a coma but she could see her if she wished. Stella decided to go to the hospital that afternoon.

Stella and Lynn had not seen each other since their father had died, now three years ago. When Stella entered the hospital room and saw Lynn lying there alone, she began to wonder how she would feel if she never spoke to her sister again. She stood next to Lynn's bed and took her hand in her own. Then she began to pray that Lynn's swelling would go down and she would wake and be well. As she prayed, all Stella could hear were beeps in the background from the machines monitoring Lynn and Lynn's light breathing through a tube.

Then Stella heard a gentle tap on the door behind her. She turned and saw Shirley. They both said hello, but that was it, neither thinking this an appropriate time for a long reconciliation conversation. Shirley found a chair and sat down in a cove set away from the hospital bed. The sun was shining through the window with a hazy effect.

After a moment, Stella whispered to Shirley, "When was the last time you, me, and Lynn were in the same room?"

"At your wedding, twenty-four years ago," Shirley said, looking down at her lap.

Shirley watched Stella as she stroked Lynn's foot and leg and bent down to tell Lynn that she loved her and everything would be all right. There was no response from Lynn, but Stella knew she could hear her. Stella eventually went over and sat next to Shirley. Nothing was said about the letter or their last situation at Stella's house.

"Stella, I don't want Lynn to know I'm here," Shirley said.

"Why? I think she knows you're here," Stella said.

"Because I don't want to hinder her healing in any way."

Shirley looked over at Lynn while Stella looked out the window at the sun shining on the shrubs outside. She had never thought such an incident would bring them all together again.

"Boy, I never realized before how much Lynn looks like her dad," Shirley said.

"Mom, Lynn needs all the love she can muster right now. I think she would be okay if you were here," said Stella.

Shirley stood up and went over to Lynn's bed. She started rubbing her foot. The nurse came in to check Lynn's vitals. "She is in stable condition, no changes, but we won't know anything until the swelling goes down; then we can check to see if there is any brain damage."

Stella sat in the chair while Shirley sat on Lynn's bed by her feet. Stella's eyes started tearing up as Shirley looked at Lynn. Stella couldn't imagine not seeing her child for twenty-four years.

"Mom," Stella asked, "how much longer are you going to stay with Lynn?"

"I'll be here until her doctor comes back in to check on her. The nurse said he will be making his rounds in about an hour."

"Okay, I'm going to go home. I'll come back tomorrow morning to spend some time with Lynn until you get here. What time do you think you'll be here?"

"I'll call you after I talk with the doctor and see what time he'll be in tomorrow. I want to be here when he's here so I can talk with him about Lynn's progress," Shirley said.

"Okay, I'll talk with you later on today," Stella said, hugging Shirley goodbye.

Stella had taken the elevator up to ICU without any problems, but when it was time to take the elevator down, she started having some anxiety and didn't want to deal with working through the symptoms, so she found the stairs and took them down to where she was parked.

■ ■ ■

Shirley called Stella that night and told her the doctor was going to move Lynn tomorrow sometime so she didn't have to come to the hospital in the morning. "I'll call you when the nurses move her so I can give you her room number."

"Okay, Mom. It sounds like Lynn is doing better," Stella said.

"Yes, she had a great night and most of the swelling went down, so she is progressing."

The next day, Stella received a call from Shirley to let her know about Lynn's progress in moving to a new room.

"Hi, Stella. I wanted to let you know that Lynn is out of a coma and the nurses will be moving her to another section of the building out of ICU," Shirley said.

"Oh, great. Thanks for letting me know. What room number is she in?" Stella replied.

"She's in room 456. I spent some time with Lynn yesterday before I left, and Lynn finally woke up and told me she was glad that I was there and that she missed having a mother-daughter relationship. I told her I was going on a trip to Scotland, but I didn't need too," Shirley said.

There was a moment of silence on the phone. Then she said, "Lynn told me to go and we would talk more when I get back."

"Mom, that's awesome that you and Lynn have had some reconciliation before you leave. Have a great time in Scotland. I'll talk with you when you get back home," Stella said.

■ ■ ■

The next morning, Stella called Lynn to talk with her. "Hi, Lynn. I hear you're feeling much better."

"Yes," Lynn said, slurring her speech.

"I'm going to come out today and visit for a while."

"Okay, I would like that," Lynn said.

After she hung up the phone, Stella wrote in her journal:

> I believe everything happens for a reason and there are no mistakes! It has been proven to me once again that healing one's soul is inevitable. Lynn isn't really supposed to still be alive. As her doctor explained, she had so much swelling and some damage to the brain tissue. Lynn has a second chance. I'm looking forward to seeing her.

Stella drove down to the hospital in Seattle in traffic and felt some anxiety symptoms, but she breathed through them and told herself she would be all right. She parked the car and went to the elevator. A few people were waiting so she stood aside to wait for another elevator she could ride up in alone. When her elevator came and its doors opened, Stella stood there for a minute until the doors closed. *Dam-*

mit. Just gather your courage and try again. You can do this! Before the next elevator came, a few people had gathered again so Stella went to the bathroom and splashed some water on her face. She stood in front of the mirror and told herself that she could do this; then she went out into the waiting area to muster the courage to try again. There were four elevators and two had just opened, so people scurried on. Stella didn't have to wait long till another one opened up and she was the only one standing there. *I can do this! I can do this!* The elevator doors slowly closed. *Fuck this shit! I'm taking the stairs.* Stella walked up two flights of stairs per floor. By the time she reached the top, she was out of breath. She found Lynn's room still out of breath.

"Why are you out of breath?" Lynn asked.

"I'm not sure why; just walking to the room," Stella said. Lynn knew nothing about Stella's anxieties. She didn't share that kind of stuff with Lynn because they didn't have a close relationship. However, today, Lynn and Stella's conversation in the hospital room was all about relationships.

"You and Mom have had solid relationships with your boyfriend and mom with spouses for so many years, but your other relationships have taken the backseat in your lives," Stella said. "You and Mom are very similar in many ways. Each of you have had fragmented dealings with your children and neither one of you have close friends."

"Yeah, that is true," Lynn said, while drinking her apple juice. "Have you talked with Mom today?"

"No, I know she mentioned the other day that she was going to be busy with packing for her trip," Stella said.

"Yeah, she wasn't going to go to Scotland, but I told her that she needed to go and that I had you to help me out," Lynn said.

"I'm here for you, Lynn."

"Stella, speaking of relationships, you do seem to have a good relationship with Gabrielle," she said slowly.

"I do. It has been my prime focus. I'm not good at relationships with guys, though. I admire you and Mom for having solid relationships with men."

Stella had had many boyfriends, and some of the relationships had lasted a few years. But she hadn't been blessed with the ability to sustain a long healthy relationship with a guy—yet. She didn't know why; it just had been that way. Stella had loved and she had even been loved many times, but her childhood conditioning had imprinted in her that she was not worthy.

Stella didn't have to live in that prison anymore. The prison represented the fear, the loneliness, from being detached. Being detached was the only way not to feel. Feelings caused pain. Pain was too scary. Falling in love with someone was too scary. The push and pull of emotions was exhausting. She had a deep desire to love someone and know that the person she opened up to loved her and made her feel safe. She did not want to feel abandoned. She did not want to feel disappointed. She did not want to feel vulnerable. But she did feel alone and scared. It was the worst place to be. Until she had met Rachel, Stella had suffered tremendously with those feelings.

Stella got up from the chair and went over to sit on Lynn's bed. "Can I get you anything before I go home?"

"No, I'm good. The nurse is coming in to help me shower," Lynn said.

"Okay. I'll call you in the morning and see what time to come out," she said, while giving Lynn a kiss on her cheek.

Stella took the stairs back down. When she got home, she called Rachel to talk with her about not being able to get on the elevator. Rachel suggested that Stella call Wendy, the energy worker, and have a healing around the anxiety to see whether that shifted anything. Stella called Wendy and was able to schedule something the next day.

■ ■ ■

It was good to see Wendy again. It had been several years since Stella's last session with her, so she was excited to experience some results. She did very well with chakra work; it seemed to be the one modality that helped with her wounds.

The session focused on her third and fourth chakras: personal will and heart. Wendy was working on her heart chakra when Stella had an incredible release of energy that brought tears to her eyes. Before the unshackling, she felt a pressure sink into her chest cavity like a block of bricks. She started to breathe rapidly until she couldn't hold the bricks any longer. Then she let out a moan of air that rattled the cage. Tears rolled down each cheek as she lay there catching her breath. She had never released energy like that during a session. Something came over her after that experience that she couldn't put into words, but its resonance would stay with her forever. She had integrated herself to herself.

■ ■ ■

The next day, Stella went to visit Lynn. She had her pink cord wrapped around her waist securely. She approached the elevator with a new lightness and waited for it to descend to her floor. A few people were waiting for the elevator so when the door opened she waited for everyone to get on, and then she walked toward the door, stepped inside the elevator, and turned around to face the doors. She closed her eyes. *I am doing this! I am doing this!* In no time, the doors opened and she stepped out of the elevator.

While she walked slowly to Lynn's room, she started to cry with excitement that she had gotten into an elevator without any symptoms. She wiped away her tears before she entered Lynn's room.

"Hi, Lynn. You look good today."

"I know. They gave me a shower. I've been waiting for you so you can cut my hair. The nurse gave me some scissors," Lynn said, holding them up in her left hand.

"Um, I'm not a hairdresser. Are you sure you don't want to wait till you get out?"

"No, please just cut the length. My hair is driving me crazy."

While Stella cut some of the length, Lynn said, "I don't like hospitals so I'm trying to get out of here tomorrow."

Stella looked down at Lynn. "Don't you think it's too soon to leave?"

"Well, I'm going to ask my doctor anyway," Lynn said, laughing while Stella was clipping some strands.

"Now that you spoke with Mom, how do you think your relationship will be with her?" Stella asked, putting the scissors back in the bag.

"We agreed to work on the relationship and not be prideful."

"That's really cool, Lynn. I'm glad you and mom are talking again."

Stella wrote in her journal that night:

> Vulnerability is a very difficult thing to experience. When you open yourself to someone and start to have feelings, it can be very scary, especially if you have abuse in your fabric. Being in a vulnerable place with someone else can leave you feeling powerless. I get this way of thinking. The residue from physical abuse extends into intimate relationships. The sense of being vulnerable leaves one feeling powerless over life. It could be looked at as a weakness, but what really occurs is a sense of powerlessness; you feel you have no power over your emotions. The fear is that you will not recover and you will lose yourself

in the process. This is the scariest thing about love. Opening up to someone when you don't know how to care for yourself regarding emotions can bring you all the way back to childhood and the vulnerabilities you felt as a child. It can be paralyzing to feel so vulnerable. It can stop you in your tracks, leave you powerless and weak because you put all your power into the hands of one person. It brings you back to the little child who was so pure in feelings, so vulnerable to the environment that was so abusive, so trapped by the powerlessness of the situation, the family environment. You detach from yourself and your emotions when they start to arise. The pain of not having yourself, the fear of losing yourself, can be so devastating it can leave one to separate from all emotions. Then you become vigilant in trying not to feel anything, not to feel love for another. Not allowing yourself to be lovable, or loved, or to love. This is the most tragic of them all—not to allow the natural feelings of being loved, of loving someone. It's like you have been cut off from all connection to love. Love is what heals. Love is what helps a person to grow. Love is the universal healing agent that brings one out of darkness into the light.

To be so vulnerable can be too much for one. It brings up the old behavior of detaching and running away. You think you're running away from the person you are having feelings for. In actuality, you're running away from yourself. Running from the old pain of being abandoned, the old pain of being so vulnerable to someone who is supposed to love and care for you, which could cause you so much pain and hurt. To return to the place that created this fear in the first place is paralyzing. So the other option is to detach. But this brings you back to the same place as before. It's cyclical—the fear, detachment, and paralyzing feeling creates the perception of being alone. You feel alone because you're detaching from the essence of what you are—the spirit of the universe—God. So you detach from life itself, from what feeds you, from what makes you whole, and what makes you feel most alive...love for yourself and others. That is what keeps you grounded in yourself.

To feel insecure is not the feeling of protection. When one feels insecure, you immediately protect yourself by detaching from others. You can't feel intimacy toward another; it's too painful and scary. Detaching from feelings and people will give one a sense of power, but in reality, it deepens the sense of loneliness and detachment from a life force. You continue to keep yourself in this circle of fear, too scared to attach, yet you have the yearning to attach. We need each other to help us heal, grow, and evolve into the person we were created to be. The universe wants that for us; that is why it presents people and situations to show up on our path so we can morph into an individual who can be alive, feel deeply for another, and know that we are all connected to the same universe, so we can love ourselves and others unconditionally.

19

"The idea is not to see through one another,
but to see one another through."

— C.D. Jackson

L ynn went home after a few weeks in the hospital. Her daughter came up from Nevada to spend some time with her while Lynn's boyfriend worked. Her doctor had told Lynn that she wouldn't be able to work at the local salon for a year. It would take her brain a while to heal from the swelling and for her to learn to walk without a cane. Following the car accident, she had been stuck in the car for an hour while the firefighters used the jaws-of-life to get her out. Lynn's left ankle bones had been crushed, so the doctor had pinned up the ankle, and she would need physical therapy to help her walk again.

Since the accident, Stella noticed that Lynn was more present with her in their relationship. Stella had read that sometimes, with a brain injury, a person can change her whole personality, depending on the location of the injury and how much damage was done. She recognized how lucky Lynn was and that the accident also seemed to be helping to heal Lynn's relationship with Shirley. Perhaps they had both needed some kind of tragedy to happen to realize how much they really loved each other. Stella remembered her earlier conversation with her mom when Shirley had said she would never see Lynn again; at one time, Stella didn't think she would see Shirley again, so now Stella saw that anything was possible. She believed in miracles. This was a miracle.

Lynn and Shirley were spending a lot of time together. After Lynn's daughter returned to Nevada, Shirley came over every day to help Lynn bathe and to help with errands and household chores. Stella kept her distance so they could catch up on the last twenty years. One day, Shirley wasn't available to drive Lynn to her doctor's appointment, so Stella drove Lynn and they talked extensively about their childhood.

"Lynn, do you ever think about the beatings Mom used to give us?" Stella asked while driving to Seattle.

"Yes. I used to get them worse than you," said Lynn. "What I remember the most is how mean Mom used to be to me."

Stella pondered what Lynn said and then asked, "Are you going to reconcile your relationship with your daughter now that she's in your life?"

"Before this accident, I had tried to contact her for years, but she wouldn't call me back."

Stella pondered the similarities between Shirley and Lynn, of not having a relationship with their daughters. In one of Stella's conversations with Lynn, Lynn mentioned how Shirley had previously reached out to her, but she wouldn't have anything to do with her.

"I didn't know that," said Stella. "All I remember is the letter Mom sent to you when you were in your early twenties, the one where Mom said she didn't want to have a relationship with you and you needed to get your shit together about using drugs; basically, Mom disowned you then."

When Stella and Lynn arrived at the hospital, they found seats in the waiting room until the nurse called for Lynn.

After Lynn's appointment, Stella took her home and they said their goodbyes.

On the drive home, Stella thought more about their conversation.

She realized they had both had similar issues about not being loved by Shirley, feeling abandoned by her, and not being worthy of Shirley's love, but they had always felt loved by Robert and worthy of his love. Since Shirley and Lynn had reunited, Stella had been very careful when she had conversations with them on the phone or in person when the other one wasn't around; she didn't want to get sucked into any drama between them. Stella wasn't used to being in this triangle relationship with Lynn and Shirley; the last time she had been in it had been when she was a teenager. She'd had to pick sides between Lynn and Shirley then, and Stella had picked Shirley, which left her without a relationship with Lynn.

■ ■ ■

It took about three months after Lynn got home from the hospital, but eventually, Lynn called Stella to complain about how Shirley was trying to control her life and tell her what to do. Then Shirley called Stella, complaining about Lynn and her stubbornness. Stella started joining in the mess and it started to become like old times until one day she was blamed for something she said to Shirley that Lynn had confided in her.

To nip this situation in the bud, Stella called Rachel to schedule an appointment. The situation was causing her to experience some old anxiety about being abandoned and feeling she had to fix things. She really wanted to honor all the work she had done to maintain boundaries in her relationships with Lynn and Shirley. She knew she now had an opportunity to change the way she related to them and that situation in the past. She was committed to the work she had done with Rachel for all those years and to herself.

■ ■ ■

Stella quietly waited for Rachel. She lay down on the futon mattress and placed a beautiful coral blanket around her. Just a few minutes later, Rachel entered and saw that Stella was staring at her with blurry eyes.

"Oh, what happened to you?" Rachel asked.

"I feel very tired," Stella said. Rachel could tell by Stella's eyes that she was not grounded.

"It takes a lot of energy to hold on to emotions," Rachel said. Stella knew why she was so tired. She didn't want to revert back to old behavior and wasn't sure how to handle the situation between Lynn and Shirley.

"What is going on with your sister and mom?"

"I haven't had a relationship with my mom and sister together for over twenty years. Actually, the last time I was in this situation was just before my mom sent that letter to Lynn telling her she didn't want any-thing to do with her."

"What happened then?"

"I felt like I had to choose between my sister and my mom. I chose my mom."

Rachel sat for a minute. "You know, Stella, you're different today than when you were younger. You have it in your power to tell them truthfully how you feel."

"Yeah, I want it to be different this time. I don't want to be placed in a situation where I have to choose again."

■ ■ ■

Stella received an email from Shirley two days later asking whether she and Lynn would like to go to lunch. She explained how it would be nice for all of them to get together after all these years of separation. They agreed on a day and time by email. In the meantime, Lynn was dis-closing email conversations with Shirley by forwarding them to Stella.

"This is what I have to put up with—Mom telling me what to do and how I should live my life," Lynn wrote in one of the emails she sent to Stella.

In all, Stella received three of these emails from Lynn. When Stella didn't respond to them, Lynn called her on the phone to complain about Shirley.

"Mom is treating me like she did when I was little," Lynn said. "That's why I would never talk to her before—because she always tries to tell me what to do."

Stella started getting anxious again and it was hard for her to breathe. She didn't say anything, though—just listened for a while.

"I don't want to put you in the middle," said Lynn, "but I feel like the shoe is going to drop here and I am getting scared. You know how Mom is when she tells you what to do and treats you like you can't take care of yourself; she cuts you out of her life."

Stella hesitated for a minute. "I know what you mean. Mom did the same thing to me after five years, and she told me three months into our reconciliation that she needed a break. In fact, that was just before you had your accident, so don't tell her everything; she doesn't need to know everything that is going on with you. And no, I don't want to be put in the middle."

"I don't want to put you in the middle," Lynn replied. "I just want this to work out for all of us."

"Thank you for understanding. I love you, Lynn," Stella said and hung up the phone.

Stella felt proud that she had told Lynn how she felt. It hadn't been easy for her; she had felt like running away. She always felt that way when she got overwhelmed and scared. She used to run away when she was little all the time, and the behavior had followed her into adulthood. It was easier not to deal with her emotions. But she knew better now—denying them only made them worse. Her work with Rachel had really helped her stay grounded with the pink cord and talk through the symptoms when Stella felt anxious and she felt like running.

After the phone call, she wrote in her journal:

> I am fifty-two, Lynn is fifty-seven, and our mom is seventy-four, so it's time for me to stand up for myself when it comes to this relationship with my sister and mom.

■ ■ ■

A few days had passed when Stella received an email from Shirley telling her the luncheon was off. Shirley explained how Lynn and she were fighting, so she had told Lynn she needed a break from their relationship. Stella read the email a few times and then started crying.

She had gone through the same thing with Shirley after their initial reconciliation so she felt bad for Lynn. She knew how Shirley would cut someone out of her life if she didn't agree with that person. Stella saw that her mother still wasn't open to giving the mutual respect necessary for a healthy relationship. It was Shirley's same old script of "I am right and you are wrong." Stella didn't respond to the email.

■ ■ ■

The next evening, Stella called Shirley.

"Hi, Mom. How are you?"

"I'm doing great—just sitting here having a drink."

"Oh, sounds fun," Stella said. Stella listened to Shirley talk about her day for a while. Then she asked Shirley why she had cancelled the lunch.

"Well, I was tired of being bullied by Lynn and had had enough. I need a break from the relationship."

Stella just listened until Shirley started to cry. "I'm sorry, Mom, that this is happening," she then said.

Shirley was so choked up that they ended their conversation. Stella hung up the phone and sat on the couch crying. She couldn't believe that Shirley would do this to Lynn again, especially after all Lynn had been through with the accident. Stella finally got that Shirley was missing the "playing the mother card" of nurturing. Stella felt that Shirley needed to rise above this situation and have some compassion for Lynn. Lynn needed all of their love and support to heal her injuries—not to feel abandoned. Stella also saw that no one needs to be bullied either. She was in the middle of Lynn and Shirley once again.

■ ■ ■

A few days later, Stella went over to Shirley's house to drop some books off to her. Stella approached Shirley and hugged her.

"Mom, I didn't sleep last night."

"Well, why not?" she asked. "I slept really well."

Stella paused for a minute and looked over at Shirley. "Mom, I didn't sleep because I was up thinking about the situation between you and Lynn. I need for you to know that I love you and Lynn, and I don't want to be put in the middle."

"Stella, you're the only one who can put yourself in the middle."

Stella wasn't sure how to respond. Shirley didn't know that Lynn was bitching to Stella. It just wasn't worth the energy to discuss.

■ ■ ■

The next day, Stella called Lynn. She didn't want to take sides, but she did want to give her sister comfort so she told her she had received the email from Shirley that their luncheon was canceled.

"Yeah, Mom and I got into a big fight," she said. Stella kept quiet as Lynn cried. "I knew this was coming," she said. "Didn't I tell you the shoe was going to drop and she was going to stop talking to me?"

Stella cleared her throat and told Lynn that everything would be okay. "I love you, Lynn."

"I love you too. You understand what I'm saying, don't you?"

"Yes, Lynn, I do, but don't worry about this. Just give it some time and she'll call you soon. Try not to worry about it. You both are very prideful and stubborn. Just give it some time."

"I know, Stella. I'm just scared and my head hurts from the accident. I just need to rest," Lynn said, still crying.

"Yeah, you've just been through a traumatic situation. You should be concentrating on healing your injuries. Don't worry," Stella said, and then she said goodbye.

Stella hung up the phone and lay down on her bed to take a nap. She was awakened by the phone ringing. It was Rachel.

"Hi, dear; how did the conversation go with your mom?"

"It went well. I told my mom that I loved both her and Lynn. Now I understand why I had so much anxiety when I was young. My mom and Lynn are so controlling and domineering that I never had a chance to voice my feelings, and I was scared of their anger and the fights between them. My sister and mom are so much alike in many ways. I was always put in the middle and forced to take sides."

"Stella, when you told your mom that you loved both her and Lynn, it was a strong message that you were not going to take sides."

"Yeah, that's so true. Thank you for giving me that insight about my mom and sister. I wasn't sure whether I gave them both the message that I'm not going to be part of their shit."

That night, Stella slept well and didn't have any more symptoms of apprehension.

■ ■ ■

The next day, Stella received a text message from Shirley. "I want you to know that Lynn and I worked everything out and we're okay now. You don't have to worry anymore about us because we worked our differences out."

Stella responded, "Thanks for the message. I'm glad you and Lynn are talking now."

■ ■ ■

A month passed. Everything seemed to be back to Lynn and Shirley having a relationship since neither one was calling or emailing Stella anymore. Stella went to see Rachel so she could make sure she was staying grounded.

"Stella, do you have any jealousy that your mom and sister are spending a lot of time together without you?"

Stella looked at Rachel for a bit and said, "No way. I enjoy not being the center of attention. I felt so obligated for many years to have a relationship with my mom. I feel off the hook for once."

Rachel looked at Stella. "That's a good place to be."

"I know. They can have each other. I'm concentrating on my own stuff. I feel really free for once. I felt so much pressure trying to cultivate the relationship with my parents. I was the only one they each had to talk to, and that brought me so much anxiety, and most of the time, I couldn't breathe, knowing that they counted on me to be their child, their only child. That is why I felt obligated and alone. Every holiday, special occasion—whatever arose—they expected me to be there. I still had the identity of my parents, and I so desperately wanted to move away and have a different life—my own life."

Rachel just sat and listened to Stella go over the situation so she could once and for all let go of the residue left in her cells from birth.

■ ■ ■

That evening, Stella was home watching a movie when Gabrielle came home from work. Gabrielle seemed pre-occupied, so Stella paused the movie and went into Gabrielle's bedroom.

"Gabrielle, are you all right?"

Gabrielle turned around and looked at Stella with tears in her eyes, throwing her phone on her bed.

"Mom, my dad is getting a divorce."

Stella paused, then grabbed Gabrielle to hug her. "Oh, honey, what happened? I can't believe it!"

"I just talked to Dad on the phone, and he wouldn't give me a straight answer. I spoke with my sister Julia, and she doesn't know much about what happened either, just that they haven't been happy in their marriage for a long time." She continued to cry.

Stella knew the divorce would affect Gabrielle tremendously because she had developed a good second family with her stepmother and siblings and spent most holidays with them. Gabrielle continued to cry as Stella held her closely.

"Mom, I need to go to bed. I'm so tired."

"Okay, sweetie. Let me know if you need anything," Stella said and kissed her on the cheek.

Stella couldn't finish her movie, so she turned off the television and went to bed. The thoughts of the conversation whirled around in her mind as she tried to go to sleep. It wasn't working, so she wrote in her journal:

> Gabrielle's emotions about her father's divorce made me feel responsible for some reason. It took me back to the time when Ashton and I were married and how I left the marriage when Ashton wanted to work on it. I didn't have the tools to be in a relationship, let alone a marriage, so I left suddenly, confusing both Ashton and Gabrielle, who was only four.

Stella lay there for most of the night, thinking about the way she had left Ashton and how hurtful it all was. She felt bad for Ashton. Even though their marriage had been over for twenty years, she was so grateful for him. If it hadn't been for her relationship with Ashton, she never would have experienced being a mom to Gabrielle. Being a mom to Gabrielle had filled her up with purpose. She had never known anything to be as fulfilling as motherhood. Stella fell asleep thinking about how much she loved Gabrielle.

■ ■ ■

The next day, Stella spoke to Rachel on the phone. "Hi, Rachel. Gabrielle told me yesterday that her dad is getting a divorce."

"Oh, that's interesting."

"The weird thing is that I feel a bit responsible."

Rachel didn't say anything for a minute. "I don't understand why you would feel responsible, but I recommend you do some work around this feeling and why you're making this situation about you."

"It's because of the way I left him."

"Again, think about why you're making this about you," Rachel repeated before she hung up.

20

"Love begins at home, and it is not how much we do...
but how much love we put in that action."

— Mother Teresa

Twenty-five years earlier, Stella and Ashton had met at an up-scale department store in Seattle. Ashton was a sales representative for a sports equipment and clothing line and Stella sold women's cosmetics. Ashton traveled a lot for his job. They had known each other casually because Ashton visited her store frequently. Stella wasn't too interested in him at first; he was tall, blonde, and had chiseled features, but Stella thought he was superficial when she witnessed how all the girls responded to him when he entered the department. She hadn't dated a lot of attractive guys and was so insecure about herself that her anxiety had taken its toll on her self-esteem. One day, Ashton approached Stella at work and asked her whether she would like to go on a date sometime. Not knowing how to say no, Stella agreed and they made plans for the following weekend to go canoeing at the arboretum in Seattle.

When that beautiful, warm day arrived, Ashton was distraught about the San Francisco earthquake that had just devastated the area because he had family down there. Finally, they did go on the date after he knew everyone in his family was accounted for; then he felt he could relax and have fun with Stella.

When Ashton arrived to pick her up, he said, "Hi, Stella. I brought us a bottle of wine and some cheese and crackers," and he bent down to hug her.

Stella hugged him back. "It's good to see you. That was really thoughtful of you to bring wine and something to eat."

They drove to the river where they were going to canoe, but when they got there, Ashton said, "Let's sit here for a bit along the shore so we can enjoy the wine." Stella agreed so he popped the cork and poured Stella some wine in a plastic cup.

"Thank you," she said as she raised her glass.

Ashton was very fit and dressed nicely. Stella enjoyed looking at him as he drank his wine. "Where are we going to get the canoe?"

"Just right across the bridge," said Ashton, pointing north.

They finished up the wine and munchies and went to fetch the canoe. A few minutes later, they had put the canoe in the water.

"What a beautiful day," Stella said as she picked up the oar and sat in the front.

"Have you ever canoed before, Stella?" Ashton asked.

"A long time ago, but I'll get the hang of it."

"Then you should sit in the front so I can navigate," he replied.

"I'll bet you're a good navigator," said Stella, turning around with a smile.

They canoed for two hours, admiring the flowers and how quiet and serene the views were. Some of the areas they passed were not so serene, like the #520 floating bridge. Soon it was time to go back and drop off the canoe. They didn't want the date to end, so Stella invited Ashton over to her apartment. Ashton lived thirty minutes south of Seattle, and Stella lived thirty miles north of Seattle. He had a roommate, so they decided to go to Stella's place. They ate some left-over pizza and drank another bottle of wine. Ashton was feeling a little tipsy then, so he asked whether he could stay overnight rather than drive home. Stella interpreted that to mean he wanted to have sex.

When they went in her room to go to sleep, Stella said, "Wow, I'm so attracted to you," and she started taking off her clothes.

"Hey, um, I don't think this is the right time to have sex," Ashton replied. "We're drunk and I want to get to know you better before we make that decision."

Because Stella mistook sex for love, she thought his response meant he wasn't attracted to her.

"Oh, okay; I get it," she said as she rolled over with her back to him. Ashton left the next morning, but he called her later that day and told her how much he liked her. They started dating immediately. Stella's style was to rush into relationships.

On their third date, Stella and Ashton were canoeing on the river near where Ashton lived. The water was still cold from the run off. They were coming around a bend in the river when the back of the canoe hit a submerged tree branch and the canoe flipped, sending them both into the water. Stella and Ashton held on to the canoe as they floated to the riverbank. As they both stood soaking wet, Stella started shaking uncontrollably "I can't believe how cold I am," she said, hugging herself.

"Let me get the canoe upright enough so we can get back in and float to the other side where the car is," Ashton said, while emptying out some of the water.

"That would be good because I can't stop shaking," Stella said, trying to form the words.

"You look pale and lethargic; I think you're hypothermic," Ashton said, while helping Stella into the canoe.

Ashton gingerly got them to the other side of the river where his car was parked. He helped Stella out of the canoe. Then he ran to open the car door to turn on the heat. Stella made it to the car and plopped into the front seat.

"I would suggest you get out of those wet clothes. Here is a long flannel shirt for you to get warm while I load up the canoe," said Ashton, getting out of the car.

Stella took the shirt, pulled off her wet clothes, and placed them by the heater. She was feeling sick and really tired, so she closed her eyes until she heard the door open.

"How are you feeling?" Ashton asked, wrapping his arms around her.

"Better."

Ashton started the car and drove Stella to her car up the river. By then, she had put her pants back on and gathered her wet clothes. She followed Ashton to his house where she took a hot shower to warm up while he made them some chicken noodle soup and turkey sandwiches. After dinner, Ashton said, "I would like you to stay the night with me."

"Okay. That would be nice. Where is your roommate?" Stella asked.

"He's gone for the night to his girlfriend's house," Ashton replied, walking over to the stereo while Stella walked into his bedroom. "I'm going to take a shower so you just relax," he added as he turned on some music.

Stella got into his bed and lay there naked for a while, trying not to fall asleep. Ashton had put her wet clothes in the dryer before he got into the shower, but she must have drifted off because she felt Ashton slide into bed and wrap his warm body around hers. *Damn, he feels so good. I love how our bodies fit together,* she thought. Ashton started kissing Stella's back as she slowly turned to face him. Then he kissed her on the lips—long and soft kissing until Stella pulled away and said, "You feel so good to me. I appreciate how you cared for me today when I was really cold and then you made me dinner."

"You're welcome. I really care for you, and I was concerned about you," he said, kissing her forehead.

Stella stared into his beautiful blue eyes as he looked at her with adoration. Their breathing and kissing got heavier and longer as their bodies moved to create some much needed warmth and slid into rhythm together. Ashton reached down and grabbed Stella's leg to wrap around his waist as he penetrated deep within her. "You're so wet," he said, kissing and probing her mouth with his tongue. *He feels so good to me,* she thought. *I wonder if I can have an orgasm. Usually it takes me some time to know a guy before I can trust enough to let go.* Stella tried to let go, but she couldn't just yet. She didn't need to fake it because Ashton had pulled out and released his cum all over her belly. They fell asleep in each other arms and woke up the next day in a hurry because Ashton had to catch a plane to go to California for business.

Ashton was building himself as a serious sales representative in the Seattle area, so when things became serious between him and Stella after six months of their spending most of their time together, he told her that he liked her a lot, but he really wanted to focus on his sales career before they moved in together. That always seemed to happen to Stella in her relationships with guys. She didn't know whether it was her desperation, or they just weren't that into her and wanted a way out.

Ashton and Stella continued to date for another year. Then Ashton asked her to come down to southern Oregon to meet his family. She agreed and drove down one night after work to meet up with him. The plan was that he was going to drive back with her on the coastal line to Seattle. Everyone was going to be there—even his relatives who lived in California. They had a great time together with his family, hiking trails in Grants Pass, having barbeques at night with music, and playing lawn darts during the day. It was a dream come true for Stella.

Ashton was one of seven children; they were very tight and always hung out with each other. He had three sisters and three brothers, all older than him except one brother who was just a year younger than him. The girls were really close and kind to each other, and the guys were funny and competitive with each other. Stella, on the other hand, didn't come from a large or close family. She felt some insecurity over how close Ashton was with his siblings and whether she fit in with his family's dynamics. Since she didn't have a close relationship with Lynn, Stella didn't understand the closeness and fun Ashton had with his family. Ashton couldn't understand why Stella needed constant attention and reassurance from him since he got all the attention he needed from his siblings.

Ashton also hadn't grown up with much money, but Stella had. Ashton was three years younger than Stella, which showed itself when he went out with his friends and they would smoke pot and stay out all night partying. Stella didn't do drugs at all. But they were both athletic and enjoyed the outdoors and traveling, spending much of their time together or with his family. When it came to their friends, they spent time with them separately.

Eventually, Ashton moved to Green Lake, a Seattle suburb, and had his own apartment while Stella still lived on the lake up north in Snohomish. Then one month, Stella missed her period; she and Ashton had always been careful, using some form of birth control, but she wasn't able to go on the pill because it gave her severe side effects. When she told Ashton, he wanted to go with her to the doctor, so she agreed. The doctor confirmed that they were going to have a baby. After the appointment, they went down to the local beach and discussed what they wanted to do.

"Stella, what are you thinking about the baby?" Ashton asked.

"I really want to keep the baby," she said, with tears in her eyes.

"Well, if that's what you want to do, then that's what I want to do too," he said, kissing her.

They didn't discuss marriage, although it was on Stella's mind. If he would just marry her, then she would feel worthy.

Stella's anxiety grew because she knew the next step would be to tell her mom. She phoned Shirley the next day to ask whether she would meet her and Ashton at the waterfront in Seattle for lunch because they had something to tell her. Shirley had already met Ashton the year before. By that point, Shirley owned her own business as a wedding planner.

When the three of them met, the conversation went well while they discussed superficial things like the weather and how work was going for Ashton and Shirley. Then Ashton told Shirley he and Stella had something they wanted to share with her.

"Stella and I are having a baby," he said.

Shirley didn't say anything for a minute as she continued to chew on her sandwich. Then she looked up at Ashton and Stella. "You are not pregnant. She is pregnant," she said hastily. "We are not having a baby; she is having a baby."

Ashton looked over at Stella. "Well, yeah, Stella is pregnant, but I'm excited for this baby."

Shirley looked down at her sandwich and pushed away the plate. Ashton looked surprised, but Stella didn't. This was Shirley's typical behavior when it came to Stella. Stella was really excited to become a mom, but when her mom responded like that, she felt like she had made the wrong decision and done something wrong. Stella became very anxious and was unable to finish her lunch; she suddenly had a stomach ache and became very quiet. Ashton didn't know how to respond to Shirley, and Stella wasn't saying much, just looking down at her lap in shame.

"I'm excited to have this baby," he repeated enthusiastically. "I'm ready to be a father."

Shirley now piped up. "Are you going to marry her? Are you going to support the baby if you don't get married?" Those were very good questions to ask since Stella hadn't asked them because she was afraid of the answers.

"Well, Stella and I feel at this time we don't need to get married," he said, taking a bite out of his sandwich.

Shirley looked over at Stella and just stared at her while Ashton talked. "We are planning on moving in with each other, and eventually, we'll get married," he said.

Once Ashton had said that, Stella knew the rest of the conversation wouldn't go well.

"Well, I'm done here," said Shirley. She got up from the picnic table and threw her lunch in the garbage can nearby.

Stella got up and hugged Shirley. "Bye, Mom."

Shirley waved at Ashton as she walked away. Stella sat back down at the table next to Ashton. She wasn't used to asking for what she needed in a relationship, so she was quiet while they sat at the beach for a while longer.

■ ■ ■

When Ashton told his family and some of his siblings, they had the same reaction as Shirley concerning the issue of marriage. They were also concerned because he was going to be leaving soon on a three-month business trip to Europe, which would be in the middle of Stella's pregnancy. Stella continued to work so she could support the baby if needed; she was the one with health insurance. She felt really secure about that part of the situation. Stella guessed that if Ashton didn't want to marry her or support the baby, Shirley would help her out like she had with Lynn, whose boyfriend didn't marry her either when she got pregnant.

Stella didn't like depending on her mom for financial support. She felt so much anxiety and shame around taking Shirley's money because Shirley used it to control and make her children dependent. She treated Stella like she wasn't able to take care of herself without Shirley's money.

A few days later, Ashton agreed to go with Stella to tell her dad about the baby. When they arrived at Robert's house, he answered the door as Susan was out running errands.

"Hi, honey," Robert said, giving Stella a hug.

"Hey, big guy," he said, while shaking Ashton's hand. He and Ashton had met a few times and seemed to hit it off.

They went into the family room since Robert was watching the baseball game on television. There was small talk between Ashton and Robert about the game, so when a commercial came on, Stella told Robert she had something to tell him. "Dad, I'm pregnant."

Robert sat for a minute staring at the TV. "Oh, that's nice."

Ashton chimed in, "Robert, both Stella and I are happy that we are having a baby."

"What about marriage?" Robert asked.

"We're talking about when would be a good time to get married. We don't feel in a hurry," Stella said.

"Well, marriage is important," Robert said as he turned back to the game.

They all sat and watched the game for a while longer until Stella said she had to go home because she had to get up early for work. Stella hugged Robert and said goodbye. Robert turned to Ashton and shook his hand. "Do the right thing," he said.

■ ■ ■

Ashton went off to Europe. He wouldn't be back until the eighth month of Stella's pregnancy. Stella kept in contact with him by phone and learned about all the places he had been and what it was like living there. Then she would update him on the pregnancy. One of Ashton's brothers and a sister also kept in contact with Stella with phone calls to see how she was doing. Shirley was busy with work, but Stella visited with her when she had time in her work schedule. Lynn knew Stella was pregnant, but she lived in Nevada and wasn't in contact with Shirley or Robert very much. Overall, Stella was pretty much alone in the process, but she was busy with work so the days went by fast.

While Ashton was in Europe, the U.S. declared war on Iraq because of the invasion of Kuwait in 1990. Stella was concerned the war might affect Ashton's return to the U.S. Stella's insecurities flared up one day when she could not get hold of Ashton. He was living in a guy's house that the agency had set up for him and the guy was really wealthy. They would always go sailing or on helicopter flights on weekends. Because a female friend often accompanied them on these adventures, Stella became very suspicious and jealous. She didn't know what to think. She was working full-time to keep her health insurance. She was getting fat and feeling lonely. The anxiety started creeping into her mind about not knowing what to expect. Was Ashton coming back to her? Would he find her attractive? Would he fall in love with that girl? Stella didn't know anything about the situation with the friend, and she didn't have the self-esteem to ask any questions.

It wasn't until Ashton called her one day and said he would be extending his stay for another month that Stella spoke up. All her insecurities and anxiety flooded in during that conversation. She was so angry with Ashton, feeling that he was being very irresponsible and not thinking about her or the baby. Stella put her foot down and told him that he needed to come home when he said he would. Ashton wasn't too happy, but he flew home when he was scheduled to.

When Stella picked Ashton up at the airport, she hugged him and said, "I don't even recognize you."

"Wow, your belly is so big. I barely recognize you, either," he said, kissing her on the lips. They were strangers in a familiar place. "Where is your luggage?" she asked. She didn't know how else to act.

Stella's anxiety was worse than ever because she couldn't breathe. "I'm going to go sit over on the chair and wait for your luggage to come," she said, waddling over to sit down. She didn't like being anxious because she knew the baby would feel the effects and she didn't want to harm him or her. Stella had opted not to know the baby's sex.

Ashton came over with his two suitcases to where Stella was sitting. "Hey, are you ready to go to the car?" he asked and helped Stella to her feet.

On the way to his apartment, Ashton asked, "Why don't you stay with me tonight so you don't have to drive home in the dark?"

They still lived apart, but that night, Stella did stay with him, hoping it would help with her anxiety.

■ ■ ■

A week later, Ashton took Stella to their favorite beach near Ashton's apartment. "I want to ask you something, Stella," he said, pulling her closer as they sat on a blanket watching the sun slowly disappear behind the Olympic Mountains.

Stella looked up at Ashton. "What?"

"I want to marry you. I don't have a ring because I want you to pick it out. Spending three months away from you and the baby made me realize that I want to make this official. I'm ready to be a husband and a father."

Stella was not expecting such words from him. "Wow, that's so awesome. I want to marry you, too. It's really important to me that we make this official, too."

Even though Ashton didn't have a ring that day, he made a promise to her, and later that week, they went to buy a wedding band. Stella wasn't into diamonds or anything; she really liked crystals, so they had a ring made out of a stone from Brazil named Blue Quartz. They also found a new apartment and moved in together.

They planned on getting married just before the baby was born, so

Shirley and Stella went to an upscale department store to find something that resembled a wedding dress that would be the right size for someone in her last month of pregnancy. Luckily, they found a cream-colored dress that fit Stella beautifully. Shirley was happy about the marriage and so was Robert. The wedding was going to be at Ashton's parents' house. Not too many people were going to be there since it had been planned pretty quickly. Some of Ashton's siblings in California and Oregon weren't able to make it because of the time frame, but they were all very happy about the news.

The day before the ceremony, Stella went into labor, and twenty hours later, she had a baby girl, seven pounds six ounces. Stella wanted to go natural, but because she hadn't dropped and she wasn't dilated, the doctor suggested an epidural. Against Stella's wishes, she went along with the injection and Gabrielle was born.

Ashton's mom flew up from Oregon to stay with them for a bit and help with the newborn. Stella didn't know a thing about babies, so even changing a diaper was going to be a challenge. Shirley wasn't good about helping Stella with Gabrielle because she said she wasn't good with babies—even though she'd had three of her own.

One night, Stella stood in the shower for a while sobbing, not knowing how to take care of a baby. She felt like she couldn't even take care of herself. *It's weird to have Ashton's mom here helping me,* she thought as she turned so the warm water would help ease her sore breasts. Then she started crying as she thought, *My mom should be here helping me, but she isn't interested in little babies. She only likes them when they can interact with her.*

When Shirley had told her that, it had suddenly made sense to Stella why Shirley hadn't had a clue about how to mother. Stella stood in the shower for a while crying until Ashton knocked on the door to ask whether she was okay. She was so anxious she couldn't speak; she felt paralyzed in the shower as the warm water rushed over her head. She couldn't breathe. When Ashton didn't hear anything from Stella, he opened the door to see whether she was okay. Stella was leaning up against the wall with her arms wrapped around herself, sobbing. Ashton rushed in, turned off the water, and put a towel around her. Stella was thinking they had never had time to develop into good friends or mutual partners. He had his friends and she had hers. The pregnancy had brought them closer, but there was still some separation in their relating to one another. Now they had a daughter together, but it didn't feel like they were a family unit.

Gabrielle was like an angel, all snuggled up in her basinet next to Stella's side of the bed. She was a good sleeper, only waking up for feedings every three hours; then she would immediately fall back to sleep. Stella ended up going to bed early that evening after Gabrielle's feeding so Ashton and his mom could visit since she was leaving in a few days.

■ ■ ■

Once Stella went back to work, Ashton spent the days taking care of Gabrielle. He moved his office home so they didn't have to put her in childcare.

They also had a small wedding ceremony at the beach where their first date was. Gabrielle and Ashton's friend attended with the pastor whom they had hired to perform the marriage, and about a hundred people showed up to celebrate at the beach club. Stella sat in the room nursing Gabrielle during the reception. Most of the people who attended were related to Ashton. Stella was jealous that he had a large family and they all got along. She was ashamed of her family because they weren't as close.

Eventually, Ashton started with another company designing surf boards. Then Stella quit her job to be at home with Gabrielle. When Gabrielle was two, they moved to Whidbey Island and rented a house on the water. Stella stopped breastfeeding Gabrielle just before she found a job at a local chiropractor's office. She also started to make friends in her community—other wives and moms, whom, unfortunately, she began to compare herself to. Then she started drinking more than usual because her anxiety was really bad. She didn't feel good about herself, and she always felt she wasn't good enough as a wife or a mother. Ashton hit all her insecurity buttons because he was smart, educated, good-looking, and had a wonderful family. She began to feel like she didn't deserve him, and that he knew it, and since he didn't suffer from anxiety, Stella wasn't able to talk to him about her feelings. She became resentful and eventually stepped outside of the marriage with a man she had just met. She felt special and good enough with him because he paid attention to her.

Stella abruptly left the marriage without giving Ashton any reason why. She just cut him off at the knees. It was an old pattern of hers in relationships with guys. Her behavior was all based around anxiety and not feeling she was lovable or enough. She blamed everyone. She made them out to be bad. Her needs weren't met. They didn't give her enough attention. She was detached and superficial with everyone except Gabrielle.

Gabrielle brought so much light to Stella's heart that it was almost overwhelming. Stella felt like being a mother was all she needed. Stella loved playing with her, talking to her, lying down next to her at night reading a story and waking up with her smile every morning. It filled Stella up so much that she had no desire to be anything else but Gabrielle's mom. All Stella needed was to love Gabrielle and have that love returned. She didn't need Ashton anymore; she showed him that, too.

Stella didn't know how to be in a marriage, let alone a relationship. She'd had some therapy after Michael had died because she'd never had anyone close die before and she didn't know how to deal with her feelings and anxiety, but none of her relationships ever lasted for more than two years. She'd always found a reason to leave. Stella and Ashton's marriage had lasted for two years.

■ ■ ■

Stella scheduled a session with Rachel after their conversation on the phone about Ashton's divorce. At the session, she explained further to Rachel why she felt upset over Ashton's divorce.

"All my intimate relationships with guys were centered around my fear of abandonment. Feeling I'm not enough and that I'm not worthy of love has caused much anxiety for me. It's not like the other apprehensions I have; it's another feeling that is continuous and lives in every cell of my body."

Rachel looked at Stella as she continued. "It's attached to my worth and not being enough in the relationship and needing for the other person to love me. I look at myself in the mirror and see a beautiful soul, a person who is worthy of love, true love. Why does this energy still reside in my being? I am worthy! I am! I don't understand why after all this healing work I have done with you and Wendy around integrating the pieces back into me, I am still left with a few of the puzzle fragments missing."

Rachel sat for a moment. "Stella, you've done a great job healing yourself, and you're continuing to heal what was lost."

"I lost myself, but honestly, there was no one to lose; I was simply not connected to me and didn't know who I was. Like I said, it was all around my self-worth," she said, wiping her tears.

Rachel smiled. "Stella, remember how I've told you that in your family you were handed crumbs in your childhood so that was all you felt you needed for survival? As long as you kept quiet, had no needs, and gave all of you to the relationship, then maybe, just maybe, someone would love you."

"I understand what you're saying. I was so afraid of being abandoned that I would always leave a relationship before he could abandon me. Doing that hasn't served any purpose for me in my relationships with guys," she said, while gathering her jacket.

"This situation with Ashton isn't your fault," Rachel said.

21

"If we can find the courage to do the things that
make us feel most alive,
we do not only owe ourselves a favor but the
world a favor too."

— Author Unknown

A fter all her work with Rachel, Stella had overcome her fear of driving in traffic, riding in an elevator, and riding on a ferry. Now she decided it was finally time to commit to flying on an airplane. Stella's daily regimen to help decrease her anxiety included taking 5-HTP and magnesium each night to help her sleep a full eight hours. She made sure that she had some kind of protein with each meal, and she drank plenty of water to keep her hydrated. She had read somewhere that being dehydrated could cause anxiety. Every morning, she did breathing exercises, inhaling through the diaphragm and exhaling through the nose, as well as practiced being grateful. She limited her alcohol consumption because it would cause symptoms of hypoglycemia, which, in turn, would make her anxious.

She called Marilyn, the hypnotherapist she had seen, to help her prepare to get on an airplane. Marilyn was an expert in EFT (emotional freedom technique). EFT uses tapping to access meridian points on the body and internal organs, and it touches on emotional and energetic effects in the area of the point. Marilyn had worked effectively with Stella in the past on her fear of elevators and driving in traffic.

However, Marilyn was very busy, so she wasn't able to schedule Stella in for a few months. In the meantime, Stella called Rachel to schedule a time to talk about her desire to fly again.

■ ■ ■

When Stella arrived at Rachel's house, she went inside and sat down on the futon. Peering through the window, she noticed how much things around Rachel's yard had changed over the last twelve years. The grapevines were at full maturity with lots of purple grapes in clumps ready to be plucked and eaten. She admired them, remembering when they were small and barely ripe enough to eat. They had grown up over the years into a solid healthy vine of radiant grapes. Rachel's office, by contrast, had remained the same during Stella's healing, which was comforting to her.

Stella had a mission with this session—to talk with Rachel about getting back on an airplane.

"I haven't seen you for a while. What have you been up to, dear?" Rachel asked when she entered the room.

"I've been busy with the house and getting ready for spring. Rachel, I'm ready to get back on an airplane," Stella announced as Rachel shifted in her chair. "I just don't know how to go about it. I'm afraid I'll have another panic attack just like the last time I was going back East," she said, looking down. "I have worked so hard to get here; I mean, even to think I can get back on a plane. I don't want to have another attack and have to start all over again." Tears rolled down her cheeks.

Rachel sat for a minute and closed her eyes. She did that a lot. She was accessing Stella's energy field to see whether she could find a block. Stella loved it when Rachel did that because most of the time she was right on in her assessment.

"Is it the fear of flying or the symptoms of anxiety that bring you panic?" Rachel asked.

Stella thought about that for a minute since she had always concentrated on the anxiety originating from the airplane.

When Stella didn't respond, Rachel offered, "I think the panic comes from the symptoms you haven't named and have moved through. You just freeze when the symptoms occur, and you don't have a resource inside to move through them on your own."

It was quiet for a moment while Stella searched inside for the truth of Rachel's observation.

"You know, that makes so much sense to me. My fear has never been about the object, whether it's an airplane, ferry boat, bridge, elevator, or traffic. It was always around the symptoms and whether I could manage those fears when I'm alone."

This was an epiphany for Stella. It had changed the playing field for her because she had always assumed she was fearing the objects outside herself when, in reality, it was the feelings that arose that she wasn't able to manage on her own. She had always reached outside herself to find comfort for those feelings—to her mom as a small child, then her sister, friends growing up, alcohol, sex, boyfriends, Rachel, and Gabrielle. Now she had a new way of looking at the anxiety. Stella felt some freedom because she knew she could manage the symptoms.

"You will need to find something like pinching yourself, tapping, or some kind of physical reminder that you can access when the anxiety arises," Rachel said. "Go down to the ferry alone and see what symptoms arise. This will be a good practice for when you get back on an airplane."

"I can ride on a ferry boat but not by myself," Stella said. "This will be a challenge, but I feel very strong about moving forward. I am not willing to sit in this prison anymore. I want to 'move about the cabin.' I want to be free of those chains—the shackles that bind me to the past. I'm ready to break free from the confinement that has plagued my life for as long as I can remember. I'm so excited I can't stand it. I'm so scared I can't stand it." Stella sat quietly for a minute while this new feeling sunk in.

"This will be good practice for when Gabrielle moves out," added Rachel.

"Yeah, I know," Stella said, looking down.

Stella started to cry as she talked about how much she loved being Gabrielle's mom and how proud she was for her own focus on raising Gabrielle and her commitment to healing. "I understand now how important it was for me and Gabrielle to do my work with you. And I really appreciate what you have done for me. I would've never been the mother to Gabrielle that I was without your love and support." Stella started to sob.

"I get it now why I made the decisions around my career and committing to heal my wounds so Gabrielle could have a good life and be healthy. I am so proud of myself for turning the page in my family on parenting. I remember when I had the epiphany that I was becoming like my mom in believing my career and status were the most important things in being successful so they were all that mattered. I could not have done this healing without you, Rachel, and I am so grateful and love you so much."

"You can do this, Stella," Rachel replied. "You're ready, and I'm here to help you make this a reality."

"That means a lot to me. Yeah, I'm ready," Stella said while hugging Rachel goodbye.

■ ■ ■

One day when Stella was leaving work, she saw a group of women playing soccer in the field across the street. It was starting to rain hard, making it difficult to drive, so she sat there for a minute, watching the girls play while she waited for the rain to let up. She remembered how she had played on a women's soccer league for ten years when Gabrielle was little; it had been the only sport besides golf that Stella had been interested in. Gabrielle used to come to every game with her and stand on the sideline rooting for her and the team. The rain reminded Stella of how she used to bundle Gabrielle up in a raincoat, hat, and rain boots so she would stay warm and dry. She could hear her little voice yelling, "Go, Mom! Make a goal!"

When Stella got home, Gabrielle was fixing herself some dinner so Stella leaned against the kitchen counter. "How was your day, sweetie?"

"Okay, Mom. I'm just fixing some dinner for us," she said, stirring the vegetables.

Between the stir fry and mixing of salad greens, Stella told Gabrielle about her day. "I was leaving work, and across the street is a soccer field where a bunch of women were playing a game," she said, with a big smile.

"Oh yeah," Gabrielle said, distracted.

"Yeah, it reminded me of the time when you used to come to all my games," Stella said, reaching up into the cupboard for plates to hand to Gabrielle.

"Thanks, Mom."

"It got me to thinking that we have been so much a part of each other's lives, and the support we have given each other has been very special, more so than in an ordinary mother and child relationship."

Gabrielle filled her plate and went into her room to eat her dinner; she loved watching TV while she ate. Gabrielle spent a lot of time in her room, so Stella always sat with her in the bedroom to continue their conversations. That had been the norm since Gabrielle had moved back home after college. Stella continued to reminisce about the old days.

"Do you remember those slightly stained green rain boots you used to wear when you stood on the sidelines?"

Gabrielle looked at her and laughed. "Yeah, they sure kept my feet dry and warm. Mom, not to change the subject, but I found an apartment with Sarah, and we're going to move in in two weeks," she said, taking a bite of chicken.

Stella had been expecting this day since Gabrielle had been born. "Oh, so soon," she said.

"Well, she is already in the apartment building, so it's a matter of moving to another unit and they have one available at the first of the month."

Stella had experienced living alone when Gabrielle had gone off to college, but when Gabrielle moved back home after college, Stella had become more relaxed. "I knew you would move out eventually, but I didn't think it would be so soon," Stella said, wiping her face with a napkin.

She didn't like Gabrielle being away from her. Stella just sat on Gabrielle's chair and listened to the excitement in her voice when she described the unit. "It has two bedrooms and I'll have my own bathroom. The apartment has a swimming pool and a balcony where we can have barbeque parties."

Stella thought she had prepared herself for this day, but she still found it difficult. She wrote that night in her journal:

> I know this won't be like the last time she left home when she went to college. This time is different. She is starting her life, and she won't be moving back home. She is finding herself and her place in the world separate from me. Gabrielle spends a lot of time up north with her dad and siblings since the divorce. Of course, she is her own person, but this is different. How do I deal with this? I know I will be okay. We have been together, just her and me, for twenty-four years. We've had each other's back, depending on each other—knowing that when either one

of us comes home, the other will be there or will be home soon. The last time I lived alone was just before I met Gabrielle's dad. I lived alone for one year. One year in my entire life. I will be living alone again. How will this be for me? I am scared and excited all at the same time—excited for Gabrielle to find her way in life and for me to find my way in life. I have been taking care of her for twenty-five years. How do I change the focus to me? I am not used to just focusing on me. I have always made someone else more important than me. Their needs were more important than mine. How do I do this? Focus on me? What are my needs and desires? I have been working with Rachel for fourteen years. I have developed tools to make this happen. Oh man, I'm scared!

■ ■ ■

The next morning, Stella told Gabrielle she was excited for her. They made a plan to figure out what she would need to take to her new apartment.

That night, Stella went to bed early and lay there while thoughts of being alone in the house and Gabrielle moving on with her life whirled around in her head, so she wrote in her journal again:

It's so ironic that Rachel and I were talking during my last session about the time when Gabrielle will move out and how I would respond to the emotions and change. It's like Rachel is psychic.

Stella tossed and turned all night, not able to turn off these thoughts of being alone. She started to cry and to chant the mantra Rachel taught her several years ago from a Hawaiian healing process called Hoʻoponopono. "I love you. I'm sorry. Please forgive me. Thank you." She repeated the mantra over and over again till she fell asleep. Hoʻoponopono's is based on a perspective of "total responsibility" for what one thinks and does. The theory behind it is that loving yourself is the greatest way to amend yourself, and with that improvement, it will ripple out to the world.

Stella got up the next day, exhausted, and called Rachel to tell her Gabrielle was moving out and to talk with her about a plan to get back on an airplane.

22

"We lose ourselves in the things we love.
We find ourselves there, too."

— Kristen Martz

Rather than discuss getting on an airplane in her next session with Rachel, Stella realized she needed to work on her abandonment issues as a result of Gabrielle moving out. During the session, she recalled how as a toddler she would cling to Shirley and sometimes was abandoned by her. After she told Rachel this, Rachel thought it would be good to uncover any remaining residue Stella had about her childhood and feeling alone. This work could unravel the core reason for Stella's anxiety with flying.

"Stella, how was it for you when you were little and feeling alone?" Rachel asked.

"It was really scary for me when I finally had a room of my own. I shared a room with my sister up to the age of eight. I remember when I got my own room, my anxiety was extreme. I would end up leaving my room in the middle of the night to find comfort with my brother or sister. Rachel, I'm starting to feel really scared."

"Okay, stay with it," Rachel insisted. "This is a memory of this time so stay with it."

Rachel asked Stella to close her eyes and go into her old bedroom that had caused her so much anxiety. "Describe the experience for me," Rachel requested.

"I am in the bedroom," said Stella. "The walls don't have any pictures; it is dimly lit with one small window, a dresser, and a twin bed."

"What are you feeling right now?"

Stella slipped deeper into the image and felt a pit in her stomach. "I feel really alone and scared. This feeling is making me anxious."

Rachel got up and moved over to Stella so she could have physical contact. "Stay with the feeling."

Stella started to cry. "I can see that my sister was for connection and comfort when no one else was able to comfort me when I was scared."

A sudden feeling of peace flooded Stella when Rachel touched her. She didn't feel scared anymore. Stella opened her eyes and stared at Rachel for a minute. "Is this the reason I was so needy in my relationships with guys?" she asked.

"Possibly," said Rachel.

"I was very controlling in my relationships, making sure the guy I was attached to would not abandon me. I was flighty in my dealings with friends, always having another person to call just in case one let me down, like by having other plans that didn't include me, and I was very smothering with my boyfriends too. I always felt abandoned. It didn't matter whether it was a friend or boyfriend; I always felt alone and scared."

"Stella, you didn't know any other way to be with yourself. You didn't have an attachment to you—to who you were and what fed you. That is why you continued to look outside yourself for comfort and connection. You didn't receive those as a child."

Stella was silent for a while, absorbing what Rachel was saying, "You make a lot of sense. I wasn't connected to me. Fuck, I didn't even know who I was. I'm really angry with my parents."

Rachel adjusted her seating so she could bring Stella closer to her.

"When I was in the room at night," Stella continued, "I used to run downstairs to my mom and tell her I was scared. When she would ask me why, I could never answer her question because I didn't know what I was scared of, and when I told her I felt alone, my mom always said to me, 'You're not alone.'"

Stella had experienced the same feelings around Gabrielle. She kept a tight rein on her. She didn't allow her to spend the night with friends when she was young because that meant Stella would be alone with herself.

Rachel mentioned the situation with Gabrielle moving out. "When Gabrielle was young, the sensation was so palpable that it felt like I didn't have any ground under my feet, like I was floating in a cloud of spinning wheels gaining speed, feeling dizzy, lightheaded, my tongue swelling enough to cut off my airway. When I was ready to pass out from extreme fear, I would reach for the phone to call someone who could bring me back to myself. Or at least it was a temporary fix."

Stella's breathing became shallow.

"Just stay with the feeling so it can move out of your cells," Rachel told her.

"Oh, man, this is hard. I hate feeling this out of control." Stella started to cry so she could release any emotion that seemed bottled up or old.

Stella felt like a freak and was so ashamed to be that way. "Why can't I grow up and stand on my own two feet? Why is it so hard for me to be with myself, alone with me? Why can't I get a handle on this fear of being alone? I don't like it, feeling so vulnerable and unable to resolve this fear and be all right with just being alone. This terror stripped me from being authentic with friends. They mainly had a purpose to fill my well, which I was unable to achieve; I was always searching for ways to satisfy the loneliness that was my fabric, my being. Of course, it was an illusion because there was never a sense of achievement; it would be a Band-Aid to cover a long-held wound that needed a different salve to heal."

Stella craved freedom from the shackles that kept her from feeling and experiencing what it was like to be at peace with herself and actually enjoying her own company.

"Stella you already accomplished this when Gabrielle went away to college," Rachel said. "Don't you remember that?"

"Yes," she said, timidly.

"I don't like it when you revert back to old ways," Rachel said.

Rachel reminded Stella of what she had accomplished and that she was ready to live alone.

"We have done so much work on you connecting with yourself. You've done so much healing around what you didn't receive as a child. I need you to remember these things," Rachel said with authority.

Rachel was right. At times, Stella entered her victim role when she felt overwhelmed.

"I am capable of being alone. It might be hard at first, but I'll get used to it," Stella said. She knew Rachel got mad at her when she did the self-pity thing. She raised her voice and tilted her head to the left, as if to say, "Get a clue." She wished some things weren't so hard—she was tired of working on her shit.

Stella went home that night and prepared herself for the big day when Gabrielle moved out by drinking some magnesium and taking a 5-HTP.

Stella heard Gabrielle come in around ten in the evening, so she went into her room and gave her a kiss goodnight for the last time in

Gabrielle's bedroom, "Sweetie, I would like to help you move tomorrow so I can see your new apartment," Stella said.

"Sure, Mom, that would be great," she said.

"I love you, Gabrielle."

"I love you, Mom."

■ ■ ■

Saturday came in like a lion. After a couple of hours, they had loaded all of Gabrielle's furniture and boxes so they were ready to drive to Gabrielle's new apartment. Stella followed Gabrielle because she didn't know where the apartment was. It was twenty minutes east of their house and in a nice neighborhood beside a trail along the lake. The apartment was large, about 1000 square feet, and clean. Gabrielle's roommate Sarah was already there waiting to help them unload. Stella had met her a few years earlier when Gabrielle would come home from college.

Everything was unloaded in a few hours so Stella started hanging up Gabrielle's clothes for her. Gabrielle was fixing up her bathroom. "Mom, do these towel colors look good together?" Stella walked into the bathroom. She felt proud of how Gabrielle had placed all the towels like they were at home.

"Yes, sweetie, they look great," she replied. Then she went back to finish hanging up the clothes in the closet.

When she finished, she went back into the bathroom and asked, "Gabrielle, I'm done with hanging your clothes. Do you need me to do anything else?"

"No, Mom. Thanks for all your help." Stella looked around at Gabrielle's bedroom and thought how much her daughter would love living on her own. Gabrielle quickly finished up in the bathroom and then walked to the door with Stella.

"Mom, I appreciate your help," she said. Stella looked at her for a moment, then gave Gabrielle a big, long hug.

"Sweetie, I'm so proud of you, moving out on your own. Let me know if you need anything."

"I'm good, Mom. I'll talk to you later." Stella said goodbye to Gabrielle's roommate Sarah and walked down the hall to the stairs where her car was parked just outside the complex. As Stella drove home, she felt calm and relaxed—not like when Gabrielle went away to college.

Stella went home and kept herself busy for the rest of the evening, vacuuming Gabrielle's room and cleaning up the kitchen from dishes left over from the night before. She was surprised by how grounded she felt and that she didn't have any symptoms of anxiety. A few days later, she still felt calm and relaxed. She was wiggling into her new way of life. It had been over twenty-five years since Stella had lived alone, but it felt very different this time. It was becoming her own space.

23

"Man cannot discover new oceans until he has
courage to lose sight of the shore."

— Anonymous

er next session with Rachel was an eye-opener. Rachel explained, "Stella you're looking at your identity outside of being a mother, and it's triggered by Gabrielle moving out."

Stella looked at Rachel. "I always had someone else's identity—my mom's or my sister's."

"You became a mother and loved it; you found your purpose and made your life around Gabrielle."

"Yeah, I made Gabrielle my new identity."

"Now that Gabrielle has grown and moved out, it's like you're suspended in air, not knowing who you are and where you want to go."

"I know that I'm moving forward, but to where?"

"That's what you need to figure out," said Rachel.

■ ■ ■

Stella had one of her sessions with Wendy. She hadn't had one for about a month, so she was excited to work with her again.

"Hi, Stella. How are things going with you?" Wendy asked.

"Really good. After our last session, I cried for two days about buying into my belief that I wasn't lovable and worthy."

"Oh, good; we really worked on your heart chakra last session so that makes sense. What are your intentions for today's session?"

"I'm working with Rachel on this negative belief that I'm not worthy and lovable. I've been working on this belief for most of my time with Rachel. I feel that I've healed, but there seems to be some residue stuck in my thinking, so I want to let that go."

"Okay. Go ahead and lie down and relax."

Stella started to relax. After a minute, Wendy asked, "Are you comfortable?"

"Yeah," said Stella, feeling calm as she lay on the warm massage table.

Most of the time, images would appear in Stella's mind while Wendy worked on her energy field: Native American animals like the eagle or jaguar, or Indians dancing in a ceremony, or a medicine man working closely on Stella.

"Okay, Stella. How do you feel?" Wendy asked when she had finished, sitting down on her stool next to Stella's head.

"I'm so relaxed. I felt so much pressure around my stomach area. What was going?"

Wendy always talked about the session and what she uncovered at this point. She'd explain what chakras were spinning and in what order and talk about images that appeared in her mind while she worked. "I've never had this happen before during a session with anyone because I work on the level of spirit in the aura field, but this time, my guide asked me to work on the level of soul, which is a deeper level of energy work. When you felt the pressure in your third chakra and heart chakra, I was working at a soul level."

"That's interesting because when you were working in that area, I had an image of me sitting in a warm, round stone bath deep in a cave-like atmosphere. I was surrounded by five or six jaguars lying down next to me and up on a podium while I bathed. It was a sudden image that popped into my mind because most of the session I was sitting on a ledge high up on a hill looking out to a sea with my little girl tucked in my lap. We were laughing and letting the wind blow through our hair and the sun was shining on our faces."

"What I picked up was the belief you were conditioned to believe as a child that you weren't lovable and worthy," Wendy said, "but now you're ready to move into a new belief system about yourself."

"That makes sense," Stella said. "I'll have to research what jaguar means in Native American belief."

Stella went home and researched what jaguar meant. She was amazed by how relevant the readings were to what she had experienced that day. Among the jaguar's qualities, the one that stood out for Stella was integration. She remembered that Wendy had mentioned her moving out of old beliefs about herself and moving into a new belief system about who she really was. The research said the jaguar represented the process of integration and learning how to apply its lessons to life. It was the process of sifting through pain so clarity could be achieved. When Stella read that, it made so much sense. In the past, she had always felt alone and separate from everyone. She didn't feel that way any longer because Rachel had shown her that she could connect with someone and that she was not alone. Stella used to be skeptical of those methods, but not anymore.

As Brene Brown said, "Vulnerability is courage." It had taken a lot of bravery for Stella to address her past, understand the core of the anxiety that had plagued her, and want a better life for herself. She realized now that she had grown up in an environment of scarcity thinking; it had carved out her existence—not only in how she viewed herself, but also in how she imagined people viewed her, so she had placed herself in relationships and jobs that fed those beliefs. She was always afraid of not being enough and being unworthy of love. Whenever it came time to ask for what she needed in a relationship with a man, she would discover he was incapable of showing up emotionally so she eventually ended the relationship.

Stella hadn't dated anyone for over five years as she focused on healing herself with Rachel and raising Gabrielle. But not long after Gabrielle moved out, Stella met a man when she attended her friend Kate's daughter's graduation party. Stella had a casual conversation with him, and then they exchanged phone numbers. The next day, she received an email for a coffee date; they conversed back and forth until they decided on a day, place, and time. He wasn't her type, compared to her past encounters; he was ten years her senior, but she was open to meeting with him, and she felt it was time for her to find someone she could connect with and hopefully share a long-term partnership with. After a few months, however, Stella slipped back into some old behavior of not feeling enough, which developed into anxiety, so she scheduled a session with Rachel to help her resolve her fear.

Rachel and Stella sat for a while discussing the fear of not be worthy. "I'm glad to see that you're open to dating again," Rachel said with a smile.

"I know. It has been a long time. I feel scared that I will lose myself in this relationship," Stella said.

"Well, you've done a lot of healing work on your self-esteem and learning to feel worthy of happiness. I'm here to help you in the process. I won't let you lose yourself."

"I'm just getting the urge to run away like I did when I was young."

"Why do you feel like running away?"

"I'm scared because it's only been a few months of dating, and I'm starting to like this man, Dale. He is showing strong attraction to me, and he wants me to go to a company function and spend Thanksgiving and Christmas with his family."

"How do you feel about meeting his family?"

"Well, he mentioned to me the other day that he could easily fall in love with me, so his wanting me to meet his coworkers and family makes me think he is serious about the relationship."

"Isn't that a good thing?" asked Rachel.

"Yes, but I'm just feeling scared, and I see some red flags."

"What kinds of red flags?"

"He drinks alcohol more than I do, and a few times when I was with him, I drank too much and felt sick the next day. And sometimes I sense that he is pulling away because he complains he's too tired and doesn't want to be intimate, like kissing and having sex."

"Well, he is in his sixties, so libido can be an issue. Just be open to the process of the relationship unfolding."

Rachel always gave her such great advice, but being patient was hard for Stella because she always took relationships fast in the beginning. This one was different, however; he had been the one who started taking it fast, but now it seemed to be going in the opposite direction.

Stella recognized that Dale was moving away from her by not calling her every day or expressing his feelings like he had in the beginning. He clammed up and became distant. At first, she felt responsible, like she hadn't done something right. She got really scared, and it felt like old wounding, where she didn't feel enough in the relationship for him to love her. She went over to his house one day so they could talk about it.

"I feel you've been so distant lately. I keep asking you why you aren't affectionate with me anymore. You complain you're tired, but I think it's more than that. What's going on?" Stella asked.

"I'm really busy at work, and I have a lot on my mind," he replied.

"I understand that you're tired, but you seem so distant and preoccupied. I was under the impression that we were getting serious because during the winter holidays I met your family and friends. In the beginning, you just seemed so engaged with me. I'm not sure what shifted."

He just looked off in the distance and said, "I'm just not as into you, I guess, as you are into me."

Those words made Stella so angry that she reverted back to the way she used to end relationships—she would cut the man off at the knees.

"Well, I don't get why you changed your mind so fast. But I'm done with this relationship," she said, as she stood up and walked to the door.

"Well, I'll contact you sometime to see how you're doing," he said, standing on his porch.

Stella turned around and looked at him. "Goodbye."

Her reaction came from not wanting to feel the disappointment and sadness of rejection. The relationship had only lasted six months.

Five months later, she met a man named Daniel by chance in a restaurant in Seattle and he gave Stella his number while she was having lunch. She was apprehensive at first because he was ten years younger, but she was really attracted to him and he was more her type: tall, funny, and intelligent. He had moved to the Seattle area fifteen years before from another state, with his former wife. They had been divorced for six years, and he was starting over in his career as a sales executive for a major corporation in Seattle.

Their first date was meeting for a drink in Seattle after work. It had been a few weeks since their first encounter in the restaurant due to work schedules, so they agreed to meet in a grocery store parking lot near the place they would go for a drink. Stella was nervous but very excited to see him again. When she showed up at the agreed spot, he was standing by his car waiting for her. She parked and got out of the car, "Hi," she said as she walked up to him and they embraced with a hug and a long, passionate kiss.

Then he stepped back and looked at her for a bit. "You're so beautiful. I'm so glad you're here," he said, and he reached down and pulled her close as he passionately kissed her again.

They eventually got into his car and parked for a while, continuing to make out in the front seat. This was the first time Stella had been so aggressive on a first date in a long time; it made her feel like she was sixteen again.

But about four months into the relationship, Stella saw signs of Daniel disengaging, and again, it started to make her feel unworthy like she had as a child. What had changed this time was she expressed her feelings upfront; learning from the last relationship and working with Rachel had given her the tools to communicate her feelings. They had a phone conversation one evening when Stella said, "I'm starting to get scared because my heart is starting to get involved."

"Maybe we should slow down; I don't want you to get hurt," he said.

"What do you mean by that?"

"I don't want you to hurt is what I meant."

"How do we slow down? What does that look like?"

"I don't know. Let's just communicate with each other on how each other feels. We can let it take its course," he replied.

After that, they talked on the phone a couple of times a week, checking in with each other. It was a lovely, respectful, and heartfelt exchange of words.

During the holiday season, after they had been seeing each other for eight months, he confessed to her the difficulties he was having with his feelings for her.

"I can't afford to have feelings," he said. "I need to feel strong, aggressive, and powerful in order to make money. Having feelings for you will just complicate things in my life, and then I wouldn't be able to accomplish my career goals."

"Feelings are part of a relationship," Stella replied.

"Feelings make me feel vulnerable and weak. I don't have the luxury to feel weak and vulnerable."

Stella pondered that conversation for a while; she realized for the first time in an intimate relationship that her partner's issues didn't have anything to do with her. She immediately drew on her compassion for him and felt complete understanding for where he was at and what his fears were all about. He was not capable at that point to show up with his emotions. It was too scary for him; being vulnerable was just too risky. This realization hit Stella straight in the heart and she started to cry. Being in fear and shutting feelings out was what Stella had learned to do in the past, which aggravated the anxiety. Being disconnected and not allowing love to be part of her life was what had made her feel alone and separate from people. But being connected and loving each other was what humans ultimately seek.

She wrote in her journal:

> I know love is risky and scary. I feel like my skin is turned inside out most of the time; all my inners are exposed, and if anyone blows on me, it will be uncomfortable or hurtful. Even with all its uncertainties, I can't imagine ever living a life without love and the feeling of being loved.

Stella kept the door open. There was no discussion of a breakup. She didn't have to control the relationship's outcome; she didn't feel like she had to end it. She didn't take on any responsibility for how he was feeling; she didn't try to do or say the right thing to make it work. She saw it for what it was: a beautiful thing. Stella sat for a bit and cried, knowing that she had worked very hard to get to this place with herself where she could believe in her worth and stand in her truth for what she needed in life in order to feel nurtured and connected to purpose. When she wasn't with him, she missed him. When they spent time together it was fun—so beautiful and lovely—and she felt like she was home. There were similarities in their upbringings and the ways they were treated as children. He had the same issues Stella did around abandonment, trust, and not being able to feel enough. She recognized it immediately when they were together, and afterwards, he would disappear for a few days. It didn't make her feel good, but she understood why he did it. It was easy for Stella to be with him, and he expressed how easy it was being with her. Stella didn't look at that as letting go of him; she was focusing on loving herself and keeping her heart open. She believed that love was the way, maybe the only way.

24

"I think that when enough time has passed, when you've
survived that which you didn't imagine you could, there's
a dignity in that. Something you can own. A pride in
knowing the pain made you stronger."

— Mia Sheridan

With all the strength she was now feeling, Stella thought it was finally time to tackle her fear of flying. How would she step forward to take the initiative and board the plane? Rachel suggested she begin by picking a place to travel to that wasn't a long plane ride.

"Yeah, I was thinking the same thing, so I searched online to see where I could go locally for a test flight," Stella said.

"Did you find a place?" Rachel asked.

"Yes, many."

"So where would you like to go?" Rachel asked.

"Arizona is only a three-hour flight, so I could go down there to get some much-needed sun and warmth. Spring and fall are the best times to travel there so that could be an option. Southern California is only a three-hour flight as well. I love the beach, so that could be a better choice. Or Portland, Oregon, which is only a forty-minute flight."

Rachel got out of her chair, walked over to her bookshelf, and grabbed a pamphlet. "I got this from my sister who works for an airline. Why don't you call the number and see if this is something you want to do?" she said, handing Stella the brochure.

The pamphlet described a non-profit organization that helped people who fear flying. Stella browsed through it and then looked up at Rachel. "Yeah, I'll give them a call when I get home."

■ ■ ■

When Stella got home, she called the nonprofit to find out what the course was about and left a message. A few hours later, a man named

Mike called and explained how it was a volunteer-based company that helped individuals get back on a plane. Mike went through the process: You meet in Seattle down at Boeing field and they walk you through the mechanics of the airplane. You board an airplane to get familiar with the seating and cockpit. They start the engines so you get used to the noises. You're assigned a companion who has already been through the program to accompany you on the short hour flight. Mike said he would be Stella's companion for the flight. As Mike talked with her on the phone, Stella started feeling stressed, so she knew instantly that this was not the right option for her. She knew that she didn't want to take her first flight by herself; she would need someone to go with her after fifteen years of not being on a plane.

■ ■ ■

During her next session with Rachel, Stella said, "I called the organization you told me about, but just talking to someone there made me anxious, so I don't want to take that route. Would you fly with me on my first flight?"

"Do you not think you can do this on your own?"

"No, I thought about it for a while and asked my friend Stacy if she would go with me. She said yes, but she travels a lot, so it would be difficult to time it."

"I would need to do this on a non-working day, but yes I will go with you. Look into the scenic flights on Lake Union. That would be a good start," Rachel said, smiling.

"Actually, I went on their website this morning and found some days and times," said Stella smiling.

Before she left, Stella and Rachel discussed the possibilities and agreed on a flight they would go on together.

Stella wrote in her journal that night:

> I imagine the day I will fly as clear as a star in the night sky, the one who shines the brightest. I have longed for this day, working diligently over decades of healing, putting the pieces of my life back together and integrating myself into all the parts of this beautiful body, mind, and soul. It's so overwhelming— the love I feel for myself and how grounded and accepting I am of this individual who is me. I have all the tools I need to take this flight. There are no more shackles that bind me to the past or to my fears anymore. I have made it to this point not only

through the love of myself but through the support of the people around me who love me, the people whom I can trust and who know I am worthy. I am ready to be free!

■ ■ ■

Stella woke up at seven in the morning the day of her first flight and began throwing up. She called Rachel and left her a message to cancel. "I feel so anxious. I can't seem to get my footing to go ahead with the flight. I know it's not a big deal, but it's a big deal to me."

Rachel called Stella an hour later and talked to her about flying.

"Stella, I'll be with you," she said.

"I know, Rachel; I'm so scared. I can't go," she said, crying.

"Can you meet me down at the dock about an hour before the flight leaves, so, say 12:30?"

"Okay, I can do that," Stella said, hanging up the phone.

Planning to meet Rachel made it easier for Stella to get moving and not stay stuck in the anxiety. Stella got dressed and made herself some magnesium tea to take with her since the drive would take thirty minutes. As she drove, she practiced breathing in for four counts, then exhaling for eight counts to help prevent her from holding her breath. It really helped. She started getting excited the closer she got to Seattle, driving across the ship canal bridge.

Stella took the Mercer exit to take her down to the waterfront on Lake Union. It was a sunny summer day, so the flight would be very scenic. The flight path went over Lake Washington, downtown Seattle, and the Puget Sound, so the Olympic Mountains would be visible.

Stella parked and walked to the pier where the seaplane was docked. When she saw Rachel standing by the gate, she started feeling anxious again, with short breaths and a dry mouth. She went over to Rachel.

"Hi, darling," Rachel said with a cheerful smile. Stella wasn't feeling fully excited just yet.

"Hi, Rachel. I am so scared," she said quietly.

They just stood there for a minute to get familiar with the surroundings. They weren't scheduled to fly for nearly an hour, so Stella and Rachel sat down outside to watch the activity of the people excited for their flight. Stella had experienced the same symptoms the last time she had tried to board a plane. She knew this flight was different and she was different, but she was so scared. They sat for a minute while Stella read the brochure. Seattle Seaplanes was located on Lake Union, a twenty-minute flight around downtown Seattle. Stella was concentrating too much on her symptoms of holding her breath and feeling dizzy. Rachel was holding her hand while Stella processed her symptoms.

"Are you ready to board?" Rachel asked, looking at Stella with her calming eyes.

"Yes, let's get this over with," Stella said, hurriedly. As they walked up the ramp, Stella slowed down a bit to let the others board first. Rachel was following her lead, so they allowed the others to pass. It was a small float plane that fit five people. Stella climbed in first and sat up front with Rachel. Stella didn't know that Rachel had called ahead to tell the pilot that Stella was nervous about flying, so he was very accommodating. The engines started and the plane was humming.

I'm not afraid of crashing. I'm afraid of having another panic attack, Stella thought as she looked out the window and practiced the mantra, "I can do this. I can do this." It had helped with elevators and ferry rides, and now it was helping with the short plane ride. Rachel reached over and held Stella's hand.

Afterward, Stella didn't remember much of the sights she had viewed from the plane; she had been too busy concentrating on staying grounded and making sure she was breathing and having a good experience with flying.

Once they had landed, she hugged Rachel for a long time and cried on her shoulder. Then they said their goodbyes and Stella went home to think about what she had accomplished that day. It had been easier than she had thought it would be. She was so grateful for Rachel. She knew the big one would be to fly commercially so the next excursion would be just that. She had tossed and turned the night before, full of apprehension all the way, so when Stella went to bed that night, she slept soundly all wrapped up in her blankets.

■ ■ ■

The next day, when Stella woke up, she thought about the day before and how she felt. She was so proud of herself, a big step for her. She had worked through the anxiety symptoms and faced the fear. She felt ready for the next step.

Stella researched the theory of why phobias begin and found that they can arise through a traumatic experience, like, for Stella, having a panic attack on an airplane. If the person avoids the phobic situation, he or she will be more likely to continue to experience it. In order to decondition the phobia, the person needs to get to the source. In Stella's case, she needed to get back on the airplane.

■ ■ ■

Four months went by since the scenic flight around Seattle before Stella called Rachel to schedule a session with her to talk about flying back East. It was October, so the fall colors would be starting to change, and Stella loved that time of year.

"Hello, dear. How are you doing?" Rachel asked.

"I feel compelled to travel back East. I felt badly when I couldn't go back to Massachusetts for my dad's funeral," she replied.

"Do you feel ready to take such a long flight?"

"I'm not sure. The fear of failing again really scares me. I have come so far with my healing, but I'm not certain I won't have another panic attack and be unable to get on the plane."

"Well, let's talk about alternatives for helping you out."

"I'm going. I'm committed to going back East, but I'm not sure if taking a plane back is the right approach."

"Taking the airplane back East is too much," said Rachel. "It's a four or five-hour flight—a recipe for self-sabotage. What about taking the train?"

"I like that idea."

"Only if you make an agreement with me that you'll take a shorter flight in six months."

"Yes, I will make an agreement with you to get on an airplane in six months."

■ ■ ■

Stella called Gabrielle to let her know they were going to take the train back East instead of flying. "Hi, honey. We're going to take Amtrak back to Boston," Stella said.

"I'm not going to take the train," said Gabrielle.

"Yes, we are because I'm paying for it. We'll go one way and you can fly back home," Stella said.

"What are you going to do?"

"I'll figure that out when I get there."

Stella researched the train route from Seattle to Boston. It would take three days to get there, and fall was a great time to travel since the prices were reasonable, and it was a good time for Stella and Gabrielle to visit Robert's grave and relatives. They had a few weeks before the trip, so Stella scheduled another session with Rachel.

■ ■ ■

"Okay, I've booked Gabrielle's and my train tickets to go to Boston, and we're leaving in a week," Stella told Rachel during their session.

"Great. This will be good practice for when you're ready to fly again. Will you be taking the train back home?" she asked.

"I don't know. I'll decide when I get there."

"Do you want to do any visualization about getting on the plane?"

"Sure, that would be good, just in case I do decide to fly home."

Stella was sitting propped up on the pillows with a white blanket wrapped around her. Rachel asked her to close her eyes so they could do a visualization about getting on the plane. Stella had done this form of visualization before with Rachel, about traffic and elevators, and she had used hypnotherapy with Marilyn, so she knew how well this method worked for her. She couldn't help but think how ashamed she was feeling around the whole anxiety about flying thing. It was hard for her to concentrate at first, but with Rachel's calming words, Stella felt relaxed; then Rachel started visualizing with Stella what she would experience at the airport. "Now, you're approaching the place where you scan your e-ticket," she said in a calm voice. "How are you feeling?"

"Um, I feel relaxed and confident," Stella said. She focused on the way she scanned her ticket and walked to the security entrance. A long line of people were waiting to pass through. Stella had gone down to the airport a month before to sit and observe the process. She had seen how people scanned their tickets and observed how the patrons shuffled through security. Rachel continued with guiding Stella from security to the gate and finding a seat to sit down on until the plane boarded.

"Okay, you're at the gate, waiting for the plane to board. Is there anywhere in your body that feels scared?" Rachel asked.

"I feel impatient, like I want to board the plane and get over the anticipation," she said.

"Okay. Practice breathing and relaxing your body more."

After a few minutes, Rachel asked, "How do you feel now?"

"I feel more relaxed and ready to get on the plane."

Rachel said, "Now over the loudspeaker, a pleasant voice is announcing that your flight is boarding. You've got your pink cord tied securely around your waist."

"I can do this. I can do this. I can do this," Stella repeated out loud. "Okay, now I'm boarding the plane. I found my seat next to the window. I'm putting my luggage in the overhead bin. Now I'm sitting down and buckling my seatbelt."

"Okay. Now what are you doing?"

"The plane is moving toward the runway. It's getting ready to take off because I can hear the engines roaring. I feel the pressure like the tension on a bow just before the arrow is released. I'm being pulled back against the seat. I feel the plane lift into the air, gaining elevation, flying," Stella said as she cried.

Rachel waited for Stella to open her eyes. "That was great, and now you're ready to fly in a plane."

■ ■ ■

The day of their trip, Stella and Gabrielle took a taxi down to the King Street Station so they could catch the train that was scheduled to leave at 4:40 p.m. Stella had reserved a Viewliner room for the long distance. It was a small room, but it would fit both of them, and it had a shower and a toilet with all the extra amenities to make their trip comfortable. Best of all, they had a large window to look out when they chose to be in their room. The lower bed pulled out and was a bit larger than a twin bed, and the loft bed was fitted as a twin. Gabrielle was going to sleep up above.

The first leg of the trip would take forty-eight hours to the Chicago station, so Gabrielle and Stella stayed in their room for a few hours to catch up.

"Mom, do you remember the time we took a train down to San Francisco when I was six years old?" Gabrielle asked.

"Yeah, I remember we just sat in a seat section and slept for the overnight travel. Much different this time," Stella said, chuckling while looking out the window as they approached the Wenatchee station.

"I wonder how long these stops are going to be," Gabrielle said, yawning.

"Not sure. Let's go get something to eat," Stella said, picking up her purse and opening the door.

They walked to the eating area and picked a table by the window so they could continue watching the sights before it got dark. Then they went back to their room and got ready for bed. Stella lay in bed drifting into a dream state created by the hypnotic effect of the train swaying. Before she knew it, it was morning and they had stopped in Montana at the West Glacier station.

The stop didn't last long, so they got ready to have breakfast in the dining room. Gabrielle ordered eggs and toast, and Stella ordered Greek yogurt and granola. The travel day was going to be long so Stella sat in the observatory lounge and read a book for most of the day. Gabrielle stayed in the room, watched a movie on her computer, and slept for a while before she joined Stella. They looked at the dry plains of North Dakota and talked about how boring it would be to live in that part of the country. They had an early dinner and went back into their room. They both squeezed onto Stella's bed and watched the movie, *Fargo*. Stella fell asleep ten minutes into the movie, and she didn't even feel Gabrielle get out of her bed and climb into her own. Next stop, Chicago.

They arrived in Chicago in the afternoon, so they decided to get off the train for a bit, stretch their legs, and get some fresh air. It would take another fourteen hours to reach the Union Station in Maryland, so they found a nearby diner, ate some greasy food, and laughed at the cramped feeling they had on the train. Gabrielle and Stella had not been in that close a space ever. Stella commented on how Gabrielle was grumpy in the morning and needed her coffee to wake up before she'd have a conversation. Gabrielle rolled her eyes as she shook her head in response. They settled in their room, and before the train took off for Maryland, at about nine at night, Stella fell asleep reading her book while Gabrielle was watching a movie with headphones.

■ ■ ■

The train stopped at the Pittsburgh station about five in the morning. Stella lay in her bed while she watched the people shuffle off the train. Gabrielle was still asleep, so Stella waited for her to wake up so they could go have breakfast before they arrived at the Rockville, Maryland Station just before lunch.

Once they were in the dining car, Stella was talking with Gabrielle about the time she went to Pittsburgh with her parents when she was little to see the Duquesne Incline. Shirley was scared of heights, so Stella remembered having to hold on to her mom's hand while they rode on a cable car up the hill. Gabrielle looked at Stella and said how she was kind of holding her mom's hand too with this train trip back East. Stella laughed at the truth.

They boarded the Union station train in Maryland, which left at 3:30 p.m. and would arrive at the Boston South Station at 11:30 that evening, so they went back to their room while Stella took a nap and Gabrielle went into the observation car and listened to music. They agreed to meet in the dining car for dinner at seven o'clock. Stella felt much rested. She noticed how well she slept on the train, probably because of the constant swaying. She felt as if she were being rocked like a baby.

Stella arrived in the dining car early and ordered a martini while she waited for Gabrielle, who eventually arrived and ordered a glass of white wine. They talked about how much the scenery changed at night because they were passing through cities. The trip up to Boston was along the seaside, so they were able to admire the city lights of Philadelphia and New York. Gabrielle was impressed by the sights and told Stella that she wouldn't mind living in New York one day. Stella smiled and said that would be a good plan for her if she really wanted to move. Then they went back to their room and started packing their bags; it would be an hour before they arrived in Boston. As they were packing, Stella thanked Gabrielle for coming on this trip with her and told her how much she loved her. Gabrielle turned around and gave Stella a hug and told her that she loved her too.

They arrived in Boston at 11:30 and took a cab to the Hertz rental center to get a car so they could go to their hotel. They woke up the next morning and drove a few hours before they got to the hotel near where Robert and Michael were buried. A group of Stella's cousins were meeting them at a restaurant near their hotel. They checked in and rested for a bit before they met everyone for a late dinner. Everyone got to meet Gabrielle, and they hadn't seen Stella for many years, so they spent hours catching up well into the night. Gabrielle and Stella were going out to the gravesite the next day so they needed to get some sleep. They all said their goodbyes and Stella and Gabrielle were told not to make it so long until the next visit.

■ ■ ■

The next morning came quickly, so Stella and Gabrielle went down to the lobby to have the continental breakfast.

"Why do they talk so differently back here?" Gabrielle asked, taking a bite of her eggs.

"The dialect is different from the West Coast. I remember when I moved out to Seattle, my friends used to tell me that I talked differently," Stella said, drinking her tea.

"Nobody has left this state from Grandpa's family, have they?" Gabrielle asked.

"No, they all still live very close together."

The drive would be about an hour, so they got into the car and set up the GPS. Then they were off. The sun was shining, and it was going to be a warm day, around eighty degrees. The leaves hadn't completely changed, but some of the trees had already turned that beautiful deep red color. Stella realized how much she missed the fall season. There was nothing like a fall season on the East Coast. She was feeling very happy. They found the cemetery and went into the office to find where the marker was. The sexton and his wife were expecting them. It was nice finally to meet them since Stella had worked with them over the phone when Robert died to coordinate the ceremony and tell them how she wanted the marker to read. Stella and Gabrielle followed them out to the burial site and walked up to the marker where Robert and Michael were buried.

Stella had never seen her grandparents' gravesite either. Robert's wishes had been to be buried at the foot of his mom and dad's marker. Even though Stella had designed Robert's marker and seen a photograph of it, it was nice to see it in person. It said Robert's full name, date of birth and death, and at the bottom, Michael's full name and below that "Beloved son." Stella started to cry, not because she missed her dad or brother, but because she had been unable to attend the funeral. Now she didn't feel any guilt, just completion.

Gabrielle and Stella spent some time talking about how Robert had lived his life. Gabrielle had some funny stories about her grandpa too.

"Well, I am ready to go," Stella finally said. Gabrielle was ready way before Stella, but she knew how important this visit was for her mom. They drove back to the hotel so they could make reservations for dinner. It had been a long day for both of them, so they went to bed early. The plan was to sightsee tomorrow, and Stella wanted to show Gabrielle where she had grown up.

■ ■ ■

They spent a few days driving around. Stella was having fun showing Gabrielle where she went to school and the first house she lived in.

The morning Gabrielle was scheduled to fly back, she asked Stella at the airport, "Mom, are you going to be okay?"

"Yes," Stella said with a smile.

"When are you going to be home?"

"I don't know. I need to take some time for me. It's going to be hard and scary, but I'm going to do this."

"Mom, I'm really proud of you. Call me if you need anything," she said, hugging Stella tight.

"I'm going to be okay," Stella said, giving Gabrielle a kiss goodbye on the cheek.

■ ■ ■

The real reason Stella wanted to stay another day was she needed to do some completion work around her childhood home. She hadn't been back there since her family had moved out west. All the work she had done with healing needed to be respected, and she thought it would be appropriate to do this on her own. She also needed to fly by herself to show that she could do it. Stella left the airport and drove directly to her childhood home. It was different; she was different. She parked across the street to see whether the family who lived there was home. She noticed a woman standing in the front yard smoking a cigarette. She really wanted to see the inside like she had for the house in Seattle. Stella mustered up the courage to approach the woman.

"Hi, my name is Stella. I lived in this house over forty years ago when I was a child." The woman looked at her and smiled. "I know this is a weird request, but could I see the inside?"

The lady dropped her cigarette and stepped on it. "I'm Louise. Come on. I'll show you the house," she said.

They walked into the small three-bedroom home where Stella had lived when she was just a small child. She didn't remember much except for the backyard and her and Lynn's bedroom. Stella walked around and quietly looked. She had been nine years old when she had left this home to move to Seattle. Memories surfaced, like when she had fallen off the swing set bar and broken her jaw when she was two. She smiled when she saw her bedroom, and she remembered how her bed had been against the wall, just shy of the door, and Lynn's bed had been over in the corner by the window.

When she had seen everything, she said, "Thank you, Louise, for allowing me to come back to my childhood home. It has been very healing for me," and she shook her hand.

Stella then walked out to her car and sat in it for a minute, soaking up what had just happened. It wasn't like the house in Seattle, but she had been able to visit the two houses that had made such an impact on her emotional welfare, and she was grateful for the blessing to be able to let the past go.

Stella stayed at a local hotel for the night. She woke up the next day and walked to the café. While waiting for her coffee, she picked up a magazine. Something in the magazine called to her. She felt it in her heart and she was going to answer it. She finished her tea and muffin and sent a text to Gabrielle, telling her where she was going. "Hi, sweetie. I'm going to go to Isle of Palms in South Carolina. I'm going to fly." Stella went to the hotel and grabbed her things; then she went to the airport to buy her ticket. As she was walking on the sky bridge to the plane, she called Rachel and left her a voicemail, telling her where she was going. Stella hung up and entered the plane, heart pounding, joyful, realizing she was not afraid.

This must be what excitement feels like, Stella thought.

A FINAL NOTE

Now that you have finished reading this book, what actions are you going to take to deal with your own anxiety? What steps will you put in place to get back on an airplane? What negative thought patterns are you going to give up? What seminars are you going to attend? What changes in your life are you going to make? I challenge you to take action! Knowledge is not power; applying the knowledge is power. I'm challenging you right now to apply the strategies and inspiration from this book to your life and to do it right away. I ask that you take a pen or pencil, and in the ten exercise lines below, you write the top ten actions you will commit to taking for yourself. Maybe it's investing in yourself by hiring a coach, finding a mentor, or attending a seminar.

Exercise:

1. _____

2. _____

3. _____

4. _____

5. _____

6. _____

7. _____

8. _____

9. _____

10. _____

Now that you have completed your list of ten wellness actions and read this book, please contact me to tell me what you liked and didn't like about this book. Most importantly, tell me where you are at in your journey and in your life. Tell me how I can help you. Perhaps email me at melissa@melissaawoods.com, or better yet, reach out to me by phone at 206-681-8335.

I hope you were encouraged by Stella and this inspirational novel about getting past anxiety and reclaiming your life. I hope this book can be a beginning for us. I hope this book can become a resource that you use in your recovery. I wish you all the success, prosperity, love, and happiness that life has to offer—all the courage and strength to pursue your greatest passions in life.

Your friend,

Melissa A. Woods

About the Author

MELISSA A. WOODS is an author, professional keynote speaker, life coach, and entrepreneur. She is a licensed massage practitioner and has been in a successful practice for over twenty years aiding people with anxiety. Melissa is a creative writer and the parent of a happy, healthy son. She discovered the gift of writing while attending a memoir class at the University of Washington. Melissa received a Certificate of Memoir from the University of Washington and has published works in *Memoir Anthology of Writing from the University of Washington.*

As a life coach, Melissa has had personal experiences with anxiety disorder. She feels your pain and knows what it's like to walk in your shoes, so when you work with her, you will not be alone in your journey to healing.

Originally from Maryland, Melissa graduated from Seattle University in 2007. Melissa lived in Seattle, Washington for more than forty years until October of 2016, when she and her partner, Daniele, moved to California.

MELISSA WOODS LIFE COACHING

Don't feel overwhelmed by the thought of getting back on an airplane or facing anxiety issues. Let author, professional keynote speaker, and life coach Melissa Woods guide you through the process with one-on-one coaching calls and unlimited email and text access.

Melissa Woods has journeyed through her own anxiety disorder—in fact, she didn't get on a plane for twenty years. She has also worked on countless clients in her massage practice who suffered from some form of anxiety. Melissa Woods will aid you in the process of conquering your anxiety and serve as your coach.

For more information, visit her website below and then text her with your name, time zone, and the best time to redeem a 30-60 minute complementary consultation by phone or Skype.

www.GettingPastAnxiety.com
www.MelissaAWoods.com
Mobile: 206-681-8335